HAPPILY NEVER
AFTER

HAPPILY NEVER AFTER

a novel by

T. WENDY WILLIAMS

Q-Boro Books
WWW.QBOROBOOKS.COM

An Urban Entertainment Company

ISBN 1-933967-00-5
First Printing January 2007
Printed in the United States of America

10 9 8 7 6 5 4 3 2

*This is a work of fiction. It is not meant to depict, portray or represent any particular
real persons. All the characters, incidents and dialogues are the products of the author's
imagination and are not to be construed as real. Any references or similarities to actual
events, entities, real people, living or dead, or to real locales are intended to give the
novel a sense of reality. Any similarity in other names, characters, entities, places and incidents is entirely coincidental.*

Cover Copyright © 2006 by Q-BORO BOOKS all rights reserved
Cover Layout & Design—Candace K. Cottrell
Editors—Chandra Sparks-Taylor, Tiffany Davis, Candace K. Cottrell

Q-BORO BOOKS
Jamaica, Queens NY 11434
WWW.QBOROBOOKS.COM

Acknowledgments

All thanks to the Creator, who is forever north on the compass of my soul. My wonderful and supportive parents: Barbara J. Williams and Terry Williams. My brilliant and beautiful sister, Tawanna Williams. Many thanks to the following who won't forgive me if I don't mention them: Grandparents; Freddie M. Gordon and Henry L. Gordon; Aunts, uncles, cousins and dear friends; Sisters in the Spirit book club of Houston, Texas; Kimmie Bennett, attorney at law; my agent; Kimberly Matthews; my sister and brother under the pen Pamela Harris and Stanley McMichael; my cheerleader and motivator; Lisa Parker; and finally, you, the reader. I love you all.

PART ONE:

HAPPILY

Chapter 1

I don't know what it is about this sleepy little town that keeps my family coming back. I'm talking about the Lacroix family, from Illinois to California, gathering each year in Opelousas to feast and catch up on one another's business. I don't think everybody here is related. When you mention Lacroix and food in the same breath, all of Opelousas comes out. I'm guessing the town has about 10,000 people, and it seems all of them are here, lined up in front of a twenty-foot-long buffet-style table. They are anxious to sink their teeth into my uncle J.B.'s succulent hickory-smoked Andouille sausage links. Their mouths are watering at the sight of icing running down the sides of a sock-it-to-me cake. I can see their eyes transfixed on the smorgasbord of barbecued chicken, hot barbecued ribs, fried catfish, baked beans, potato salad, rice dressing, collard greens, and cornbread.

I'm serving fresh-squeezed lemonade with lemons hand-picked from my papa's bustling backyard when I look up to see two guys standing before me. One has skin the color of fresh baked gingerbread; the other, slightly taller one, looks like a handsome young Harry Belafonte.

"I believe I've died and gone to heaven," Gingerbread says to me. When he smiles, I see nearly all of his teeth. He doesn't look like anybody in my family. My cousin Tiny—who is 4'11", feisty, and fiery with red hair and freckles to match— squeezes between the two of them.

"They giving you trouble, Dorothy?" she asks.

"Not yet," I respond.

"Watch this one," she says, pointing at Gingerbread.

"What do you mean, watch this one?" Gingerbread fires back. He takes my free hand and kisses it. "Jerome West. Delighted to meet your acquaintance, Miss . . ."

"Lacroix. Dorothy." I blush and tingle from the texture of his lips.

"You're holding up the line, Jerome," Tiny says. She looks at Harry Belafonte. "And why are you so quiet, David?"

I glance at him. He is a sight to behold in his sky-blue shirt and khaki pants. He glances back at me and extends his hand for me to shake. "I'm David Leonard. Tiny can't possibly be your cousin."

"What are you trying to say?" Tiny gives him a playful shove.

"Say, Dorothy, why don't you take a break and join us for a spell?" Jerome says with a smile lingering between sly and irresistible.

"Who's gonna pour the lemonade?"

My other cousin Claire, whose family drove all the way from California, happens to walk by. Tiny grabs her hand and gives her the lemonade ladle.

"Dorothy says she feels some hives coming on from all this acid in the lemonade. Can you pour for a minute until she feels better?" Tiny gives her a minute to let it all sink in.

Before Claire can utter a response, the four of us are strolling across the park headed for a 1963 Impala convertible. The car is a deep, sensuous blue.

"You have a nice car, Jerome," I say.

"Thank you," David responds. I hear the clink of keys in his pocket. Inside the car, Tiny's boyfriend Mike adjusts the dial on the radio. The song "Heat Wave" by Martha and the Vandellas plays. It couldn't have come at a more appropriate time because in some aspects, it accurately describes my feelings. With all the excitement of meeting David and Jerome, I neglected to treat myself to a cup of lemonade. David motions for Mike to get out of the driver's seat. Mike reluctantly gets up, still biting on a rib bone.

With family walking around looking at us suspiciously, I don't want to appear like I'm courting, so I stand a few feet away from Jerome.

"Come here. I won't bite," he says.

"I'm fine." I notice Tiny and Mike making sweet eyes at each other. "So you and David go to school with Tiny?" I ask Jerome.

"Yes."

"That's nice. I don't know very many Negroes—I mean, people—who attend college."

"Times we live in, I guess. That's all about to change, though."

"Why?"

"I believe Kennedy is just what Negroes have been needing."

"You mean to say we'll be equal to white folks?"

Jerome chuckles. "I don't know about equal. They make that impossible. I'm just saying, use David and me for example. Him, me, and Mike are in Tulane medical school. Your cousin Tiny goes to law school there. There have never been that many Negroes at one time at Tulane. Imagine what it'll be like twenty years from now."

"That'll be very nice." I glance up and notice David staring at me from the reflection in the side mirror. He winks.

"You're very pretty," Jerome says, reaching out to touch the tip of my chin. "That's what I love about Louisiana. You can never get enough good food and pretty women."

"Where's your girlfriend?" I ask.

"I'm looking at her," he fires back. "Dorothy Lacroix." He says my name like I am making a grand entrance at a cotillion. "I love Creole women."

"Why?"

He touches my cheek with the back of his hand. "For one, I love the color of your skin. I like that it's not just black or just white or just Spanish or just Indian. It's all that mixed into one, like gumbo. You can't help but think how good that is."

"You like gumbo?"

"Hell, yeah. I can eat it every day."

"No you can't."

"Oh yes I can." He takes his spoon and licks potato salad from it. I turn away so he won't notice me blushing.

"My, my, my, Dorothy Lacroix. You are fine. You got skin soft as felt. If God made anything better than you, I'm glad he kept it to Himself."

I laugh in a giddy schoolgirl sort of way.

"I got a lot more, if you want to hear it."

Claire appears, spoiling my mood. "I see your hives cleared up." She gives me the lemonade ladle.

The park clears out around eight that evening. The smell of barbecue has slowly simmered down, as does the smell of pies and beer. The music from the cars has ceased, and the last of the Lacroix clan is loading up chairs and tables onto the back of their trucks. Voices echo out their last goodbyes until the next time. My younger sister Ophelia and I give our cousin Claire one last hug.

"When are you coming to California?" she asks.

"Sooner than you think," I say, when the truth of the matter is, I'll probably never even see California. Ophelia and I wave to more cousins until we no longer see them wave back.

"I'm glad we don't live in California," Ophelia says.

"You got that right," I reply.

HONK! HONK! I see Tiny sharing a ride with Mike in his Oldsmobile. Behind them are David and Jerome in the convertible.

"Bye." I wave.

"Who is that?" Ophelia asks.

"David and Jerome, Tiny's friends from Tulane."

Ophelia's eyes widen. "Fancy car. You know them?"

"Dorothy, you and your sister stop lollygagging and come on," my papa yells from the car. He revs up the engine of his yellow Buick. My sister and I hop in, filled with excitement.

Chapter 2

I am in desperate need of a ride to the college. Ophelia and I sit around Papa's house, just looking at each other with our faces a mile long. The thought of taking the car comes to mind, but then I think, *I'll never hear the end of Papa's punishment. Instead of him sending me back to Gentilly on the bus, he'd be sending me back in a coffin.*

I go to sleep at night thinking of Jerome. I want so much to see him and be beside him and have him tell me all the wonderful things he was telling me at the reunion.

I don't see or hear from Jerome until four days later, when he stops by Papa's house unexpectedly. I am sitting on the couch, all sweaty and damp, when I hear a voice.

"Hellooo." It nearly scares the life out of me when I see him standing there wearing a light blue shirt with a dark tie and dark blue cuffed trousers. He is strong and firm looking. All I can do is sit on the couch and stare at him to make sure what I am looking at is truly him. How did he find me? I bet Tiny told him.

"What are you doing here?" I look over his shoulder to make sure Papa isn't coming.

"I figured you wanted to see me."

We are separated by the screen door. I smell the refreshing scent of his cologne.

"Can I come in?" he asks.

I laugh, you know, to break the tension I feel mounting up inside of me.

"I'm not really supposed to have company when my papa's not here."

"How old are you, Dorothy?"

"Eighteen."

"The state of Louisiana says you're legally grown."

"You think my papa cares what the state of Louisiana says?"

"You know, I had to spend three dollars on gas to come all the way to Slidell. Don't make me turn around."

I think it over for a moment. *Should I, or shouldn't I? If I let him in, will he get fresh? And what if Papa comes in and sees us?* The thought of it makes me back away from the screen door.

"Don't make me have to turn around and drive back," he repeats, as if I didn't hear him the first time.

"So why haven't you called?"

"I lost your number," he replies.

"Oh," is my response. "How 'bout I sit with you on the porch?"

"Come on out, then."

I slowly unhook the door and push the screen wide enough to walk outside. Jerome steps back with one foot on the top step and the other on the porch. I sit down on the nearest chair. He sits down on the top step.

"How did you know where to find me?"

"I asked Tiny. Is that a problem?"

"Yes. I mean, no, no, no, it was okay." I laugh. He has this way of making me feel goofy and giddy. Jerome looks around the yard like most people do when they come to your house for the first time.

"Nice place," he says.

"I would show you inside, but . . ."

"I know. I wouldn't want your ol' man to think I was getting fresh with you."

He smiles. He has such pretty teeth and nice round lips—not to mention nice ebony eyes. When they meet mine, they tell me more of what Jerome is thinking than words ever could.

"You thirsty?" I ask.

"I just stopped by to see if I could take you out to lunch."

I run my hands through my mess of hair. "I'm not dressed."

"Go inside and change clothes. I'll wait here for you."

"I'm not supposed to leave when my papa's not here."

"Is your papa at work?" he asks. I can sense a tinge of edginess in his voice. "If he is, I can have you back before he gets off."

"Okay, wait right here. I'll be right back." I rush inside, closing the screen and front door behind me. I lock it and peep through to see Jerome's reaction. He looks kind of demure all slumped over on the porch. I don't want to take long, but I really need to look presentable if I'm going anywhere with him.

When I open the door one hour later, Jerome is lying on his back, snoring. I tap him. "Wake up."

He looks around to take in his surroundings and looks at me before he remembers who I am.

"Sorry I took so long." I have on my sun hat and my white linen sundress. I don't want to look too desperate or too care-free. Jerome looks at me like I'm a double scoop of chocolate ice cream.

When we arrive at the diner we are reminded of our status. A "Colored Only" sign hangs from the door. Jerome and I find a booth near the rear.

"What's the matter?" he asks. "You don't like the place?"

"It's okay, I guess." I take off my hat and place it next to my pocketbook. "So what kind of doctor are you studying to be?"

"I'm thinking anatomy."

"What kind of anatomy?"

"Dorothy's anatomy." He winks at me with those playful eyes.

"You're too much," I say.

We order our food. He orders a king-size hamburger with large onion rings and a milk shake. I order a hamburger and take one bite out of it before I notice the pink meat. I gag and spit the rest into my napkin.

"Now what's the matter?" he asks, looking concerned.

"Nothing." I take a bite out of my fries.

"You don't like it, do you?"

"No."

"Then why'd you order it?"

"I don't eat rare meat."

"Give it here." He briskly takes the soggy bun off my plate and puts it on his. "Didn't anybody tell you that rare meat is good for you?"

He bites into it and chews fast with his mouth open, churning bread and red meat simultaneously into a pink goo. He slurps on his milk shake then primps his lips to let out a small but audible burp. I can't finish my fries so I slide them over to him.

"I can't believe I wasted two dollars and fifty cents on you."

I am turned around by his rude attitude. I am about to say something when David walks in with a girl. I assume she's his steady because his arm is snaked around her waist. They look like they had just been to church or city hall. She slides into the booth and bounces up a couple of times before settling in.

"Hello, Dorothy," he says.

"Hi, David."

"Dorothy, this is Bettye." He points to his friend like she is more of an object than a human being. Bettye is pretty, even with her red glasses. Her black hair bounces with every turn she makes.

"You attend Xavier?" she asks me.

"No, but I'm going to Baton Rouge in the fall."

"LSU?"

"Southern."

"I suppose it's a good school," she says, burying her nose in the menu.

David eyes me with those piercing browns of his. I notice him staring at me a lot. He looks at Bettye to see if she notices. For whatever reason, she seems to be in her own world. David is kind of cute. I like the color of his skin—golden brown and flawless. His hair is trimmed nice and neat with tight curls gripping the corners of his forehead and nape of his neck. He looks about 6'1" and 200 pounds. I could easily mistake him for a basketball player, or an actor like Belafonte.

"Did you enjoy the food?" he asks.

"I would if the meat was well done."

"This is my last time taking her anywhere."

"Please don't do me any favors," I hear myself say. I feel sweat tingling underneath my arms.

David gives Bettye a dime for the jukebox.

"What do you want to hear?" she asks.

"Put on Sam Cooke or Ray Charles."

She searches until she finds Sam Cooke's "Bring It On Home to Me."

"You like that?" she asks David.

"How can you not like Sam Cooke? You like Sam Cooke, Dorothy?" David asks me.

I glance at Bettye, not sure if I should respond to David's question. I wonder if she senses him flirting with me. "My papa has most of his albums, even when he sang gospel," I respond.

Jerome finishes off my burger and sits back, rubbing his stomach. He opens up his wallet and drops three dollars on the table.

"I told Mike I'd have his car back in two hours, and here it is three and half hours later. I gotta go." He jumps up. "David, you and Bettye take her home for me."

I look at Jerome and shake my head. I am so embarrassed, my face turns a bright, beet red. He doesn't say goodbye or see you later before he dashes out of the place.

"Typical, very typical," Bettye says, sipping her shake.

"Don't worry. Bettye and I will take you home." He brushes his hands over my drumming fingertips. Bettye glances at David, not saying a word. David glances back at Bettye. "What's wrong with you?" he asks. Her throat is bobbing.

"Nothing," she replies.

I feel uncomfortable. I don't want to make eye contact with either of them, so I glance at my watch.

"Where do you live?" David asks.

"Just off the loop. It's about fifteen minutes away. I can walk there from here."

"That's not a good idea. We'll take you home."

"Thank you kindly. I really appreciate this." I finally glance at Bettye. She doesn't look happy about the invitation.

I ride home feeling disappointed in Jerome and more so in myself for allowing him to treat me like trash. My feelings are hurt, but I'm not going to give him the benefit of my tears.

David turns on the radio, and a smooth, melodious voice comes over the air saying, "Today's high is 89 degrees. Who loves you, New Orleans? This is yours truly giving you the best of the hits. Here's an old tune from Frankie Lymon and the Teenagers. It was number one in 1955—'Why Do Fools Fall In Love'—enjoy."

David moves his head to the music. Bettye sits in silence, staring out the window. David looks at her.

"Not speaking to me again?" he asks.

Bettye is silent.

"That's fine. I'll just talk to Dorothy." He adjusts the rearview mirror and smiles at me. "So, Dorothy, what are you majoring in once you get to college?"

"I haven't decided."

"Let me know if you need help."

I notice Bettye glaring at him. He stares back with a look on his face that says, *What the hell are you looking at?* If looks could kill, Bettye would be dead. I don't quite understand the private communication between them, but the mood is so intense that I can't wait to get out of the car.

David and Bettye drop me off at 617 Mulberry Street. I get out and apologize for any inconvenience.

"You be sure and tell Jerome that I never want to see him again," I say to David. "Bye, Bettye. It was nice meeting you."

She smirks and turns her head before the car makes its way up the street, turns right at the stop sign, and disappears from view.

"What's ailing my princess?" Papa asks.

"Nothing," I reply.

"Yes it is. You've been walking around here, moping with your mouth hanging down a mile. You won't eat, and you know it's not like you to turn down my smothered chicken. Talk to your papa."

I don't want to tell him I'm having boy problems, but then maybe he'd be the most qualified person with whom to discuss this matter. He could get to the gist of things. After all, he was young once. He too thought the world revolved around him. I want to ask, "When is the best time to fall in love? Is it before or after you have sex with them?" But I don't dare ask.

"Are you thinking about a certain young man?" he asks.

"As a matter of fact I am."

"Do you like him?"

"I don't know."

"Is he Catholic?"

"I don't think so."

"Don't marry a Catholic. You'll be miserable for the rest of your life."

"*Mère* was Catholic."

"And you see how we turned out."

"Were you in love when you married her?"

"I'll be honest with you, princess. I married your mother because the Church said I had to. Marry or burn. Let me tell you this: Don't ever marry anyone just out of obligation. You marry for love. Make sure he loves you more than you love him. I was just nineteen, on leave from the service when your mother got pregnant with Katherine. What did I know about love at that age?"

Papa coughs. It sounds like an old car engine rattling in his lungs. He puts our conversation on hold for a minute. I get up to rub his back. I can feel his whole body shaking and vibrating. He assures me it isn't anything that a good dose of castor oil couldn't cure; he'd get over it in no time. Papa's been telling me that for the past year. He wipes his nose with a white handkerchief before stuffing it in his pocket.

"Now, when I was nineteen . . ." He coughs again. "Now, when I was nineteen, all I cared about was running the town. I didn't know the first thing about love or a child. I wasn't but a child myself." He leans forward to retrieve a cigarette from inside the coffee table drawer.

"No wonder you sound bad," I say. "Remember what the doctors said."

He proceeds to smoke like he doesn't hear me. "I know what they said, and I told them doctors like I'm telling you— the day I give up my cigarettes will be the day y'all put me in the ground." He thumps his ashes into a nearby ashtray and makes a speech I've heard a million times about all the things that are bad for your health. On television is a news segment mentioning Medgar Evers, a civil rights leader who was gunned down a little over a week ago in front of his home. Papa stops to watch the talking head in the round black-and-white tube. I assume our conversation is over so I get up to leave.

"Dot, where you going? I'm not finished." His eyes are still on the television. I find a spot on the sofa next to him. "Get your sister. I want to talk to her, too."

Ophelia is in her room, drawing and sketching with her pencils when I walk in.

"Papa wants to talk to you."

She looks at me with frightened little eyes. "What did I do?"

"Just come and see what he wants."

Ophelia follows me into the family room. "Yes, Papa?"

"You and Dot sit down. I got something to tell you two about love."

Ophelia grimaces. "Love?"

"Just listen to what I have to say," he insists.

Ophelia looks at me and teases me, singing, "Dorothy's in love, Dorothy's in love."

"Stop it." I say.

Papa puffs on his cigarette. "Ophelia, I was just telling your sister that you should never marry out of obligation. You marry for love."

"Why are you telling me this, Papa?" She looks at me. "Are you getting married?" I want to slap my sister for being so anxious to jump to wild and crazy conclusions.

"No, silly. Papa was explaining to me about his relationship with *Mère* and when was the right time to fall in love." This time the look on her face gets even crazier. I knew what she was thinking: *Y'all interrupted my drawing for this?*

Papa begins, "I want you girls to not be afraid to talk to me about anything that's bothering you. If you want to talk about boys, I can tell you all you need to know. Another thing— don't ever let a man disrespect you or your household, you hear me?"

"Yes, sir," Ophelia and I agree in unison.

"I never hit your mother. Lord knows I wanted to, but hitting a woman is the worst thing a man could ever do. He won't hit his mother, he won't hit his sister, so how in the hell does he figure he can hit you?"

Just talking to Papa lifts a burden off my shoulders. I can talk to Papa better than I can *Mère*. In fact, when I started my period, it was Papa who found out about it, and he took me to the store to get the sanitary napkins. I have friends who swear their fathers are the last people on earth they can talk to. They rarely see their fathers, let alone talk to them.

I often hear some people say that when you return alive from a catastrophic event, like a war, you're a changed person. You've either changed for the better or for the worse. I think the war made Papa change for the better. I think seeing all those people wounded and killed changed his outlook on life. It made him appreciate his family and friends more because when it comes to his family and friends, nobody can out-love him. If I'm hurting, he's hurting, and he makes sure that we never go lacking. Now *Mère* is a different story. I love her very much, but she gave up too soon on Papa. He wanted to please her, but trying to please her broke him. The last straw before they separated happened when Papa bought a house he could afford out in Slidell. *Mère* didn't like it. She complained every day how she hated the long drive into town, and she always found something wrong with the house. Because the Church forbids divorce, *Mère* left instead. I was eleven when they separated, and it was the saddest thing I had ever seen. It was the first time I saw Papa cry. It wasn't a sorrowful cry, but more like a cry filled with anger. For the next seven years my sister and I made sure we spent our summers with him. To tell you the truth, those were the best months of the year.

"I can tell you about love all day and night, but remember this. The only people who truly love you are me and your *Mère*."

Ophelia pretends to cry. "Oh, Papa, that's so sweet." She gives him a hug and a big kiss on the forehead.

Papa sits back in his chair and takes one last puff of his cigarette. "I'm serious," he says. That night, I go to sleep feeling a little better.

Chapter 3

Jerome's hands are trying to ease their way into my blouse. I push them away. He moves in closer and starts wiggling his slimy tongue in and out of my ear.

"Jerome!"

"What?" he responds, irritated.

"Don't."

"Don't what?"

Marvin Gaye's "Stubborn Kind of Fella" plays on the radio.

"You know better."

Jerome eases off and stares ahead. I turn my head to see David and Bettye hugging and kissing on the trunk of the car. Their bodies are pressed together and Bettye's long legs are wrapped around his waist.

Jerome takes my face in the palm of his hand. "What are you looking at? We could be having just as much fun." He leans in to give me a kiss. I quickly turn my head.

Before this point, I had kissed only one other guy. I remember not liking it because he wanted to fill my mouth with his tongue. Besides, I was angry with Jerome from the last time at the diner, and I wasn't going to let him think he could dump me and then try to pretend everything was all right.

"Dorothy, come on," he whispers.

"No. Don't ask me again."

"Come on now."

"No!"

"Forget this."

He opens the door with fury. I thought he was going to rip it off.

"Of all the beautiful women in Louisiana, I end up with a woman like you, a nun. Won't give me none, ain't had none." He shuts the door and walks toward the forest, ranting and raving like a madman. I see him stop to pick up something. He holds it in his hand a while before he throws it out into the darkness.

I don't want to leave the car because Louisiana in the dead heat of summer attracts all kinds of night critters. Besides, my legs can't stand the bites from the bird-sized mosquitoes. I rest my head against the window. I recall a conversation I had with Papa, remembering what he said about boys and love. Papa said don't believe it when a boy says he loves you. If he says he wants to prove it to you, don't fall for it.

I feel the car bouncing and rocking like a boat on the Mississippi. I turn around to see Bettye holding on to David. Her long legs are spread eagle, and her bloomers dangle on the heel of her right shoe. Her arms are wrapped around David's neck while his focus appears to be elsewhere. The light from the moon provides just enough light for me to see the intense look of pleasure fixed in his eyes. Instantly, our eyes connect. Feeling ashamed, I look away. Jerome is still throwing rocks in the pond, shaking his head, disgusted that he isn't getting any action.

Then I hear Bettye scream out, "David!" Then I hear David scream out, "Oh God!" Next thing I see is David running into the woods near Jerome with his pants around his ankles and a silhouette of urine pouring into the pond. I can't believe that people carry on like that with company around. The door opens and Bettye sits in the front seat. Her once neatly pinned French roll looks like a ravaged bird's nest on top of her head. She looks over her shoulder and is stunned to see me in the backseat.

"How long have you been sitting back there?" she asks.

I feel dirty all of a sudden, like some peeping freak whose nasty deed has been unmasked.

With one hairpin stuck in her mouth, she points at me with another one.

"Let me just say this . . . David and I are getting married, so you can give it up. He's mine and I don't plan on sharing him."

What is she talking about? I wasn't thinking about David, and I totally lost respect for him and for her after what just happened not even five minutes ago.

"You don't have anything to worry about," I say to affirm her. "I wish you a lot of luck."

"What are you talking about?" She narrows her eyes to the size of two slits.

"Marriage is a big thing. It's a lifetime commitment."

"What do you know about commitment, little girl?" she asks.

The door opens and Jerome pops his head in, startling me.

"Hey, what's your problem?" he shouts.

"You, if you don't stop screaming in my ear," I yell right back.

"Move over."

"I will, if you ask me like a lady." I fold my arms and remain still.

"Look, I'm trying very hard to be a gentleman right now."

"Could've fooled me," I respond. I notice his temples jumping.

"Yeah, you'll think I'm crazy if I put you out of this car."

I want to see if he is galled enough to do it, so I am as still as a church mouse. "Well, I'm waiting."

At that point David opens the door and starts up the engine. "If y'all don't hurry, I'm leaving both of your asses out here. You got that?" David looks at me. That is the second time I see that killer look in his eyes. Without a word I move over, and Jerome gets in.

"Good looking out, man," Jerome says. He gets in and rolls his eyes at me.

The ride home is a long one with me recalling just how this day started. I had gone to the college campus to help Tiny move into her new dormitory when I saw Jerome, David, and Mike passing by in the convertible. Tulane has a strict policy— there is absolutely no coed mingling in the dormitories, so I reluctantly followed Tiny to the curb so she could talk to Mike. Meanwhile, Jerome struck up a conversation with me, as if he didn't walk out the last time. He invited me to the drive-in to see my favorite actor, Sidney Poitier, in *Lilies of the Field*. How could I turn down his invitation? I absolutely adore Sidney. Besides, I was willing to give Jerome another chance. Big mistake! All during the movie he kept trying to put his hand on my leg. And to make matters worse, he ate most of the popcorn.

I look outside, and high above the Spanish moss rests a full moon.

"I'm going back to Houston for the summer," Jerome says, breaking the twenty-five minutes of silence.

"What time are you leaving?"

"Tomorrow, around one."

"Have a nice trip," I say as if I don't care. The light from the porch comes on, and Papa's huge silhouette appears in the doorway.

"That's your father?" Jerome says. I hear a slight quiver in his voice.

"Yes."

"He's a big man."

"Would you like to meet him?"

"You told your father about me?"

"Yes. He's dying to meet you."

I roll down the window.

"Is that you, Dot?" he asks, leaning forward. "Nice convertible. Who's the driver?"

David waves.

"David, you and Bettye can come in if you want."

"We'll just stay here and wait on Jerome," David insists.

Jerome looks at me. It's the first time I actually see him nervous. He pretends to chew gum, though he doesn't have a trace of it anywhere in his mouth.

"Are you getting out?" I ask, opening the door to the car.

Jerome hesitates. When he approaches Papa, I notice Papa looks him over thoroughly.

"Who are you, young man?" Papa asks.

"Jerome West," Jerome announces in a formal tone.

"I'm Vince Lacroix. What's the matter with the rest of your friends, Dorothy? Why won't they get out?"

"Papa, they can't stay very long. They have curfews."

Papa frowns. "I cooked some black-eyed peas and steamed rice with okra and Creole tomatoes, and I'll be really upset if you don't come in and eat."

Jerome looks at me, his eyes almost pleading for me to say something to convince Papa to change his mind. Before I can say anything, Papa puts his arm around us and walks with us inside.

Ophelia is sitting at the table, eating from a steaming hot bowl of okra and Creole tomatoes with stuffed mirliton.

"Smells good in here," Jerome declares.

"Ophelia, this is Jerome. He's a friend of Dorothy's," Papa says.

Ophelia nods and says a quick "Hi" to Jerome before burying her face in her bowl.

"Ophelia's my baby girl," Papa says to Jerome as they sit down at the table.

I grab a plate and scoop up a helping of steamed rice, and cover it with okra and Creole tomatoes. I use a fork to stick a piece of stuffed mirliton on the side and set the plate before Jerome.

"Papa, you hungry?" I ask.

"Yeah, *bèbe*. Make mine small." He smiles at Jerome. "Dorothy's gonna make some man a fine wife."

"Indeed." Jerome scoops up some food and blows it before eating. "Hmm, this is good."

"So what are you studying?" Papa asks.

"Medicine."

"Is that so? What kind of doctor are you studying to be?"

"A gynecologist, sir."

"Oh yeah. You like bringing *bèbes* into the world?"

I am beginning to enjoy this little conversation. Papa can more than likely get a decent conversation out of Jerome, which is more than I can say for myself.

"Have you ever witnessed natural childbirth?" Papa asks.

"Yes sir, I have."

"I tell you, it ain't a pretty sight to see a woman in that much pain, but it's nothing short of the Creator's miracle when you hear that baby crying."

Jerome chuckles and blows. "It amazes me, too."

"Yeah, I witnessed all three of my girls coming into the world." Papa looks at me. "My Dot here scared the hell out of me when she was born." He looks at Jerome. "The midwife had hell trying to pull her out of Cleo."

I get a visual.

"Then Ophelia, my youngest, she wasn't a problem at all. She took no time getting here. But Dot fought it. She came here kicking and screaming, like she knew something we didn't."

Jerome eats and glances at his watch.

"Can I call you Doc?"

"Sure." Jerome nods.

"Tell me this, Doc. I bet you witnessed a lot of surgery."

"Yes sir. I witnessed open-heart surgery once. The patient was suffering from arteriosclerosis—that's a disease in which the arteries become engulfed in fat. You get these fat deposits that end up blocking the passageway of the blood traveling away from the heart."

Pretty impressive, I think as I listen to him speak.

"You know," Papa begins, "a man I used to work for had to get that surgery you're talking about."

"Do you remember his diagnosis?" Jerome asks.

"All I remember is he had it done a couple of years back. It was so much money, he had to put his land up to cover the costs."

"Very unfortunate, but only the truly wealthy can afford it."

"Why don't you study that?" Papa asks.

Jerome laughs. "You have to be a genius to be an open-heart surgeon."

"You say so, huh? Where did you receive most of your schooling?" Papa asks. He starts coughing again. This time his shoulders shake, and his face turns beet red. "'Scuse me," he says between coughs.

"Here." I give Papa a glass of water. He drinks it with a sense of urgency.

"You okay, Mr. Lacroix?" Jerome stops eating and stands.

Papa pulls out a handkerchief and holds it to his mouth.

"Papa, you need a checkup. Don't you think so?" I ask Jerome.

Jerome nods. "Sounds like it's compacted in your lungs. Do you have difficulty breathing sometimes?"

Papa's coughing ceases. His eyes are watery, and his nose is red from the pressure.

"Good gracious," he says, trying to sound lighthearted. "You hear all that rambling and wheezing, Doc?"

Jerome nods. "If I had my equipment, I'd give you a checkup myself. I don't want to jump the gun and diagnose you, but it sounds like bronchitis to me."

"Oh, it ain't nothing. I got a bottle of castor oil." Papa clears his throat. Whenever I start coughing, I just go in there and take me some."

"Papa, you always say that," I say. "Go get a checkup."

"I don't need to go to the doctor. They don't do anything but look at you, take your temperature, and charge you an arm and a leg."

I give up trying to convince him. Papa slaps Jerome on the shoulder. "I bet when you get established, you'll be charging colored folks an arm and a leg too, won't you, Doc?"

Jerome smiles. "It's what you call a necessary evil. It costs money to maintain a practice. Especially if you have plans like I do, to go into private practice. There are so many fees that sometimes, you have to charge a lot to your patients so you can stay in business."

"Even us poor folk?" Papa asks.

"Not unless you have insurance, and let's face it. Most colored folks don't."

"Where you from, Doc?"

"Houston, sir."

"What part of Houston?"

"Third Ward, sir," Jerome replies in a boasting tone.

"I'm familiar with it. My cousin Vera graduated from Texas Southern." Papa nods. "She's doing all right out there in California. She's a pharmacist."

I observe Jerome. It's funny to see him act civilized for a change. Then, out of nowhere, Papa asks Jerome, "Do you love my daughter?"

Jerome, who finishes up his okra and rice, looks quickly at me, and then Papa. I must admit, Papa's question catches us both off guard. I know Jerome doesn't love me, so I have to defend him. I blurt out, "Papa, Jerome and I aren't steady."

"Why not? A nice young man brings you home after nine o'clock in the evening, and you don't call him a steady?"

"Not how you think it is, Papa," I say, glancing at Jerome's reaction.

Papa strokes his chin, and I can tell something is on his mind because he has that look. He blinks continually, and he sucks his teeth. "Umm-hmm," I hear him say with a hint of doubt.

"I ask you that because I love my daughter. I love all my daughters, and I don't tolerate anyone mistreating them. Do you understand me?" When he says that, his voice shifts to a serious gear.

"Yes sir," Jerome replies. He's sweating so much underneath his neck and around his temples that he reaches in his back pocket and pulls out a handkerchief to wipe his face. Jerome laughs at me. "It's hot, sir," he says and continues to wipe sweat.

"I mean *well* what I said," Papa concludes.

"Papa, it's time for Jerome to leave."

Papa stands and Jerome stands with him. Jerome extends his hand. "Pleasure meeting you, Mr. Lacroix. Thanks for the food. It hit the spot."

"Pleasure's been all mine, Doc. Do you go fishing?"

"Oh yeah, I love to fish. You let me know when."

"Will do."

When I walk outside, I realize how much cooler and refreshing it is compared to inside. Papa says goodnight and shuts the screen door, leaving the front door open. I walk with Jerome toward the car.

"Whew," he sighs. "Your pops is one helluva man."

"I'm glad you met him."

"He cares a lot about you."

"I don't know why he just came out of the blue and asked you that question," I say.

"He's just concerned, that's all. I know if I had a beautiful daughter, I'd be constantly cleaning my pistol."

"You will one day," I say.

Suddenly all I hear are the crickets chirping.

"I had a good time talking to your father." Jerome opens the door to the car. David and Bettye are asleep in the front seat. They both sit straight up when Jerome slams the door shut.

"I'll be seeing you around," he says to me.

"Take care, and goodnight." I look over at David and Bettye. "Good night, y'all."

Without a word David starts up the engine and drives off.

When Ophelia and I arrive at *Mère*'s house in Gentilly, we find her sitting on the couch with a swollen belly between her legs. She is fanning and cursing about the heat and how her thighs rubbed a rash.

"Hello, my *bèbes*," she says with a warm smile. Although my oldest sister Katherine is twenty-two, Ophelia is sixteen, and I am eighteen, she still calls us babies.

"How is your father?" she asks, looking like an exotic Creole queen with her long black hair pinned on top of her head, sitting on a carmine Victorian settee with purple satin curtains behind her.

"He asks about you," Ophelia says. Sometimes she lies, sometimes she tells the truth. The last time *Mère* saw Papa, it was nine months ago when she invited him over to fix a few things around the house. Ophelia and I were wishing they'd get back together, and it seemed all signs were pointing in that direction but, like always, *Mère* found fault. But she must have taken a little time to find something he was doing right. She's pregnant with Papa's baby. She makes us swear to never tell him about the baby, but Papa's not stupid. He knows about it.

"You didn't tell him, did you?"

"Not after you threatened to cut our lips and sell them on the black market. No way, *Mère*."

"Your papa fooling around?" she asks.

I want to tell her, for her information, Papa is beyond the fooling around and playing games stage. He wants stability. Sometimes I find *Mère* in poor taste. That's why I always run away to my Aunt Ruby Jewel and Uncle Herbie's house. My aunt's house is peaceful, and I get along with her and Uncle Herbie. Sometimes I wish Papa had married Aunt Ruby Jewel instead. She is a simple woman with simple wants and needs, like himself. Aunt Ruby Jewel is *Mère*'s older sister but of the two, she looks much younger and is in excellent shape. She can't have children, despite having been to several doctors. She told me her womb is too small to bear children. She says if she was to have a child, it would kill her. She reminds me all the time that God blessed her with beautiful nieces. Uncle Herbie feels the same way, and they spoil us considerably.

"I spoke with Aunt Ruby Jewel," *Mère* tells us. "She says she and Uncle Herbie are moving to Beaumont."

"Why?" I ask.

"Herbie's got a job, working on ships."

"What's wrong with the shipping jobs around here?"

"His brother works there, and he says it pays more." *Mère* leans forward so Ophelia can prop a pillow behind her back.

"When are they leaving?"

"Ruby says in a couple of months. They're gonna stay with a brother until they get a place of their own."

"Sure is gonna be lonesome around here without them."

"It won't be so bad." *Mère* rubs her stomach. "Once I have the little one, we can go spend some time with Ruby on the weekend."

Beaumont, Texas seems so far away.

Chapter 4

My older sister Katherine calls us to say that Papa has lung cancer. When I hear the news, my heart flutters, and for a moment I picture Papa lying in a pearly white casket. I pray to God to make him better. I can't imagine my life without him.

Mère has the baby, a little five-pound girl named Jacqueline. I wasn't around when *Mère* gave birth, but Ophelia was. She told me Father Montague and the Devereaux sisters came by. Father Montague decided to read a scripture from the Bible before the sisters, who are midwives, proceeded with the delivery. Ophelia told me through laughter that *Mère* was cursing and screaming right there in front of them. The sisters did their Hail Marys. She said after a while, she heard *Mère* singing, "Swing low, sweet chariot, come and take my big ass home." Then she heard the baby crying. I told Aunt Ruby Jewel, who was packing for her move to Texas, about *Mère* and the new baby.

"I don't know why she won't tell Vince about it. I always tell her, pride goeth before a fall. She ain't doing nothing but hurting herself."

I fold an apron of hers and place it in a suitcase with the rest of her clothes.

"Cleo was always different from the rest of us. Always thought she was a society queen. I don't know who she's fooling, but people here know a bumpkin from Opelousas when they see one."

"Why are you leaving me, Aunt Ruby Jewel?" I ask.

"Oh *bèbe*, come here." She gives me a tight hug before looking into my eyes. "I'm not gonna be too far from you. Beaumont's just a five-hour drive from here. Every chance I get, I'm coming home to see you." I feel a cold breeze rush through me.

"Why you shaking, *bèbe*?" she asks.

"I'm scared, Aunt Ruby."

"What are you scared of?"

"Papa's sick. Katherine says he has cancer."

"You know, my Bible tells me that nothing's too hard for my God. He can cure your papa's cancer. All you got to do is believe in Him."

"You better call me when you get there." I give her another hug. She excuses herself into another room. I glance at the bare walls that were once covered with pictures. There were pictures of people in my family that dated back to the turn of the century—lots of Creoles dressed in their Sunday best, with complexions ranging from the fairest of skin to visibly black. I have a lot of good memories in this house. I sit by the window and stare at a bed of carnations leading a pathway into a thick forest. I used to play hide-and-seek with Katherine and my other cousins, and we'd get lost among the thickets. In the spring, when the weeds and flowers reached their tremendous heights, Uncle Herbie usually cut them down to burn. We pouted because we didn't want him to level our emerald fortress. Aunt Ruby Jewel also had plentiful magnolias and azaleas, and smelling them reminded me of clean, fresh

Louisiana air. I was going to miss this place. I later find out in a roundabout way that Uncle Herbie and Aunt Ruby Jewel never owned the place, and that they were renting from a white man Uncle Herbie worked for. The man recently died, and now his children are claming their share of the land, which means Uncle Herbie and Aunt Ruby Jewel have to leave.

I spend my days sitting by Papa's bed, listening to him talk. Sometimes he makes sense, and then there are other times when I hear him speak of talking with his mother.

"I'm not a child. I don't have Confession this week," he mumbles. Katherine, who is a nurse, checks his temperature to make sure he doesn't have a fever.

"I'm proud of you girls," he says to us.

"I'm proud of you too, Papa," Katherine says as she gives him a kiss on the forehead.

"Why won't they admit him to the hospital, Katherine?" I ask.

Katherine takes me into the other room and closes the door behind her. "The doctors say that his condition is so bad that they can't treat him."

"So they send him back home to die?"

"Let's be positive, Dot."

I close my eyes and brush back tears. "Just a couple of months ago he was fine. Laughing and smoking his cigarettes."

Katherine wipes away the tears forming in her eyes. "The only thing we can do now is pray and hope that he hangs on just a little longer."

I grab a brush and start brushing Papa's hair. He is forty-three years old and already has amassed fine locks of salt and pepper.

"How is your *Mère* and that new *bèbe*?" he asks with his eyes closed.

"You know about the baby?" I ask.

"A father always knows."

I wonder who told him? "How do you know?" I ask.

"I was there when it happened."

"She had a little girl she named Jacqueline."

"That was my mother's name," he says with a smile.

I massage his temples with the tips of my fingers; already I notice a slight weight loss.

"Papa, I'll be heading off to college soon."

"Yessuh . . . you're going to Southern so you can get your learning. That's the greatest gift you could ever give to yourself: knowledge. That's the key that opens all the doors for you."

"I don't know what I want to do once I leave college."

"Don't worry about that. You keep your focus on right now. Get in, get your lesson, pay attention, meet new people, join a group so you can learn how to deal with people."

"You ever wish you went to college, Papa?"

"Yes, sometimes. It's not too late for me. I'm gonna beat this cancer nonsense, you watch. I'll be taking classes with you."

I stop massaging and give him a big, warm hug. He opens his eyes and gives me a smile. "Don't ever give up on a Lacroix. You come from a long line of survivors. I watched your uncle J.B. get stabbed with a butcher knife once. Now look at him."

"You are a survivor, Papa."

"I know it."

I am enjoying my life at Southern. I met a girl who reminds me of Tiny; her name is Joan St. Julian. We're in the same civics and history classes. Joan is pretty and, like Tiny, speaks her mind and doesn't hesitate to tell you how she feels. We are in civics, talking about the March on Washington and how Martin Luther King's "I Have a Dream" speech made us feel.

"I'm from D.C., and I went to the March," Joan says. "I saw all those people and I thought," she gestures with her hands, "it's a shame that one hundred years after the signing of the Emancipation Proclamation, that Negroes in America are still talking about dreaming." She shakes her head. "It's time we stop dreaming and start waking up. Why are we the only people still dreaming? Immigrants can come over here with nothing and build multi-million-dollar corporations. We've been here over four hundred years and can't even build decent schools for our children." Everyone in the room rallies with her.

"Negroes must wake up and stop relying on the other man and start relying on each other."

Professor Bourgeois nods. "Excellent." he says in northern baritone voice. I look at Joan, whose face is red and warm from her heartfelt speech. Looking at her, I think that she really will make a good lawyer.

There is a gathering at the student union. Southern's chapter of the Student Nonviolent Coordinating Committee is having an interest meeting. Joan tells me what it's about and that she's joining it. I remember what Papa said about being active and involved, so I give it a shot. Tiny informs me that a certain sorority is holding an interest meeting in the home of an alumna. I inform Joan, who declines on the basis that sororities promote elitism. She says they're superficial and she wants no part of it. So I attend the meeting with Tiny, who introduces me to the twelve other ladies in the room. We all sip tea and eat cucumber sandwiches. The alumna, a professor at Southern, is both gracious and elegant in her fine apple-green suit. A majority of the girls here are from the downtown districts of New Orleans. Most of them were educated at Xavier

Prep but decided to come here because they had absolutely no interest in a scientific field. I feel a little odd, being a working-class Creole, but there are some members of the Lacroix family living downtown—like Tiny's, for example. I've learned so much being around her mother, Carolyn, whom I call a New Orleans society maven. In spite of her pedigree, she remains very down-to-earth. *Mère* tries to imitate her, but it comes off as ostentatious.

"I believe you left a really good impression," Tiny says once we leave.

"I was a little nervous."

"About what?"

"Being around all those snooty girls."

"They aren't any better than you. Besides, half of them are legacies."

"Meaning?"

"Their mamas and grandmothers were in the sorority, so more than likely they end up joining."

We get in the car that she's borrowed from David. "How did you manage to get this car without Miss Bettye knowing?"

"Their little ice cream castle is melting."

"She told me they were getting married."

Tiny lets out a big guffaw. "When did she tell you this?"

"A couple of months back."

"I don't see a ring on her finger, and besides, David is too busy asking about you to be concerned with her."

"I don't believe you." My heart flutters at the news.

"Jerome is going steady with some girl from Xavier. He doesn't think anybody knows."

"I don't really like him," I say, recalling the couple of times we've gone on dates. "He moves too fast for me and he likes to kiss with his tongue."

Tiny covers a giggle with her hand. "Dot, that's how it's supposed to be done."

"But they don't do it that way in the movies."

"Oh, come on now, Dot. Kissing with the tongue is the most sensual part of the act. The way a man kisses determines whether he goes to second base."

"I don't like it."

"You just haven't found the right kisser."

"Is Mike a good kisser?"

"He makes my big toe shoot up."

"Has he ever gone to second base?" I ask.

"Oh, lots of times."

"You know, the Church says you have to get married once that happens."

"The Church doesn't have to know."

"But God knows."

"I'll just pray forty times for forgiveness and ask the Lord to give me a clean slate."

"I invited my friend Joan, and she said she doesn't want to be a part of this elitist, superficial group."

Tiny takes her strawberry-red hair and pins it on top of her head.

"It's usually people who don't have a chance of getting in anyway who say that. Where is she from?"

"She's from D.C."

"What part of D.C.?"

"I don't know."

"Probably the ghetto. Let's face it: elitist groups are just that, because they encourage the growth of elitist individuals. Our circle is a tight one and in order to preserve it, you get those who share your backgrounds and your beliefs."

"I wish you could meet her. She reminds me a lot of you. She has a lot of fire and spunk."

Tiny smiles. "You think your cousin has spunk?"

"Of course I do."

"I'm gonna be mud if I don't get this car back to David before curfew."

Joan is reading when I walk into the room. She looks up momentarily before she looks down again into her thick book. I notice she has shelves of books with titles like *Native Son, Invisible Man,* and *The Mis-Education of the Negro* sticking out.

"What are you reading?" I ask.

"The teachings of Karl Marx."

"Who is that?" I ask, taking off my shoes.

"An interesting person with thorough knowledge on class."

"Never heard of him. Is he like Martin Luther King?"

"I guess you can say that. I mean, both men are independent thinkers."

"You ever read any of those books?"

"Of course I have. Read most of them by the time I entered high school."

"I don't believe you."

"Some I've read twice, some three times," she says with a confident smile.

I grab a book at random from the shelf and open it. A picture falls out to the floor. I reach down to pick it up, and it is a black-and-white photo of a group of girls, all white except for Joan.

"Where was this, Joan?" I ask.

"It was in Virginia."

"Were you at school?"

"Yes."

"You went to school with white girls?" I ask.

"I hated every minute of it."

"You went to prep school?"

"It was more like a boarding school. I hated it. They made every possible minute miserable for me."

"Like what did they do, call you names?"

"Not only that, it's the way they look at you and the condescending way they talk to you that lets you know that even if your father is the only Negro chief surgeon of a major hospital and your mother is the great-great-great-granddaughter of the founder of an elite institution of higher learning that, may I add, most of their parents had the privilege of attending, that I will always be second class."

"So you're not from the projects?" I ask, shocked by the news.

"You assumed that because of my outspokenness about poverty conditions that I was from the ghetto?"

"Yes." I shrug.

"You don't have to be from the ghetto to be concerned about it. Just like you don't have to be privileged to feel you have to join up with an elitist group. I'm all about change and seeing Negroes rise up. I don't have time for labels."

I stare at the poster she has on her wall of a colored man with a goatee and horn-rimmed glasses. Underneath are the words *By Any Means Necessary*. She follows my gaze. I close the book. I don't even glance at the title before I stick it back on the shelf.

Katherine and her husband, Ricky, are visiting Aunt Bridgette, *Mère*'s youngest sister. Katherine wears no makeup, which I think is strange seeing as she never leaves the house without it. The moment she looks at me and shakes her head, I assume the worst.

"Papa's not doing good." Her voice cracks.

My heart thumps and pounds against my chest. I feel a sudden ringing in my ears.

"He's giving up. He's not taking his medicine, he's not eating."

Ricky clears his throat. "We've tried everything."

"Don't say that," I tell Ricky.

Katherine looks exhausted. There are dark circles shaped like coals around her eyes and her hair is pulled into a frizzy ponytail. Ricky doesn't look any better. He needs a good shaving, not to mention a haircut.

"I'll go out and spend some time with him," I say.

"No," Katherine insists. "You focus on your studies. Aunt Naomi and Aunt Theresa are helping me."

Aunt Bridgette sets glasses of lemon tea before the three of us. Katherine rests her head in the folds of Ricky's arm. With her eyes pressed shut, she forces a smile. "With all this going on with Papa, I haven't had a chance to see the baby."

"The baby is fine. *Mère*'s been feeding her a lot so, she's all plump and such. She's got the Lacroix mark." I point to my widow's peak.

"That's how you know we're his children. All of us got that Lacroix mark." Katherine chuckles when Ricky points to her forehead.

Katherine and I go to *Mère*'s when the rain clears. *Mère* is happy to see Katherine.

"Hello there, stranger. I forgot I had a daughter your age," *Mère* says when she embraces Katherine. Seeing them embrace each other is like watching someone embrace her reflection in a mirror.

"Where's my little sister?"

Mère smiles. "Sleeping," she says before plopping down on the sofa. She sighs the exact same way as Katherine. It's amazing how they act so much like each other.

"This was much easier when y'all were *bèbes*."

"You think so?" Katherine asks.

"Yes, Lawd," *Mère* declares. She grabs a coin purse from a nearby coffee table. Reaching inside it, she pulls out a cigarette. She places the thin white stick between her ruby-red lips and lights it up. She puffs twice before exhaling a cloud of smoke into the air. I watch as it swirls about the room and I think, *Why on earth would anyone inhale all that smoke?* I imagine it swirling in her lungs, and I think of Papa. It swirled a million times in his lungs, too. Swirled so much that it's built a crusty black monster whose job is to suffocate the life out of its victims. It has them breathing and panting and wishing for cleaner air. I look at *Mère* taking another drag. She has that smoking-a-cigarette look. You know, the one when the smoke gets in your eyes and you frown with your lips half parted.

Katherine reaches into her purse and, to my surprise, she pulls out a cigarette.

"You too?" I ask, disgusted at the sight of her with a cigarette in her mouth.

She cups her hands around the cigarette to keep the flame from flickering out. "Yes." She holds the cigarette between her slender fingers. "Don't look at me like that, Dot."

"Do you want to end up like Papa?" I ask.

Katherine thinks on it, takes a drag, and blows out a cloud of smoke before smashing it in the ashtray.

"Well, I'll be," *Mère* begins. "Katherine, I know you're not gonna sit there and take shit from her. You're a grown-ass woman. Shit. Smoke your damn cigarette if that's what it takes to calm your nerves." *Mère* opens her coin purse and hands Katherine another one. "Don't let this child tell you what to do."

"*Mère!*" I'm appalled that she's encouraging Katherine.

Mère thumps her ashes. "Go to hell, Dot. Leave your sister alone. Let her smoke if she wants to. Ain't nobody gonna end up like yo' papa. Shit, that man's been smoking since he was two."

I don't want to continue with *Mère* because both of us are stubborn and bickering gets us nowhere. Meanwhile, Katherine sits with the unlit cigarette between her fingers. "I just started smoking. Like you say, it calms my nerves."

Mère studies Katherine. "Let me get you some cucumbers for those bags under your eyes. Where's your makeup?" She gets up, walking stiff-legged into the kitchen.

Katherine unties her ponytail and runs her hand through her shoulder-length black tresses.

"Between my hours at the hospital and running out to Papa, sleeping is a luxury I can't afford to have."

"*Bèbe*, at the rate you're going, you're headed for trouble," *Mère* yells.

Katherine places the unlit cigarette on the table beside an old picture of the family in the early fifties. *Mère* returns with a couple of cucumber slices with hints of olive oil on them, and places them on Katherine's eyelids.

"*Mère*, you ought to go see about him. Let him see the baby," Katherine says.

"I ain't going way out there."

"It's just thirty minutes away. It's not like you're driving to Opelousas."

I hear a cough followed by a sharp cry. It's the baby crying in the other room. *Mère* puts out the cigarette and runs into the room. She returns, holding the baby in her arms.

"Look who just woke up."

Mère holds the baby so Katherine can see her heart-shaped face. Katherine's mouth falls open with awe. She reaches out to hold the baby.

"Do you know who I am?" Katherine kisses the baby's rosy red cheeks. "Oh *Mère*, she's so pretty. Hello, precious."

Mère's eyes sparkle. "She's a doll, isn't she?"

Katherine kisses her cheeks again. "Let Papa see her. I don't know why you won't."

"I'll wait until she gets her shots," *Mère* says, taking the baby out of Katherine's arms.

"What are you afraid of? So what if y'all are separated? He's still your husband and this is his child. Let him see her before . . ." Katherine stops herself and bites her lip. She picks up the cigarette. I guess she remembers what I said and drops it back on the table where she found it.

Sunday, a feeling of melancholy hits me, and I realize this may be the last time I ever see my father alive. I arrive to find him on a breathing machine. Aunt Naomi sits nearby.

"How is he today?" I ask.

"He was awake for about thirty minutes," she says softly. She rubs his widow's peak.

"Has he eaten?"

"Yes. He still has an appetite."

I take his bony hands that were once strong and huge and hold them next to my lips.

"Papa, I told you to leave them cigarettes alone . . . now look at you."

His breathing is shallow. I look at a man who was once six foot two and a brawny 225 pounds dissolve into two-thirds of the man he used to be.

"I want to thank you for being so good to me. I'm in a couple of groups at the school, and I'm doing well in all my subjects. I know what I want to major in; I want to major in history. My roommate told me that if I don't educate myself on my history, I'm doomed to repeat it. I'm gonna go, okay, Papa? I love you." I shower his frail forehead and cheeks with light kisses.

Back at school, Joan and some members of the SNCC group are outside the dormitory. I try to walk by without them noticing, but I sense Joan's eyes following me into the building.

Once inside my room, I put on my nightgown and slip into bed. Five minutes later I'm sitting at my desk, crying about Papa. My knees are shaking, and I feel so helpless. I get out *Grandmère*'s rosary beads and repeat *Our Father*, *Hail Mary*, and *Glory Be*. I finish with a sign of the cross and sit at my desk to start writing. I think about a lot of things, the oddest being David. So I start to write him a letter.

Dear David,

How are you? I hope you are doing fine. How is medical school? I'm sorry to hear that things aren't going well for you and Bettye. I always thought you two were the ideal couple. I am sitting at my desk in Baton Rouge, a little sad because I'm not closer to home. My papa is ill, and it appears that his days are uncertain. He is the light of my life, and it hurts to see him wasting away. When you study, think of him and think of ways of finding a cure for cancer. It is a beast and it wipes out the strongest among us. Keep him in your prayers.

Yours truly,
Dorothy

A week later I receive a letter from David. I sit on my dorm floor and proceed to read it.

Dear Dorothy,

I was stressed out, but your letter made everything all right for me. I don't usually write letters, but when I received yours, I had to make an exception. I know I don't have the best penmanship in the world, but how many doctors you know do, for that matter? So all I can say is make out what you can of my writing.

Jerome saw the letter you wrote. He wondered why you chose to write me instead of him. He wanted to know if you and I were going steady. I told him that if I got the opportunity, I was going to take you out. He pretended he didn't care, but it obviously bothered him seeing as it's been a week since we spoke last.

Enough with Jerome. In your letter you said you were stressed out due to your father's illness. All I can say is be there for him, and try to expect the best. If there's anything I can do, let me know. I know words can only go so far, and in situations like yours, good family support definitely helps. Speaking of family, your cousin Tiny is a very nice person; I don't care if she is short and noisy.

I'm sure you've heard by now that Bettye and I aren't together. For five years I thought the sun rose and set around her. I had known her since our undergraduate years at Xavier. Well, I thought I knew her, but I realized that the person I grew to love was still a stranger. Do I still love Bettye? I do care about her still, and I hold no ill feelings toward her. It's just in the case with Bettye, the magic has worn off. Will I ever go back to her? I don't believe so this time around. We've separated on many occasions and reconciled, but this time it's over for good. Did Bettye try to hurt herself? Yes, she did, and that's something I am very bitter about. When we broke up, we agreed we were not going to be childish and there weren't going to be any hard feelings. So we left it at that. About a day later, I get a call from Bettye's parents. Her father is cursing at me because he's heard only her side of the story. So I drive to the hospital—mind you I have exams and I'm in the middle of studying—and her parents are giving me a difficult time. So I tell them my side of the story. I explain to them that Bettye told me how she felt. I told her how I felt, and she appeared to take our breakup well. Big mistake. Her parents don't believe me, and they're threatening to call the school and have me expelled. That's where I drew the line.

Dorothy, I'm glad you decided to write me. I wish I wasn't studying so that I could see you. If you find some time to come up for air again, don't forget to keep in touch.

Sincerely,
David

David has a lot on his mind and like me he needs someone to talk to. Once I get on line with the sorority I think I'm going to bubble over like a pot of boiling hot water. I need a network to express my feelings. I find one in David, because for the next three weeks, we write each other back and forth. His words get me through hell week. When it comes time to cross the burning sands, I am able to do so with confidence with the assurance there is a letter of good cheer waiting for me once I get back to the room. He is a great advisor, very wise and intelligent to be so young. I am looking for someone like that.

I let Joan read my letters. "Impressive, once you sift through the handwriting."

"I used to date his best friend. You don't think there's anything wrong with that?"

Joan thinks about it for a second. "That depends . . .give me some details and be honest." Joan sounds like somebody's parent.

"I used to date Jerome, and to be honest, we only went on two dates. It wasn't serious. Besides, we've never even kissed."

"Who do you like the most?" she asks.

"David, only because we've been corresponding with each other."

"Then that's who you should go with . . . you want somebody who will listen to you. Communication is key to a good solid relationship."

"That's exactly what my papa said." Melancholy takes over when I think about him.

"Does David make you laugh in those letters?"

"Lots of times."

"Does he make you think?"

"Always."

"Then get your man," she says.

"Why don't you have a steady?" I ask.

"I'm too busy getting ready for the revolution," she says.

"I see," I respond, not quite understanding what the revolution is. The funny thing that comes to mind is the war that's going on. I know she's not talking about going to war.

Everyone is talking about Kennedy's assassination. It's on every channel and graces the front cover of every newspaper out there. Not once did I see anything on Papa's death, not even in the daily newspaper's obituary section. Papa died on the twenty-third of November around nine in the morning. Katherine called and told us. She said when she went into Papa's room, she noticed his eyes were pressed shut and his face was still and solemn. When she called out his name he didn't answer, so she called out his name once more, but still no answer. As she told me, I could see a picture of sun rays beaming down on Papa's bed, and I could see his spirit rising from his body and him vanishing into the rays. After calling his name for a third time, she checked his pulse and felt nothing. She said she held on to Papa's corpse and cried.

Mère and I were going to see him this weekend with the baby. I feel drunk, nauseated, and I want to throw up everywhere. It has to take some time to sink in, but when it does, I explode. Papa? Dead? It's unbearable to mention it in the same breath. Now the hardest thing for me to do is go home and face Ophelia and *Mère*. When I arrive at home, *Mère* is sitting in the living room listening to Mahalia Jackson, of all people. She doesn't look at me when I walk in. The room smells like bourbon. I notice on the floor next to *Mère*'s foot is a half-empty glass decanter with the remains of the bubbling brown liquid in it. Ophelia is sitting across from *Mère*, absorbing Mahalia's voice. Listening to her sing is haunting. Her voice sounds like she, too, is mourning Papa's death. When Ophelia sees me, she stands up. I see tears glistening in her eyes. She's sobbing as she walks toward me. I embrace her and we both sob. Listening to Mahalia sing doesn't make the situation better; she only is adding to the sorrow.

"*Mère*'s not talking," Ophelia says between each sob. "All she's been doing is drinking." I look at *Mère*, who's sitting with her back to us, staring out the window. Her silky black hair is down, and her shoulders are slumped over. I can't tell whether she is crying but from the way she sways left and right, I can tell she is hurting. I know that for sure because she plays Mahalia whenever someone dear to her dies, like *Grandmère*. I walk toward *Mère*, but something tells me to leave her alone with her thoughts.

The first of the Lacroix family arrives around eight the morning of the funeral. By ten o'clock there are so many cars lined up in front of the house and craziness inside. Katherine arrives, dressed all in black, with her husband, Ricky. We embrace. I try to hold back the tears with a smile, but I can't. All around I hear muffled voices and Katherine's voice trying to soothe me.

"Where's *Mère*?" she asks, her eyes moist.

"In the room getting dressed."

She touches my crimson cheeks. "He's gone to a better place. I know it."

I touch her hand and hold it next to my cheek, crying. Katherine tries to fight back tears by biting her bottom lip. "Come on, now. Papa wouldn't want us carrying on like this."

I nod and wipe away tears. I watch as she walks through a crowd of our relatives. Everyone tries to hug and console her, but she doesn't stop to talk. I can tell her mind is on *Mère*.

Claire, my cousin from California, enters the room, decked in black. I know as soon as we embrace I will start crying again. Her mother Vera, who is Papa's second cousin, embraces me. She cups my face in her hands. "Be strong," she says. I wish I could.

I look at the front door and notice as Tiny and Carolyn enter, both looking fabulous with their hair pinned identically, and both wearing eye-catching pendants over their black suits. Tiny and Carolyn both embrace me. They are refreshing. Carolyn takes my hand. I look into her eyes and notice they are the color of the sky on a clear day.

"I'm so proud of you for being such a wonderful daughter. You always knew that your papa deserved the best." Before I can say anything else, she moves on to the next person, offering good cheer in her refined, elegant, and kind way. Confused, I look at Tiny.

"What is she talking about?" I ask.

"Oh, don't worry about it," she says, taking my hand.

At the funeral, I sit and my mind wanders. I see the priest's lips moving, but I don't hear anything. I know Papa was a good man and a devoted father who bragged to the world about his girls. I know Papa served his country with honor in World War II. I know Papa was a devoted church member of St. Mary's Catholic Church, up until the very end.

I look at *Mère*, sitting on the corner holding two-month-old Jacqueline, who is sound asleep. The black veil covers her face so I can't see her eyes. I remember when we left home, she was wailing about how hard it is for her to make it. She never stopped loving Vince Lacroix. We recite the rosary and sing the *Gloria Patri*, but Papa's favorite was "I'll Fly Away." I remember when I was younger, Papa used to take us to this little diner near Elysian Fields to hear his favorite band play. They played "I'll Fly Away," but I remember it having a secular feel to it and people grooving to it like a blues tune. I'll never forget how the people were dancing, and some started to shout. Papa was dancing, too. It was surreal and bizarre at the same time. I glance at Papa's pearl white casket and picture him dancing around heaven, making the people laugh the way he made me and Katherine and all these people laugh.

I can't stop crying at the end of the service. My mind keeps saying, *This is it. This is the last time.* My sisters can't calm me; my cousins can't calm me. I flinch every time someone touches me to comfort me.

Then, out of nowhere, I feel a great abundance of warmth. I look up and, to my surprise, I see David. When he embraces me, I collapse in his arms. He feels warm, tender and, secure. When we release ourselves from each other, I see something in David's eyes that I had not seen in any other man's eyes. I see a look of assurance, a look that says to me, *Dorothy, you don't have to worry anymore.* David takes a soft hand and gently wipes away a tear streaming down my cheek. He doesn't have to say anything to make it all better for me; his touch is enough.

Dear David,

  Thanks for everything. I wasn't expecting you to come down. It was an overwhelming surprise, and I can't stop thinking about it. I wish we could've spent more time together. Thanks for the pink roses and the conversation. I wish you could've known my papa. He would have loved you, David.

Yours truly,
Dorothy

Chapter 5

The fall session is over, and everyone has left for the holidays. I spend the majority of the days with Katherine and Tiny, helping to clean up Papa's house. He has old pictures that look like they've been around since the days of slavery. I show them to Tiny.

"My papa has that exact same picture," Tiny says, taking it and wiping the dust away from it. "It's our great-great-grandparents."

The man in the picture is wearing an 19th-century tuxedo, and he is flanked by a woman whose corset is tied so tight that her waist appears small in contrast to the rest of her attire.

"This must've been taken in the 1800s," I guess.

"*Gendes de colour libre*, is what Papa said to me." Tiny sits the picture next to an old faded picture of a grand house. "They had a lot of land in Opelousas. They also had slaves, too."

"Slaves?" My eyes widen with discovery of the news.

"Yeah. Our family owned slaves."

The news stuns me. "How could we own slaves?"

"Our family owned land with a free and clear title, and had been owners of the land since the early 1800s."

"How do you know all this?"

"My mother. She's working on a book about our family."

"I would never have imagined black people owning slaves."

"It was more common than you think."

We stop for a moment to sit. "I wonder what David is up to," I say.

"Probably somewhere picking out some flowers for you," she says with a smile.

"You think I should go out with him?"

"Of course. He's available and let me tell you, if you don't go out with him, there are a lot of girls who will."

I feel myself blushing.

"You're all he talks about, Dorothy."

I squeal, "Really?"

"He talks about you so much that he puts me and Mike to sleep."

"I don't know. He and Jerome are best friends. They think alike."

"No, they don't," Tiny responds quickly. "David knows how to treat a woman, and you don't have to worry about him seeing other girls. He is twenty-three years old and very sure of himself. He knows exactly what he wants and I tell you, it isn't Bettye," Tiny says with conviction.

"How do you know this?"

Tiny takes off her shoes and rolls her feet. "I do my homework."

"He told you to tell me this?"

"Of course not," she says, fighting to keep a straight face.

"Tiny, I'm scared."

"Scared? Who are you scared of? Jerome?"

"No."

"Then why are you scared?"

"Things could get serious."

"Don't you want that?"

"Yes, I do, but I'm scared that David might end up treating me like Jerome did."

A look of disgust is on Tiny's face.

"What?" is all she says. It's like she can't believe I thought that way about David. She laughs. "Oh, cousin, you are dealing with the wrong type of guy. Not every man is like Jerome West." She rolls her feet counterclockwise. "From here on out, I don't want to hear any more excuses. You need to go steady. Work on your M.R.S. degree."

"What's that?"

"You know, a Mrs. degree—that great big American dream—the husband, the two kids, a dog, and a great big house with a white picket fence."

Later that night, Tiny, David, Mike, and I ride around gawking at Christmas lights while listening to Nat King Cole. David looks so handsome in his black Botany 500 jacket and tie. He's dressed like the preppy white boys I see in the J.C. Penney catalogs. His cologne, intertwined with aftershave, smells like he's been in the shower for hours. I'm nervous. I haven't seen David since Papa's funeral, and I'm anxious for a conversation, anything to break the silence and small talk.

"David, every time I see you, you're dressed so nice."

When he smiles, I notice a small dimple near the corner of his chin.

"Only the best," he says, keeping his eyes on the road. I look outside my window at the rows of houses and Christmas lights.

"Dorothy, you look beautiful tonight," he says. "Of course, you look beautiful all the time."

"Wheeew!" I hear Tiny squeal from the backseat. She and Mike find it amusing.

"Cool-Hand David has a way with the ladies," Mike adds from the backseat. David smiles, only a little. I notice he has a habit of licking his lips to keep from laughing.

"I meant every word of it," he says, staring at me. His eyes sparkle from the incoming traffic lights. My heart starts pounding, and I begin to perspire underneath my arms.

"David, you remember Norm from Xavier?" Mike asks.

"What about him?"

"He's back in town from Meharry. Told me he's having a little soirée tonight."

"Parents out of town?" David asks. He licks his lips again.

"Gone for the winter. Norm was supposed to go with them, but he fed them some lie about taking a job during the break."

"Do I remember Norm?" Tiny asks, feeling a little left out.

"He took civics with us," Mike says.

"Always fell asleep in the back of the class?"

"Slept his way through Xavier. Folks just paid top dollar to get him into Meharry."

"He won't last through next semester." David rounds the corner and parks the car.

"Since when did they start letting Negroes live in the Garden District?" I ask. I watch as David walks around the car and opens the door for me. I take his hand, and I am amazed once I get out. The first thing I notice is the Boston ivy covering the wrought-iron fence. I can't help but touch it.

"You always had Negroes living over here," David says, "except they don't think they're Negroes."

Mike helps Tiny out of the car. "They call themselves Creole," she says, finishing his sentence. The gate to the place is locked, and outside I see three preppy guys—two Negroes and one white—in the courtyard smoking funny-smelling cigarettes.

"Norm," Mike yells from behind me.

The guy named Norm takes one long drag of his cigarette and acknowledges us with a quick nod. He doesn't appear to be in a hurry to unlock the gate by the way he drags himself over. He's crooning, all the while trying to puff on that funny-smelling cigarette. He unlocks the gate.

"Where's y'at? Where's my girl?" he asks Mike and David, slurring his words. His breath smells like he's been cocktailing Sazeracs. He looks at me. "I don't believe we've met." He reaches out to shake my hand, but David intercepts him.

"Whatever it is you've been drinking, you need to ease up on it," David says, looking Norm square in the eye.

"No disrespect. I didn't know she was yours." Norm moves back, holding up his hands, indicating he may have crossed the line. His eyes change lickety-split from dazed to upbeat with a glimmer. "You got to let me know something. *Laissez les bon temps rouler*," he chuckles before leading us past the other, two who stand with their hands in their pockets, smoke whirling from their nostrils.

Norm offers Mike his funny-smelling cigarette. Mike takes it. After a long drag, he offers it to David, who looks at me and then back at Mike before he declines. Mike offers it Tiny who, to my surprise, grabs it and takes a long drag. She gives it back to Norm.

"Good stuff, just off the boat," Norm says before opening the huge Spanish-style door of a home packed from wall to wall with people. Chubby Checker's voice is telling everyone to twist, and they don't hesitate. I see a lot of arms swinging, skirts twisting, and feet shuffling. I hear a lot of good-time laughter and singing with the music. Girls are squealing while the guys bask in the glory of their skirts. David takes my hand, and we manage to find a seat near a corner of the room.

"This house is jumping tonight," David says. "Can you dance?"

"I've been known to cut a step or two." He glances at me as to say, *I'm scared of you, Dorothy Lacroix.*

"Can you dance?" I ask.

"Yes, I can dance."

"You're gonna have to prove it to me," I say.

Staring at me with handsome brown eyes, he nods. "I will turn this place out."

On the floor, Mike and Tiny are all into the music; they move all the way down to the floor doing the twist. Tiny looks so cute in her pink cashmere sweater, twisting all over Mike. The expression on her face says, *You can't mess with me when we twist. Honey, I made this gig.* I check out the room and notice a lot of girls dressed in their cashmere sweaters and the guys looking dapper in slacks and shirts with ties. Everybody is so lively. It could be the music, it could be the alcohol or those funny-smelling cigarettes lingering in the air. I think I speak too soon because Jerome stumbles through the crowd, looking like a lost animal with his lips hanging down a mile and his eyes a sulky mess. Two girls walk by him. He revels at the sight of their wiggling hips.

"Guess who's here," I say to David over the loud music. He follows my gaze, spotting Jerome in the center of the room, laughing out loud and hugging Mike. I notice Mike grimacing.

"Stay here. I'll be back." David walks to the floor.

When he leaves, Norm sits in his place.

"Hello. You never told me your name."

I clear my throat. "It's Dorothy."

"Dorothy, like in the *Wizard of Oz*, right?"

"That's right." I glance around the room, taking in the crowd. All at once, I feel shy talking to him.

"Where's your drink?" he asks, leaning in closer.

"I don't drink," I say affirmatively.

"Where are you from?"

"Gentilly."

"Gentilly people drink. My folks let me drink from the time I was three years old. I know good wines, been all over France. I got a bottle I want to share with you."

I fidget uncomfortably, waiting for David to get back so he can leave. "That's okay," I say.

"You nervous?" He covers my hand with his.

"No." I quickly remove it.

"I won't bite. Though I'm not gon' lie. When I saw you earlier, you know what you reminded me of?"

"I'm afraid to ask."

"I'll tell you . . . Bananas Foster. It's the God-honest truth."

He moves in a little closer. I inch farther away. I feel half of me hanging off the edge of the chair.

"So you're David's new girl?" He chuckles.

"What's so funny?" I ask, almost in David's defense.

Norm brushes the fine hairs forming on his top lip with his finger. "It's just that I invited a lot of people here, and when I say a lot of people, you might get unlucky and run into somebody you might not want to see tonight."

"Like you." I stand and make my way through the crowd. I hear him shouting behind me, but I pay no attention.

"Dorothy, where are you going?" I hear a familiar voice. The place is so crowded that I didn't notice I had walked past Jerome and David.

"Jerome," I shout back.

Jerome grabs me and holds me in his arms. I feel his lips touch the side of my neck and when I try to pull away, he pulls me back to kiss his lips. His breath reeks with alcohol.

"C'mon now, Dorothy, give me one right 'chere." He puckers his lips. I glance quickly at David. I can't understand why he isn't stopping it.

"Dorothy, I haven't seen you in so long, girl. Can we go

somewhere and talk for old times' sake?" He puts his arm around me, stumbling, "You look so pretty tonight. Doesn't she, David?"

"That's enough," David finally says.

Jerome releases me and just stands there. "I can't believe you took my girl. She was my girl." He points to himself for emphasis.

"Let's talk about this outside," David says, cool and calm.

"I don't wanna talk. I want my girl back." His jaw bloats and his chest heaves like he might hurl on Norm's mama's cypress floor.

David grabs him. Mike comes over and they both escort him outside.

"Let go of my arm. Ain't a damn thing wrong with me," he shouts. I follow them outside, with Tiny close behind me.

"Why did you show up here with my girl?" Jerome shouts in David's ear. I see precipitation from the moist air coming from his lips. He keels over and hurls pinkish white-and-yellow vomit on the sidewalk and all over David's shiny black shoes.

"Son of a bitch!" David knees him in the side.

Jerome ups and surprises David with a punch to the stomach. Mike runs over to intercept the next punch.

"Break this shit up! Y'all know NOPD is hell on a Negro 'round here."

Jerome wipes away the sweat pouring like a leaky faucet down his dark brown skin.

David, with one hand holding on to his stomach, points at Jerome. "You better be glad he got here."

"Ah come on, fellas," Tiny says, sounding diplomatic. "Be civil and hash it out in the morning."

"There ain't gonna be no hashing out in the morning. I want this out and settled right here," Jerome shouts.

"What are you trying to do, ruin the night for us?"

"I want my girl back," Jerome shouts.

"My cousin doesn't want you. Look at you. You are one pathetic-looking Negro."

"Stay out of this, Tiny," Mike says, taking her hand, "and take Dorothy back inside."

"I hate that my cousin ever got mixed up with the likes of you in the first place."

"What the hell do you mean by that?" Jerome starts walking in our direction.

"I said, take Dorothy back inside. We'll handle this." Mike nods in the direction of the house.

"Come on, let's go," Tiny says, still glaring at Jerome. "I feel a drink coming on."

Inside, a bartender pours us a glass of red wine. Tiny takes a look at the bottle.

"Umm, '61 that was a good year." She sips. I still hold on to mine, not yet taking a sip, not sure if I'm gonna like it.

"Can you believe the nerve of him, trying to pick a fight? '*I want my girl back*,'" she says, mimicking Jerome's voice. "Let me tell you something about Jerome. He tells everybody that he's from this part of Houston called the Third Ward, and he wants everybody to think he's like us. Quiet as it's kept, Jerome's mother is actually the Leonard family help. They don't know where the father is. David said they hired her when Jerome was a little boy, and they sort of grew up like brothers. But Jerome was always bothered that David got handed everything and he didn't. But, he's the son of the help, and unless the Leonards include him in the will, he ain't much."

I set my drink down and watch as two couples slow dance in front of us. They are necking like nobody's business. I tap Tiny on the arm. "Look at those two."

Tiny shakes her head. "That's a shame. They might as well go home."

We giggle.

"So, Dorothy, what do you think of David?"

"He's a gentleman."

"He comes from a good family, and he's really good people. Mark my words, in two years you and David are walking down the aisle."

I feel myself blush as I picture that moment.

"Two years?"

"It could be sooner or could be later, whatever. I'm getting some really good vibes."

"When we do, you'll be the first to know."

"I better be."

"I'm going to the powder room. Hold my seat, please." I place my wineglass on top of the bar.

"Don't be long. They're playing my song and I want to dance." She snaps her fingers.

I move in slow motion through the crowd upstairs to where there are couples kissing in the hallways. In another room is a group of men and women engaging in a card game. I walk farther down the crowded hall, asking for the bathroom until I find it. It is rather large with gold-handled faucets and a free-standing tub with a sheer wrap-around silk shower curtain. I move the curtains back just out of habit to make sure no one is there. Just as I open my purse to look inside for my lip rouge, the door opens and in the reflection of the mirror, I see Bettye, David's ex-girlfriend.

"I thought that was you," she says.

"Hi," I respond, and for the strangest reason I feel nervous.

"I was just on my way out when I saw you passing by." Her voice is calm and strangely soothing.

I don't know what to say, so I reach into my purse and pull out my lip rouge. I don't know what state of mind she's in, but I'm prepared for anything.

"Are you happy now?" she asks.

I'm still speechless.

"For Christ's sake, say something."

I take a deep breath. "Bettye, if you think I had anything to do with you and David breaking up, I swear to you, I didn't."

"Ever since that day in the diner, I could sense things between him and me were not going to be the same."

"I'm sorry, Bettye."

I see a tear glistening in the corner of her left eye and her bottom lip trembling.

"Just a word of advice to you, Dorothy."

"Yes?"

"Beware. Things aren't always what they appear, and that's all I have to say to you." The tear begins to fall down her cheek. I feel like crying myself.

"I wish you the best of luck. Make a better man of him. God knows I couldn't."

She grabs a tissue nearby and removes her glasses. I watch in silence as she wipes away tears and walks solemnly out the door. I want to grab her and say, *Stop. Please come back and tell me more*, but something inside urges me to leave well enough alone. I feel a sudden numbness and my arms are trembling. I feel like I'm in the twilight zone and everything, including me, is moving in slow motion. I gather my things and walk back out into the hallway, hoping I can catch a glimpse of her. I search high and low for her, but I don't see her. I find Tiny dancing and having a good time.

"Hey Dot, remember this song?" she asks, snapping her fingers and moving up and down like she's on a seesaw.

"Yes, girl," I say, pretending to sound upbeat and in high spirits.

David and Mike arrive twenty minutes later. David is looking the room over.

"Tiny, I see David and Mike by the door. I'll be back."

When David sees me finally, we hug like we never have seen each other before.

"Where's Jerome?" I ask.

"I don't know, and right now, I don't care."

"Is he going to be okay?"

I feel a stinging glare from David. He doesn't answer and I don't push the question any further. I quietly take his hand and lead him to our seats. He and Mike pull up a couple of chairs.

I can't help but wonder if he ran into Bettye on his way in. I can't get her words out of my mind, and what really shocks is how she managed to stay calm.

"Come on, let's dance," I hear David say to me. I take his hand and follow him to the edge of the dance floor where it isn't crowded.

"I like this song," David says. It's the Inkspots' "I Only Have Eyes for You." I wait until David leads the first step before I follow. He holds me, and I relax and rest my head on his chest. Now and then I look up into his eyes. He smiles and continues to lead me along. I like the way we move. I don't want the song to end.

We leave that night, listening to Nat King Cole and joking about everything.

"Mike, is it true?" Tiny asks out of the blue.

"True about what?" Mike responds with a puzzled look in his eyes.

"I saw Eunice de Mille at the party tonight, and I heard you two had a little history together. True or no?" She looks him straight in the eye.

Mike shakes his head. "No."

"Liar."

"Honest! I swear on a stack of bibles and my *Memère*'s grave."

"She was sure giving me the evil eye tonight. I thought I was gonna have to give her a piece of my mind."

"If she was giving you the evil eye, it was because you kept staring at her, urging her on," Mike says.

"Did not."

"Did too."

"Did not."

David laughs so hard that he nearly chokes. I've never seen him this lively before.

"What's so funny, David?" Tiny eyes him suspiciously. "You want to share with us? Heck, I want to laugh, too."

Mike starts to snicker to himself. Tiny slaps his arm. "Stop laughing. You're working my nerves."

Mike stops and fights his laughter with a phony smile.

"I still say you're telling me a tale."

"Okay, Ms. Christine Lacroix, answer this. Did you key my car and put my tires on flat?"

Tiny sits there silent for a second. "What kind of woman would do a thing like that?" I can't tell if she's being serious or not.

"The kind who thinks her boyfriend is cheating, that's who."

"I-I-I . . ."

"I-I-I my foot, you did it."

"Prove it."

"Don't come here with that legal bull. I know you."

"No, you don't. I let you know what I want you to know."

Mike waves his hand. "I don't want to hear it. Besides, I'm tired of you anyway."

"I'm tired of you too, now." Tiny sticks out her tongue like a young, immature schoolgirl. She glances at me. "So what's gonna become of you two?"

I look over my shoulder to see her smiling, her chin resting on top of the seat. David glances at Tiny.

"None of your business," he says, licking his lips.

"My cousin is my business," Tiny fires back, sticking out her tongue. "Why don't you two kiss and get it rolling here?"

Mike taps her on the arm. "Stop instigating."

Tiny bounces up and down like a kid. "My cousin has never been with a man before."

"Shhh." I feel slightly embarrassed.

"That's nothing to be ashamed of. I would take back my virginity in a heartbeat." Tiny says. She rolls her eyes at Mike.

"Tiny, what did you have to drink tonight?" David asks.

"Don't get off the subject. I want you to kiss my cousin."

"I'll kiss her when she's ready and with fewer people around."

"You two ain't no fun." Tiny pouts and falls back to the seat.

Once we come to my house, David stops the car and shuts off the engine.

I hear Tiny and Mike kissing in the backseat.

"Good night, David. I had a good time with you."

"I plan to see a lot of you."

"Me too."

He takes my hand and holds it. "You know," he begins in a low and sensuous voice, "I like you. I really, really like you. You're beautiful, you're smart, and you're a very classy lady."

"You think so?"

"Yes." His expression is so intense I feel it burning through my blouse. He moves in closer and touches the tip of my chin with his finger. He looks into my eyes, and without a word, he kisses me . . . sweet and gentle and full of emotion. When we stop he looks at me. "How do you feel?"

I think about Bettye and what she said, and I erase my doubts.

"I feel really warm inside."

He plants a tender kiss on my forehead. I forget about Tiny and Mike in the backseat. We hold each other in a tight embrace before he kisses me again, and again, and again. On the radio Nat King Cole sings, "Unforgettable." *Oh yes, that is my song. Our song.*

Chapter 6

Time sure does fly when you're in love. I mark an X through the day on the calendar when it hits me that David and I have been courting for a year and a half. Today he graduates from medical school, and this will be the second time in a year that I see his parents. I met the Leonards last year when they came to New Orleans for a visit. My first impression of the Leonards? Very aristocratic.

I felt Mrs. Leonard fall in love with me the moment we met. She hugged me and whispered, "Welcome to the family." She is beautiful; her flawless *café au lait* complexion has a glow about it, reminding me of Dorothy Dandridge. She moves with grace and spunk like Eartha Kitt. She was a serious dresser with impeccable style. David gets his sense of style from her. His father, on the other hand, is a stocky man of medium height with a loud voice and a boisterous laugh. He has all the characteristics of a prestigious doctor: a clean bald head and mustache-free look, which makes him look a lot younger. He was very affectionate with me, which made me feel uncomfortable at first, but then I realized it was part of his charm. I also noticed he was flirtatious with his eyes—winking at the white hostess when we walked in and nodding and smiling at a table full of Creole ladies, decked out in their Sunday best. We met for dinner at a restaurant on the lake, and his parents already had us married and living near them in Houston. I don't like Houston. The town doesn't have a sense of charm like New Orleans does.

I sit next to David's parents at his graduation ceremony. *That's my man*, I tell myself when he glances at me and his parents. Mrs. Leonard dabs her eyes and puts on her most dignified pose. In that moment, she and I both share a spot on top of the world. I glance at David's father. He has that nod of approval. I notice his eyes are pressed shut underneath his glasses. It looks like he is praying: *Thank you, Jesus, the tradition lives on*. A tradition, I discovered, that dated back to the turn of the century with David's grandfather. Dr. Alfred C. Leonard was the son of a wealthy white benefactor who had an affair with a young Negro teacher. Alfred Leonard went on to become president and founder of the Texas Board of Negro Physicians. His two sons—Alfred C. Leonard II and David Claude Leonard, Sr.—soon followed in his footsteps.

After the ceremonies, Norm's family, the Prejeans, host a soirée for David and Mike in their home. I never thought I'd stop smiling and posing for pictures. After three hours of it, I am plum exhausted. I find a guest room upstairs and convince myself that all I need is twenty minutes of shut-eye. I curl up on the Louis VXII chair facing the fireplace and close my eyes. Somewhere between dreaming and reality I hear laughter. It's very familiar laughter, the high-pitched giggling of a female commingling with the sound of someone blowing his nose.

"You think she'll like it?" It sounds like David's voice.

"Of course she'll like it. I'd take it if you weren't marrying her."

"Emma, it wouldn't work out." It is David's voice. I hear sniffing sounds. "You and I are too much alike."

I peek over the top of the chair and see David sitting on the edge of the bed. Norm's sister, Emma Prejean, stands in front of the door holding the knob. The light from the lamp casts a sad aura over her pasty white face. David is hunched over the nightstand, sniffing.

"I'm glad you're marrying her and not Bettye. She was sneaking with Norm, anyway."

"Have you seen Dorothy?" David rises up before falling back slowly across the width of the bed. I notice his lashes batting like crazy.

"You okay?" Emma walks over and takes what appears to be a mirror out of his hand. "Son of a bitch, you damn near used all of it."

"Go find Dorothy for me."

"Fuck you. Go find her yourself." She falls on the edge of the bed next to him and begins sniffing from the mirror. I turn around to face the fireplace. My heart is racing like the speed of light, and I want to make a sound to let them know that they're not alone in the room. I have a better idea. I get up and walk to the edge of the bed. Emma screams, tossing the small mirror on the floor, shattering it to a million little pieces. White powder is everywhere, even on the tip of her nose. David stands to his feet. I see sweat pouring off the sides of his face.

"What the hell is going on?" I hear myself say.

"How long have you been in this room?" David ignores my question.

Emma takes my hand. "It's okay, Dorothy. We were just talking. It's nothing, seriously."

"Emma, just go and let us talk, okay?" David ushers her to the door.

"But who's gonna clean up this mess?" I notice she is sweating, and white spit is forming on the corners of her mouth.

"What do you want to talk about?" I begin once he closes the door.

"What I have planned for us."

"How do you expect me to feel when I see you here with another girl?"

"I'm sure you heard everything we said."

He comes closer and starts kissing me. "I promise you, tonight was the first and the last time. Now, give me some love."

That night David checks us into one of the finest colored-owned bed-and-breakfasts in New Orleans. I'm quiet and trembling, wondering what I've just gotten myself into. He opens the door to a room with white satin sheets, white sheer lace curtains, and a white sofa with an ottoman. The walls are painted a yellow pastel color and fresh flowers and a bottle of red wine are on the nightstand.

"I'm gonna take a shower. You ought to come in and join me." He flicks on the light to the bathroom and turns on the shower. Today is my twentieth birthday, and I should be feeling more upbeat, but after what I just witnessed, my spirit feels broken. I hear the shower gushing water and splashing what I imagine to be David's naked body. In the year and a half we've been dating, I've never seen David without a shirt, let alone naked. I lie stretched across the bed until I feel something wet and slippery slithering against my legs. I turn around and there he is, dripping wet and wearing nothing but a smile. I can't help but smile.

"You satisfied, now that you got me all wet?"

Without a word, he gets on top of me and begins to unfasten the buttons on my dress one by one. He studies each button carefully as though he's examining a patient in the hospital. *Oh God, I think this is really gonna happen.*

After he unbuttons my dress, he takes me in his arms and removes the rest of my clothing. I feel the tickling effect of the water dripping from his flesh onto mine. I feel goosebumps. My backbone arches, and my spine tingles from the touch of his fingers. He picks me up and carries me to the bathroom and pulls back the shower curtain. Once inside, we kiss and wash each other's bodies. The warm water feels so good beating against my skin that I don't want to get out. After we shower and dry each other off, we stand in the doorway of the bathroom kissing and occasionally glancing at the reflection of our naked bodies in a full-length mirror.

"You are my world," he whispers, holding, squeezing, and kissing me from the doorway to the bed. We collapse on top of the covers, which feel so cold against my naked body. He takes my hands and kisses them. "These hands, these hands, these soft and delicate, beautiful, gentle hands."

"What about my hands?" I ask.

"I want these hands to hold me." He kisses each of my fingers. "Now and years from now. I want them to warm me. I want them to feed me. I want these same beautiful hands to chastise my children when they fall out of line."

"What are you talking about?" I ask.

"I think you know what I'm talking about."

My heart starts pounding against the walls of my chest.

"Dorothy, I can't see my future without you."

I swallow so hard, I nearly strangle on my own saliva.

"Will you marry me?" he asks, and before I respond he slips the largest, prettiest, and shiniest diamond ring around my slender finger. I'm at a loss for words.

"Here." David pours me a glass of red wine. I drink quicker than he can blink.

"From the moment I met you, I knew. I used to wake up in cold sweats thinking about us. I want to shower you with a love that you've never even felt before."

I think back to what Papa said. *Dorothy, nobody's gonna love you more than your mother and me. Always remember that.*

I taste salty, bitter tears on my lips. I want unconditional love, like the one my papa and *Mère* give, and David has me convinced that he's more than qualified to give it to me, so I forget about him ever being with Bettye and catching him in the room snorting white powder with Emma Prejean. I say yes. I close my eyes, and I receive his kisses. They overwhelm my throbbing body, and I forget about waiting until the night of the wedding. I discover the nature of an orgasm and the feeling of euphoria it brings to me.

The next morning over breakfast, we share the news with our parents. My mother is unusually quiet while the Leonards smile cordially.

"Well, Cleo," Mrs. Leonard says to my mother, "it looks like you and I have a lot of planning to do."

"I look forward to it," *Mère* says but her facial expression tells another story.

"So, do you have a date in mind?" the elder Dr. Leonard asks.

I fix my mouth to say the words when I hear David say, "We were looking to get married in the next six months."

Mère clears her throat. "What about your schooling?"

"She's gonna finish at TSU." David speaks for me again.

"TSU?" *Mère* looks confused. "Where is that?"

"In Houston." David sips his coffee and continues to eat like nothing's wrong.

Mère looks at me with eyes full of questions that I know I can't answer without giving cause for her to be alarmed. David notices and he stops to rub *Mère*'s hand.

"Don't look so worried, Mother Cleo. I'll make sure she finishes and graduates; makes us all proud."

His words don't ease her expression, and although I should be feeling happy about getting married and moving on to a new phase in life, those angst-like, melancholic feelings set in.

"What's your major, Dorothy?" Dr. Leonard asks.

My scrambled eggs feel more like bricks in the pit of my stomach. "History," I respond.

"The chair of the history department is our neighbor. Let's see if we can get you enrolled by next spring."

"In the meantime," Mrs. Leonard gets up and takes both my hand and *Mère*'s, "the three of us have got a wedding to plan. Starting with the guest list."

For the next hour and a half, *Mère* and Mrs. Leonard argue constantly over how big the wedding should be. *Mère* suggests a quiet and simple backyard wedding, with a priest and only a handful of guests. Mrs. Leonard is quite the contrary, saying the wedding should be in a cathedral with a priest and about three hundred guests. *Mère* wants winter white as the color and nothing else. Mrs. Leonard suggests the winter white be offset with European red. I suggest my sorority colors. My God, the faces they make when I say that. Even David's face shrivels. *Mère* makes another suggestion of turquoise and pink. Mrs. Leonard turns up her nose. Definitely not. I finally decide on turquoise and fuchsia. At that moment I see an array of sunshine in the room; everyone seems to like the combination. Mrs. Leonard proudly takes credit for it, but *Mère* begs to differ. "Elizabeth Leonard, you wouldn't have thought of it if I hadn't suggested we use turquoise in the first place."

Mrs. Leonard suggests setting up committees: a guest list committee, an invitation committee, a fashion committee, an entertainment committee, a food committee, a decorating committee, an usher committee, a security committee, and a transportation committee. She even suggests a beauty committee, which is a trio of her acquaintances: one is a hairstylist, one a manicurist, and the third is a makeup artist.

"What's with all these committees? I'm paying for the wedding, and I think we should keep it simple." *Mère* puts her foot down.

"I never do anything simple, Ms. Lacroix. Now traditionally, you are responsible for the cost of the wedding, but this is not some ordinary backyard barbecue. This is my son we're talking about."

"You think I don't want a nice wedding for my daughter? You think I can't put together high quality with my meager ends? Don't belittle me."

"Dorothy, I haven't heard a peep out of you," Mrs. Leonard says. *That may not be by accident.* "Honey, tell us what you want."

I want to tell Mrs. Leonard to back off, but I'm not one to start confrontations. I want to appease everyone, even if it means I go lacking in the long run.

"I want a big wedding with lots of guests, and I want my colors, and I want everybody to be happy for us."

Mrs. Leonard walks up and plants a little kiss on my cheek. "You are so sweet and wonderful. You must be so proud of her, Cleo."

"I am," I hear *Mère* say. My heart warms over when I hear her say that.

I get on the phone to call Aunt Ruby Jewel.

"What did the woman do now?" I've been calling her so much that she already knows the subject matter.

"I just wish this was over."

She laughs, and it's a soft, refreshing, throaty laugh. "You think you're ready to be a part of the family?"

"They've already got my life all planned out for me."

"What do you mean they've got your life all planned out? You can't let them run all over you now. You've got to put your foot down at some point."

"But I don't want to cause a hassle, you know."

"Honey, you better. People will run all over you if let them. Now tell me about this wedding."

"We've got four hundred guests."

"You don't know four hundred people."

"Most of them are David's guests. His family knows people all over the world."

"What's the main entrée?"

"I really wanted a traditional Creole flair, but Mrs. Leonard wanted her guests to have options."

"I'll say, are you getting married or is she getting married? Honey, you'd better open your mouth and speak up."

"Are you coming to the wedding?" I ask, cutting her off.

"Of course you know I'm coming. Everybody's been telling me about your fiancé, saying how nice he is and how handsome he is. Everybody's gotten the opportunity to meet him except me." Aunt Ruby Jewel pretends to sound upset.

"You will."

"And I'm told he's a doctor, too."

"Yes, he is."

"You're a beautiful girl. I always knew you would find a wealthy man to take care of you."

I can hear Uncle Herbie's voice in the background saying something.

"What is Uncle Herbie talking about?"

"He's upset because you haven't been to Beaumont to see about us."

"Tell him that I'm coming to Houston in a few weeks, and I'll make sure I'll stop by to see him."

"*Bèbe*, she said she's coming through and she's bringing the fiancé so we can break him down." He tells her something else. "*Bèbe*, I'm not gonna keep passing messages back and forth over the phone. Here she is if you want to talk to her."

I laugh and listen at them yell back and forth to each other.

"Darling, your uncle says he can't wait to walk down that aisle with you."

"Tell Uncle Herbie that I love him and I can't wait, either."

After I hang up, I think about the wedding again and fall back against the sofa. The thought of it and moving to Houston exhausts me.

Chapter 7

"Dorothy, you need something blue," Joan, my room-mate from Southern says, looking over the items in front of me. Already I have something old, something borrowed, and something new. Tiny enters the room and stands behind my chair. She stares at me in the mirror.

"Oh girl," she cries, "you got something blue all right." Tears fall from her eyes. I try holding back my tears, but I can't. Soon every girl in the room is a crying mess.

"Stop it, all of you. Stop it before you make me ruin my mascara." I start dabbing my eyes with a tissue. Everyone in the room starts to laugh. The hairstylist takes my silky mane of hair and twists it on top of my head. She takes hairpins and proceeds to pin, allowing curlicues to fall to the nape of my neck.

"Dorothy, don't wear your hair like that. It makes you look old," Tiny says.

"Umm-hmm." I hear other voices agreeing with her.

The hairstylist takes out the pins and proceeds to brush through my mane of curls. There's a sharp knock on the door. Everyone *oohs* and *ahhs* when Mrs. Leonard enters. She is decked in a fuchsia double-breasted suit with hat, shoes, and purse to match.

"How's the hair coming, Miss Beverly?" she asks, gazing at Miss Beverly's reflection. Miss Beverly smiles and pins the top part of my hair. "Dorothy has such a lovely head of hair and lots of it, too."

Mrs. Leonard smiles at me. "You look fabulous, honey. Let me see your nails." I hold up my right hand. "You didn't want the French manicure?"

"No, ma'am. I wanted to go with clear." Mrs. Leonard examines my nails with a keen sense of detail, like I had seen David do before. "Nice. I'm glad you decided to go with clear."

I point out *Mère's* old brooch, the borrowed strand of black pearls, and the new pair of white nylon gloves.

"I see you have something old, which is your grandmother's brooch, right?"

"Yes."

"Now which one of these is borrowed, and which is new? Don't tell me." She points to the strand of black pearls. "These are borrowed and the gloves have got to be new, right?"

"You're right again," I say.

"You're missing something," she says, looking around the room.

"I need something blue," I say.

"Right."

"Mrs. Leonard, you should have seen our faces earlier," Tiny says. "We had something blue all right."

Mrs. Leonard's smile is so wide all of her teeth are visible. "How cute. Anyway, Dorothy, I have a blue leather wallet you can use. You know blue is my favorite color."

"Great, then I'll have everything I need," I say, staring at my hair. It's turning out to be beautiful.

Joan and Tiny, who met for the first time at the rehearsal dinner, are examining each other's dress. The dresses are fuchsia, designed with a strapless bodice and V-shaped waist-line. Underneath they wear petticoats to give the dresses a Victorian look. I have *Mère* to thank for that. Speaking of which, she enters adorned in her fuchsia- and-cream-colored suit. She has Jacqueline, my adorable little flower girl, with her.

"Oh Cleo, she's so precious," Mrs. Leonard says to *Mère*. Jacqueline pretends to be bashful, which makes her even more adorable. Katherine and Ophelia enter the dressing room, smiling brightly at me.

"In fifteen minutes," Katherine says, "my little sister will be taking that long walk, and honey, I do mean long walk, down the aisle. Honey, that walk will be so long, you'd swear you were walking to the border."

We laugh and watch as she talks and makes silly exaggera-tions with her face. "Honey, be prepared for it. You may need to do away with those pumps and put on some walking shoes."

I laugh. "Katherine, you're so crazy."

Miss Beverly is teasing my hair in the back with her brush.

"That's pretty, Dorothy," *Mère* says.

"Thank you."

I notice her fighting back tears with a smile. "I bet Vince is upstairs right now smiling down at this very moment."

My heart flutters when I think of him. I can hear him say-ing, *Baby girl, you've done mighty good for yourself.* I also hear him say, *Marry that man because he loves you. Stand by him, and honor him. He should be the first person you see when you wake up in the morning and the last person you see when you lie down at night. And another thing . . . don't marry just for the sake of marriage; marry for love.*

Miss Beverly stands back to examine my hair. "You like?"

I nod. "Yes." I turn to examine it from the sides. "Just how I pictured myself looking on my wedding day."

Katherine approaches me. "Now Dorothy, let's see if you can wiggle your hips into this size four." She retrieves my wedding gown. Ophelia holds my veil while Katherine and Tiny help me into the gown. Once it's on and fastened, Ophelia places the cap that contains my veil on top of my head. Everyone stands around me wide-eyed, as if I am a shrine and they came to worship. I am adorned from head to toe with embroidered rosettes and pearls; even my ten-foot-long train is trimmed in pearls. I imagine myself as a goddess, like Aphrodite, the goddess of beauty and love.

"Oh, Cleo," Mrs. Leonard cries. "My son's marrying a princess. Oh, I can't wait to see our beautiful grandchildren."

Everyone, including me, gives her the once-over. Katherine places the veil over my face. I hear *Mère* and Mrs. Leonard telling the girls to get in their places.

"Where're your other bridesmaids?" Mrs. Leonard asks, referring to my sorors, Whitney and Alexis.

"They went to get some Calla lilies."

"Well, they need to hurry. The wedding's going to start in five minutes." Mrs. Leonard is back to her Dragon Woman role, just giving orders and breathing fire everywhere. *Mère* gives me a hug. I can't remember the last time we hugged each other.

"I'm not going to cry," she says, blinking her eyes. "I've been through this before with Katherine."

"*Mère*, if you cry, then I'll start crying, and right now I don't need to cry with this mascara on."

We both laugh. Then she removes the veil to touch my face. She stares into my eyes for a moment before she mouths the words, "I love you."

"Oh, *Mère*," I say. My lips tremble and I burst out crying before I know it. I look around the room, and to my surprise everyone is dabbing at their eyes with tissues and blowing noses. Katherine takes *Mère*'s hand. "Come on," she says softly. *Mère* wipes her eyes with her handkerchief and follows Katherine out of the room.

"Dorothy, check your mascara," Tiny says as she starts to dab at her own.

"I don't know why we put on mascara," Joan says. "We knew this was going to happen." Whitney and Alexis walk in holding their Calla lilies.

"We were just about to send an APB out for you girls," Mrs. Leonard says. Whitney and Alexis ignore her. An usher sticks her head in the door. "Are you ladies ready to take your places?" When she sees me, her eyes widen. "You look gorgeous in all your splendor," she says.

"Thank you," I say.

"You must've spent a fortune on that dress."

Mrs. Leonard clears her throat and looks at the usher. "My husband and I spent a fortune on it."

The usher only stares at Mrs. Leonard before closing the door.

Uncle Herbie and Aunt Ruby Jewel are standing outside in the foyer, waiting for me, when I walk out.

"Well, here she is," they say in unison.

"She's too beautiful and I'm not worthy," he says underneath that glowing smile of his. Aunt Ruby takes my hand and looks into my eyes. "You are a precious little jewel." I see tears in her eyes. "You deserve only the best." She gives me a kiss on the cheek.

Although the doors are closed, I hear my cousin Jacqué's mezzo-soprano blessing the guests with "The Lord's Prayer." I am trembling. Uncle Herbie notices and begins to rub my arm. "It's okay, baby girl."

"What if I trip coming down the aisle, or . . . or forget the vows, what if they forget the ring, wh—."

"Stop that nonsense. That's not going to happen. Your uncle will make sure of it."

"I'll try not to think about it so much."

He turns me to face him. "Now you listen to me, young lady. Stop all that negative thinking. Your papa wouldn't want you thinking like that, now would he?"

"No, sir, he wouldn't."

"Now you build up some confidence."

I love it when Uncle Herbie comes to my rescue.

Soon the doors of the church open, and I see Katherine walk out, followed by Tiny. I close my eyes until Uncle Herbie and I are the only two standing in the doorway. The organ starts up the wedding march and I hear the congregation stand to its feet.

"This is it, baby girl," Uncle Herbie whispers. "Your last walk as Dorothy Lacroix."

I squeeze his arm and hold on to my bouquet of fresh Calla lilies. Off we go down the aisle; all eyes are on me. There are so many people that their faces are just blurs. As I near the altar, I look to my left and see *Mère* and the rest of the family smiling and crying. I look to the right and see the Leonards and their family and friends. Mrs. Leonard is dabbing her eyes and smiling at David. I see David at the altar, standing tall and majestic. Standing next to him is Jerome, who leans forward and whispers something to him. David smiles and steps forward.

I arrive teary eyed, still trembling, while my heart turns cartwheels. Sweat is inching its way down my spine, but I hold on to Uncle Herbie. I remember his words and I remember Papa. When the music stops, there is a brief moment of silence except for the occasional flash of a camera. The priest opens his book to begin.

"Dearly beloved, we are gathered here today before the sight of God to unite this man and this woman in holy matrimony . . ."

As he talks, my mind wanders to David standing on the other side of Uncle Herbie, and the flames burning from the candles nearby. My eyes are filled with tears, and it seems like the flames are a mile long.

"Who gives this bride away?"

Uncle Herbie says, "I do." He releases my firm hold, and David takes his place. David looks straight into my eyes and smiles, warming my heart and easing the nervousness. The priest begins, "If there is one here who does not see why this man and woman should be joined together, speak now or forever hold your peace."

David turns to face the congregation. He looks the room over with a hand pressed against his ear. "Hark! Do I hear anyone?" The congregation laughs. I glance at Jerome; he barely cracks a smile. The priest waits until the laughter ceases before he continues with the ceremony.

My mind drifts off again. Catholic weddings are just like Catholic funerals: boring and ritualistic. I think back to last night's rehearsal dinner and the bringing of our families together, and that David had everything all planned out for us. I shared this information with Tiny, who thought it a good thing for him take such initiative. Joan, on the other hand, asked me how I felt. I told her that I couldn't wait to move on and see what married life had to offer me in Houston. I moved all my things out of her room, and I told her that I wasn't coming back to Southern come January. She nodded and, being so wise and kind, she told me something that stayed with me. She said, *Dorothy, don't lose yourself.*

The priest says to David, "Do you, David Claude Leonard the Second, take Dorothy Lacroix to be your lawfully-wedded wife, to honor and cherish her, for better or worse, through sickness and in health, for as long as you both shall live?"

"I do," he replies.

"Do you, Dorothy Lacroix, take David Claude Leonard the Second, to be your lawfully-wedded husband, to honor and cherish him, for better or worse, through sickness and in health, for as long as you both shall live?"

"I do," I reply.

"The rings, please."

David slips an eighteen-karat gold band around my finger. I, in return, slip a size eleven eighteen-karat gold band around his.

"By the powers vested in me by the state of Louisiana, I now pronounce you husband and wife. You may kiss your bride."

"May I?" David asks jokingly.

The priest closes his book and takes off his reading glasses. "Yes, you may."

"You're not kidding me, are you?" David asks once more. The church is laughing again. He lifts my veil. I hear the church stand to its feet when David and I kiss.

The organ starts up the exit march, and I am bombarded with hugs and kisses. The church feels like Carnival, with cameras flashing, rice being thrown, and people whom I've never seen before, applauding. The chauffeur opens the door to our Bentley.

"Whew," David shouts once we're inside. I'm speechless. It hasn't quite sunken in just yet that I'm married.

"Why the dazed look?"

"Pinch me. I mean it, pinch me."

"I've got a better idea." He takes my bouquet and places it on the floor. He takes me in his arms and kisses me with one of those paralyzing kisses.

"Whew," I shout after we come up for air. "You should've kissed me like that at the altar."

"The church couldn't have handled it."

I want him to kiss me like that again; I think I heard fireworks explode after the last one.

A photographer snaps shots of David and me with our families. I don't think I will ever stop smiling. The photographer takes pictures of me with the bridesmaids and David with the groomsmen. More pictures of the family posing for a huge portrait, pictures of David and me cutting our three-tiered, nine-layer pineapple cream cake, pictures of David and me drinking from each other's champagne glass, pictures of me with Jacqueline and the ring bearer, and pictures of David and me sharing our first dance.

Near the center of the room is a small band of musicians playing both classical and modern music. When they play our song, "Unforgettable" by Nat King Cole, David and I take center stage. Everyone clears the ballroom floor for us. David takes my hand in his and leads me around to the slow tempo of the music.

"David, do you remember the first time we kissed?"

"How could I forget?"

"This song was playing on the radio."

"This is our song, then." He holds me close as we slow dance around the room. For some strange reason, I think of Cinderella and the handsome prince. I hear David trying to sing. His voice sounds horrible.

"Stop laughing."

"I can't help it," I say. "Stick to your day job."

"Ha, ha, ha. Thanks a lot," he says underneath that bright smile of his.

After the dance we sit down to a gourmet feast of roasted duck nestled atop steaming hot vegetables, seafood étouffée,

Beluga caviar, fresh-cut fruit salad, and bottles of red and white wine.

"Dorothy, it's time for the bouquet toss," Mrs. Leonard says. She's beginning to get on my nerves again, telling me how to organize my wedding. *Don't start eating until after your uncle proposes a toast. Don't slice the cake until after the main course.* She's flapping so much that it's starting to get on Dr. Leonard's nerves.

"Liz, this a wedding, not the Barnum and Bailey Circus."

Mrs. Leonard excuses herself from the table. "Dorothy, I will see you in five minutes on the far side of the room."

After she leaves, David whispers in my ear, "You don't have to go over there if you don't want to."

I wipe the corners of my mouth with my napkin. "That's all right," I say calmly. "I'm finished eating, anyway. Besides, I wanna see the woman who's bold enough to catch my bouquet." David helps me out of my chair. "Do you want to come and see?"

"No, honey, there's only one woman I want to see holding your bouquet."

"That's right, sugar." I peck him on the lips.

Mrs. Leonard gathers almost every single woman in the ballroom. She's barking out orders like a Catholic schoolteacher, telling them to stand behind some imaginary line and don't step over it until the bouquet is up in the air.

"Now, Dorothy, you turn around and stand here." She takes my arm and places me over some imaginary dot. Although my back is to the ladies, I still recognize the voices daring one another to catch it.

"Are you ready?" I shout.

"Ready when you are," they shout back.

I toss the bouquet over my head. There are a few screams, a little scuffling, but someone finally catches it. I turn to see that "someone" is a girl whom I don't recognize. She looks sixteen or seventeen. She is a gorgeous mahogany-colored girl, who holds the bouquet high above her head like a trophy, shouting "I caught it! I caught it!"

I approach this girl. She stops shouting and holds it like a mother protecting her young from danger.

"What's your name?" I ask.

At that moment, Whitney, my soror, introduces her. "Dorothy, this is Chanel, my half-sister—unfortunately."

"Chanel?"

"Yes."

Chanel stands there holding the bouquet in her hands, admiring it like a prize of money. "These are beautiful," she says.

"So who's the lady bold enough to try to take my wife's place?" David asks, walking up behind me.

"Chanel," I reply.

David stares at Chanel. "You're not twenty-one, are you?" he asks jokingly.

Whitney clears her throat. "Excuse me, but I don't think Dorothy is twenty-one, either."

To that remark, David replies, "You hear me complaining?"

Whitney playfully rolls her eyes at him. David takes my hand. "Excuse us."

On my way to the powder room, I see Jerome standing near the balcony sipping on a glass of champagne. He sees me and motions for me to come join him. I point to the powder room and tell him I'll be back as soon as I can. Inside, Tiny and Joan are powdering their faces.

Tiny takes a tissue and dabs around her nose. "I just can't stop sweating."

I notice my lip rouge wearing thin. "You can't stop dancing either."

She laughs. "You know me."

Joan runs her hands through her hair. "Dorothy, you know the girl who caught your bouquet?"

"My soror's half-sister." I apply rouge to my lips. "She looks pretty young."

Tiny finds it amusing. "A young one, you say?"

"Yes, about sixteen or seventeen."

"What business did she have out there, anyway?"

I purse my lips together. "I don't know. You should've seen her. She was waving it around like a million dollars."

"Oh yeah?" Tiny stops dabbing and puts her hand on her small hip. "Dot, I don't mean to disrespect your new mother-in-law, but that woman . . . I could strangle her."

"What happened?"

"She always has something to say to me. Check this out. I was on the dance floor dancing and having a good time with the band you know? She comes waltzing her stiff-legged behind out there and says to me, 'What's going on here? You shouldn't dance that way. I'll have you know there are Christians at this reception, and I will not tolerate this display of obscenity.'"

"Seriously?" I ask.

"Joan is my witness."

I look at Joan, and she nods in agreement.

"And Dot, when I cut two slices of the groom's cake, she says, 'Christine, I'm ashamed of you. You're eating like a hog. You need to stop and lose the weight you have.'" Tiny imitates her voice. "I started to tell her, 'Honey, if you don't get out of my face you are going to be eating this cake before I do. And I guarantee it won't be a pretty sight.' But that's your mother-in-law, and I realize this is a formal setting, but just that moment, girl, I was ready to nail her behind."

"Oh, don't pay her any mind. Just ignore her."

Tiny stuffs her coin purse with tissues. "She's got one more thing to say to me tonight."

Joan begins to chuckle. "Poor Mrs. Leonard."

"Somebody has to set her straight. Knock her in the head a couple of times."

I think about Jerome. "Tiny, I saw Jerome on my way in here."

"And?"

"He asked me to join him on the balcony."

"What did you say?" Joan and Tiny both watch me closely.

"I told him I would for a few minutes."

Tiny picks up her purse and flings it over her shoulder. "Remember those vows and that ten-thousand-dollar ring."

Joan grabs her pocketbook. "Don't fall for those I'm-not-so-sure-I'm-over-you lines."

Tiny replies, "Yeah, and the I'm-lonely-and-can-we-go-somewhere-private-to-talk lines."

"That's what I'm talking about," Joan says before she and Tiny leave the room. I follow them and notice Jerome still standing by the balcony sipping on his champagne. I run my hands in front of my gown and smooth the wrinkles as I walk calmly in his direction.

"Hello, Dr. West. Are you enjoying the evening?" I ask.

"Yes I am," he replies. "You look really pretty standing up there."

"Hmm?"

"I said you look really pretty standing up there. Where's David? I'm surprised the two of you managed to get separated."

"He's somewhere having the time of his life."

"He's one lucky man."

I'm thinking of a way to end this conversation with a topic other than the wedding.

"What time is it?" I ask.

He glances at his watch. "It's five before midnight."

"The new year'll be here before you know it." I notice his expression is dazed. "You going to join the rest of us and toast off the New Year, right?"

He chuckles and shakes his head. "No, I'll just stay right here and relax."

I clear my throat. "Stop being antisocial and join us." I grab his hand.

I hear David's voice behind me. "Dorothy! Jerome!"

I turn around and smile at him. "Sweetheart," I say before giving him a kiss. I look into David's eyes, but they are still on Jerome.

"What's going on over here?" he asks in an accusatorial tone.

"Nothing, honey. I was about to bring Jerome in to toast off the New Year with us."

"Don't worry about me," Jerome replies, tilting his champagne glass to us. A comical smirk is on his face. "Here's to a fine marriage and a happy New Year," he says before taking a drink. David quickly grabs my hand. I think I'm getting rushed back to the ballroom, but instead he pushes me inside the men's restroom. I shriek when he slams my body against the cold tile wall.

"You must've forgotten this is our wedding night."

I look into his eyes, searching for an answer to his outburst. "I don't understand what's going on. What are you talking about?"

"I'm talking about you and Jerome. What were you doing alone with him?"

"I-I was just talking to him." I smell David's breath, but there is no trace of alcohol.

"About what?"

At that moment my mind freezes and my knees become weak. I take a good look at David's eyes, and they are like daggers piercing through my body. The pain and the humiliation I now feel is so unbearable, I feel as though I'm dreaming.

"Please let go of my arm. You're hurting me," I plead.

David slowly releases my arm and backs away from me like I am a total stranger. In the background I hear the sound of our wedding guests counting down the hour. Tears come to my eyes as I think of how sweet it would have been to bring in the New Year on a happy note. Instead, I bring it in staring into the eyes of a stranger who not five hours ago sealed a vow to love me for better or worse with a kiss.

"I'm sorry." He comes closer and cradles my face in his hands. "I'm so sorry."

I wipe away tears with my hands. "Why would you accuse me of doing something I didn't do?" I listen as sobs butcher my sentences.

"I don't want you around him, okay? I don't want to lose you." He kisses my lips.

I don't like how this is going. Something is amiss. Then I think back to that night with him in the room with Emma Prejean. She is here and maybe they went off somewhere to snort some more of that white powder. Out of nowhere, Bettye's words come back to haunt me. *Things aren't always what they appear.* I think I'm in for a rude awakening.

PART TWO:

NEVER

Chapter 8

"How was the honeymoon?" Tiny's voice was inquisitive and quick like lightning. She couldn't possibly and wouldn't even conceive of her cousin's condition on the other end. A bluish-red bruise the size of a grape stung Dorothy's right arm. Rubbing it, Dorothy tried to convince herself that if she didn't think about the pain, it would go away. Why didn't she see this in the beginning? Or had she seen what she wanted to see? How can a person be so naive and not notice the signs?

"My first and last time on an airplane."

"Come on now—was it that bad?"

"With all the turbulence, there weren't enough Hail Marys for me to shout out."

"So give me some details. You don't sound excited. Did you have a good time?"

Dorothy held the phone away from her lips so that Tiny couldn't hear her sigh of distress.

"First of all, it was storming when we boarded. I was apprehensive about that, but the stewardess kept saying the storm wasn't as bad we thought."

"Who was she kidding?"

"There was an older couple sitting a few rows behind us in first class. The woman was having chest pains, so the stewardess gets on the PA and asks if there is a physician on board. David raises his hand. Turns out he's the only one on board. So he tries to offer his assistance. Her husband tells him no thank you, he'd rather wait until they land."

"Stupid son of a bitch."

"The plane got diverted to Miami, but it was too late."

"She died."

"Tiny, it was awful. David couldn't stop thinking about it."

"I'm sure you more than made up for it."

"You know I did."

"I'm scared of you."

"David was too."

"Go on with your bad self."

"It works all the time."

"Yes it does . . . tell me about St. Thomas. Was it anything like you'd imagine?"

"The sight of the water, Tiny, it almost takes your breath away."

"Nothing like the Mississippi, huh?"

"Please. I could've stayed in the water all day; the turquoise color, the white beaches, the cute cottages, and people riding mopeds on the opposite sides of the road."

"You told me David has relatives living there."

"Used to. I found out one of his great-aunts, and his cousin, were missionaries. They built a school and a church there."

"That's fascinating."

Dorothy tried to get up but felt a sharp pain in her lower back. She fell back on the sofa.

"So did you eat good? Get plenty of plantains? Rice? Okra?"

With eyes closed and body throbbing like a hot magnet,

Dorothy forced herself to speak. "We tasted everything the island had to offer."

"Tell me about the concert."

The *concert*. Dorothy held her composure. It was part of the reason she was in the shape she was in. A friend of the family gave her and David tickets to see Miles Davis. David was a big fan of Miles—had all of his albums and tried to go to all his concerts. Dorothy couldn't understand why Miles stood with his back against the audience. She kept thinking that if she had paid to see him, she would've been real angry. The crowd was eight thousand deep and just above them, lightning bugs circled the open air. Later that evening, while strolling through the lobby, checking out a local band cover "Lady from Impanema," Miles noticed Dorothy at the bar. He put the trumpet to his lips and started tickling the valve pistons with his right fingertips. The bell of his trumpet was just inches away from her heaving chest. He riffed, turning her complexion two shades redder than her *café au lait* skin. He removed the trumpet from his lips. Dorothy nervously diverted her glowing green eyes to David, standing at the other end of the bar.

"If beauty were a disease, you'd be fucked up," Miles said to her then walked off, strolling past David. He saw Dorothy standing at the end of the bar, looking pensive. Faster than a light switch, he was in her face.

"What did he say to you?" The accusatorial tone of his voice had Dorothy on edge.

"Nothing."

"Why are you lying?"

"He didn't say anything."

David studied her for a moment, looking at the form-fitting yellow cotton dress that accentuated her size-five figure. Her neckline was kind of low, showing just a hint of cleavage. He looked closely and noticed the outline of her nipples hardening against the yellow fabric. He couldn't take her anywhere without someone staring or making a comment on her flawless beauty. She needed to stop wearing her hair like that, for it showed the sensuous nape of her neck. The lip rouge had to go because it drew too much attention to her full lips. They had a natural soft pinkness to them, and when she covered them in red, they invited stares from males. Her form-fitting dresses need to be a little looser and the neckline nonexistent. He understood how Miles could pinpoint her. In a room of black, white and gray, she was the color of spring.

"Let's go." He grabbed her elbow. She flinched. Trying not to draw attention, David waited until they got outside the hotel. With his large fingers he pinched her skin, twisting it until her eyes gushed with tears.

"The concert was nice . . . everything was nice." Dorothy forgot all about Tiny on the other end.

"I swear, getting information out of you is like watching paint dry," Tiny said. Little did she know, Dorothy was on the other end in tears. "Did you have a good time?"

"Yeah." Dorothy tried to sound normal.

"I hope you took pictures."

"Yes, we took some."

"Any nude ones?"

"Perhaps."

"My cousin, the *Playboy* centerfold. See, I knew you had it in you."

"So, when are you and Mike going to tie the knot?" Dorothy asked, anxious to change the subject.

"When he grows up."

"No telling how long that's going to take."

"We both still need to get our acts together. Me personally, I'm not all the way committed to Mike, and I know damn well he's not committed to me."

"Tiny, I never really talked about this with anyone, but do you think David and I kind of rushed into the marriage?"

"That's a question only you and David can answer."

Dorothy sighed, thinking, *Yes, I did rush into it. I should have given myself a little more time.* David seemed like such a good gentleman. Maybe the pressures at the hospital were taking a toll on him, and once he completed his residency, things would be back to normal.

"Dot, let me ask you a question."

"What is it?"

"Do you love David? I mean really, really love him?"

"Of course I love him." And she honestly did.

"A lot of times we convince ourselves that it wasn't the money or status that made you his wife in the first place. It was love. But Dorothy, let's be realistic. Love alone does not pay the bills."

Dorothy laughed. "No, it doesn't."

David arrived, carrying a load of books.

"I'm gonna let you go. Guess who just walked in?"

"Tell him I said hello."

"I will. Bye."

David took off his medical coat with his credentials on it and hung it by the door. "Who was that?"

"It was Tiny," she responded and watched as he sat down on sofa, unbuttoned his cuff links, rolled up his sleeves and flashed one of those devious smiles.

"Aren't you glad to see me? Come here." Dorothy moved in closer and received his probing tongue. She often forgot just how sweet his kisses were, even if he wasn't. Feeling bashful from the way he was sizing her up, she picked up one of his books and read the words *Masters and Johnson: Guide to the Woman's Body.*

"I must be the luckiest man in the world to come home

every day to a face like yours." David stared ever so admir-
ingly at her before he opened a notebook, mashed the button
on his Cross pen, and proceeded to write. Dorothy picked up
a sheet of paper that he had written on. There were so many
editing and proofreading marks where he had replaced common words with complex medical terms. Dorothy read the
first line, "God made Adam and gave him the breath of life,
seeing that Adam was lonely, God gave Adam a wife."

"David, what is this?" she asked.

David scanned over it. "The intro page to the book I'm
working on."

"Sounds like poetry to me."

He laughed. "The opening sentence must've caught you
off guard."

"I think I know what you're trying to say."

"Good."

"David, honey . . ." Dorothy browsed randomly through
each page in the manuscript finding words like *IUD* and *Pa-
panicolaou*, medical terms that every woman had come across
at some time or another. "Ever considered getting this published?"

"Yes."

There must've been over two hundred pages in Dorothy's
hand. "How many pages do you plan to write?"

"Until I see fit that I've written enough."

"Are you the only person working on this project?"

"No. Do you remember Dr. Corbin from the wedding?"

"Yes, I think."

"He's my co-author."

"You've been working on this for a while."

He pulled out a pair of reading glasses and placed them on
his nose. Although David was only twenty-five, those glasses
made him look much older.

"Almost two years." He continued to read a page in the manuscript.

"Are you hungry?" Dorothy asked. David kept reading as though he didn't hear.

"Yoohoo, honey, I'm talking to you."

He looked up. "You see I'm busy."

"I just needed to know if you wanted me to cook—"

He interrupted, "Dr. Corbin and I ate already."

"What did you have?"

"Grilled fish, vegetables, the works." He reached into his bag and pulled out a bottle of chardonnay. "See, I was thinking about you."

"Thank you." Dorothy took the bottle. "You know, lately I've been having these cravings."

"Cravings?" He stopped reading.

"No. I'm not pregnant."

He put aside his notebook and began to check Dorothy's temperature. "You know Mother Nature works in mysterious ways."

"I'm not pregnant."

He lifted her blouse and pressed against her pelvis and breasts. "Does that hurt?" he asked.

He caressed her breasts in a circular motion, and for a moment Dorothy was getting really excited. Dorothy took her hand and clasped it around his. "No, but it really feels good."

"Nope, you're not pregnant."

"I want to start really soon."

"I know, but right now is not a good time. I'm doing my residency, I'm writing this book, and you need to finish school. When are you going to do that?"

Dorothy couldn't think about school and having to transfer her classes. It was much too complicated, and besides, she needed a break to concentrate on finding ways to be a better

wife. David's moods could be so unpredictable. One minute
he was showering her and her family with gifts—after Hurri-
cane Betsey flooded the neighborhood, David bought Dorothy's
mother a five-bedroom house near Tulane. Then there were
times when he came in from a backbreaking day at the hospital, swearing and throwing things all over the place, like the
time he smashed their Tiffany lamp on the floor when she
didn't have supper ready.

"As soon as I talk to your father," she said, knowing good
and well she wasn't going to.

"What's he got to do with anything?"

"Remember, he said he knew someone who could get me
in?"

"You should've been enrolled by now." He inspected their
apartment. "Make me a cup of tea, will you?"

When Dorothy talked with her mother, she kept reminding
Dorothy how grateful she was to David for buying her a new
house. While they talked Cleo Lacroix admired a diamond-
encrusted watch, another gift from David.

"How's my favorite son-in-law's manual coming along?" she
asked.

"How did you know about David's manual?"

"I talked with him a couple of days ago. He called to see
how I was enjoying my new home."

"How's Ophelia?"

"I don't know if your sister is on drugs or what, but she's
been acting real spaced-out here lately."

"Did she say where she wanted to go to school?"

"She's talking 'bout Chicago. Now who in the hell does she
know in Chicago? I told her hell no, her spooky-acting ass is
staying right here with me."

"If she wants to go to Chicago, I'll see to it," Dorothy said.
At least someone she knew was motivated to get away from
New Orleans.

"Listen to you, Miss Money." Cleo lit herself a cigarette. "How's that mother-in-law of yours?"

"Fine. She does a lot of bid whist and tea parties."

"Sounds like Carolyn to me. You know Katherine's pregnant."

The news of her sister lightened her spirits. "When did she tell you?"

"She called late yesterday afternoon." Cleo thumped her ashes in a nearby porcelain flower pot. "I can't believe I'm gonna be called *Mémère*."

"Me a tante," Dorothy cooed in Creole.

"How do you like living in Houston?"

"I hate it, *Mère*."

"Give it some time."

"When are you coming to see me?" Dorothy sounded like a small child.

Cleo thumped her cigarette in the porcelain pot. "We'll come and see you on a weekend. Surprise you and that ol' Mrs. Leonard."

Dorothy forced a smile before saying goodbye to her mother. She looked at the light shining on the floor from the living room. David was still up, and in a few minutes he was coming to bed to fondle, kiss, and spread her legs high over their bedposts. She loved it the first time they made love; it was everything she had ever imagined. Even the second and third times were enchanting. The night of their wedding he all but kissed her, and when he was done, Dorothy cuddled up like a fetus on her side of the bed and cried herself to sleep.

Chapter 9

"Dot, where do you want me to hang this portrait?" Dorothy searched the family room over. "Over the fireplace."

Ophelia took the portrait she painted of her sister and hung it next to the large framed photograph of the family at the wedding. Dorothy's family room in her new house contained a photograph of almost everything and almost everyone. There was Dorothy's baby picture taken when she was just two months old, lying on her stomach with a horrified expression on her face. There were old pictures of her father, even old pictures of great-grand relatives that once belonged to her father.

David moved them out of the small garage apartment they shared just behind his parents' home to a four-bedroom, three-and-a-half bath split-level home with sunroofs, a small pool out back, and a greenhouse built to nurse Dorothy's green thumb.

Ophelia held up an old black-and-white photo of her parents, taken the day of their wedding.

"I forgot all about that picture. Let me see it," Dorothy said. "You know, there was a lot of love in this picture."

"Tell me about it." In the picture, Cleo wore a straight A-line dress over her small frame, and had a smile that reminded Dorothy of Katherine. Cleo's arms were wrapped around Vince Lacroix's shoulders with her face next to his. Vince, on the other hand, had a mellowed-out, relaxed look, which gave off the impression that as long as he had Cleo Montague-Lacroix by his side, everything was all right.

"I think this will look perfect next to our wedding picture." Dorothy placed it right next to hers. She also had Katherine and Rick's wedding picture on the mantel.

"I won't unpack too much. There's no telling when you and David'll move again."

"You got that right," Dorothy said.

She inspected the room as the doorbell rang. "Ophelia, will you get that for me, dear?" Dorothy couldn't get over the number of boxes she had yet to unpack.

"Hello, Dorothy!" It was Mrs. Leonard, wearing a loud yellow polka-dot two-piece set.

"Hello, Mrs. Leonard. You're looking just lovely, as always. Where are you going?"

"To do some shopping. I stopped by to ask you along, but I see you have your hands full here." She looked around the room and at the ceiling. "Exquisite indeed. I just love a home with a sunroof."

"There's one in the washroom and in our bedroom as well."

"How lovely. I hope you and David are satisfied with this house. It's eccentric, not bad for a colored neighborhood. Our neighbor Sylvia is throwing a dinner party to celebrate your homeowner status."

"That's nice."

"Her husband Solomon and my husband attended medical

school together. Sylvia and I were pregnant around the same time. They're just like family to us."

Mrs. Leonard opened the glass sliding door to the patio and surveyed the backyard. "Just fabulous. Though you have to be careful with my grandchildren around this pool."

Dorothy glanced at her sister, who was perched against the fireplace sipping on a bottle of Coke. They both shook their heads.

"Dorothy, I think it's about time for you and David to start a family, don't you think?"

"I'm ready, but your son doesn't see it happening right now."

Mrs. Leonard waved her hand. "He isn't getting any younger. He'll be thirty soon. I wonder what's the problem."

"Ask him when you get the chance."

She closed the patio door behind her. "Believe me, I will." Mrs. Leonard eyed the family room once more. "This room would look a lot better if the walls were cream instead of white. I think cream walls look so much better." She glanced at Ophelia. "I was told you had an eye for art. What do you think?"

Ophelia shrugged. "It doesn't matter to me. White or cream, they both look good."

Mrs. Leonard opened her purse and pulled out a small carrying case. She held up a pair of brown tinted cat-eyed glasses and placed them on her nose. "Well, I'm off to do my shopping. Dorothy, is there anything you'd like? You, Ophelia?"

"No thank you, Mrs. Leonard." Dorothy walked her to the car.

Mrs. Leonard placed her hand on Dorothy's shoulder. "Now, you've known me long enough to address me on a first-name basis. I'd rather you call me Liz."

"How about Mrs. Liz?"

"Just call me Liz, honey. Oh gracious, this humidity is killing my hair and makeup." Dorothy noticed small beads of perspiration forming underneath Mrs. Leonard's nose. "I should cut my hair. At least my neck wouldn't sweat." She pulled out a handkerchief and dabbed underneath her nose and neck. Dorothy opened the car door for her.

"Bye, honey, and don't forget: Sunday night, dinner with Sylvia and Solomon. Go mingle with Sylvia. She's just dying to meet you." Mrs. Leonard pulled out of the driveway in her vintage Jaguar convertible and sped off. That was one more reason for Dorothy not to like Houston. Mrs. Leonard lived over on the next street, which gave her reason enough to visit more often than she should, with or without her car.

David was still at the hospital, and had been since nine the previous evening. He received a phone call that one of his patients was getting a premature visit from the stork, so he left without finishing the candlelight meal Dorothy prepared for him. It was now three in the morning, and Dorothy was lying in bed, alone, with the rain beating against her bedroom window. That only frustrated her. She tossed and turned. She even made up crazy fantasies of her and David running outside naked in the rain with the drops pounding their bodies. She opened her eyes and saw the empty place where David's body should've been. Seeing the empty pillow reminded her of the empty feeling she got on her birthday the year after they married. They had made plans to drive to Surfside, but David got a call from the hospital. Dorothy got in the car and followed him because she decided there was no way she was going to spend her birthday alone. She sat in the lobby of the hospital and waited. She bugged every nurse that passed and sent countless messages, hoping they would somehow reach him. She read every magazine on the rack and talked with everyone who waited, until David sent her a dozen roses through an orderly. The card attached, scribbled in someone else's handwriting, said,

Dorothy,
Uncertain as to how long it will last. I'm sorry about your
birthday. I love you and I'll make it up to you soon. David.

Dorothy took the roses, locked herself in the bathroom, and cried quietly to herself. When she got home, she called her mother. "Shut the hell up. Since you've been married, all you do is complain."

Since David bought her a house, *Mère* had become his biggest cheerleader. Negative talk about David was off-limits as far as she was concerned. So Dorothy turned on the lamp and got out of bed to slip on her robe. When she walked near the window, a flash of lightning lit the sky so bright it cast her shadow against the wall. She opened the door and walked down the hall to the room where Ophelia slept. Her door was open. Dorothy peeked in. Ophelia was sound asleep. Dorothy went downstairs to the kitchen to open the refrigerator and saw the candlelight dinner staring back at her. She lost her appetite after David left. She didn't want salmon, so she poured a glass of water, closed the refrigerator door, and sat down at the table. It was 3:45 in the morning, and the smell of the rain brought about an uneasy frustration.

David's brother Marcus arrived early the next morning to find Dorothy and Ophelia sitting at the table eating breakfast.

"We got enough here for you, come and sit," Dorothy offered him the chair across from her.

"No thanks. It smells good, though," he said in a low tenor voice.

"How are your mother and father?" Dorothy asked.

Marcus was eyeing Ophelia. "They're okay." Dorothy noticed a small mustache outlining his top lip. Ophelia continued to eat quietly. She wiped the corners of her mouth and cleared her throat.

"Ophelia, I'm sorry. This is David's brother, Marcus. You met Marcus, haven't you?"

Ophelia couldn't remember. "Marcus, weren't you at the wedding?" Ophelia asked.

"Yes."

"I didn't know David had a brother," Ophelia said, trying not to study Marcus.

"I thought you knew."

The telephone rang. Dorothy picked it up to hear David's voice on the other end.

"Hey, I'm on my way home." He sounded exhausted and distant.

"Are you gonna make it?"

"I'm a big boy. Make sure you have my cup of coffee ready when I get there."

"Okay, and what else?"

"And a half-dozen pancakes with melted butter, swimming in a lake of maple syrup." Dorothy heard him yawn.

"Are you sure you can make it?"

"Yes."

"You positive?"

"Yes, now stop worrying and start cooking."

"I love you, David." Dorothy figured if she started saying it enough times, it would ease the tension.

"Yeah, me too." David hung up immediately.

"Poor thing. I don't know how he does it." Dorothy grabbed pancake mix and a mixing bowl. "He hasn't slept since yesterday."

"That could not be me," Marcus said. "You know a man's got to know his limitations when it comes to work." Marcus cut his eyes to Ophelia.

Ophelia eyed Dorothy. "Do you hear this, Dorothy?" Ophelia said.

"I sure do."

Ophelia rolled her big brown eyes to the whites and smiled bashfully. Dorothy couldn't believe that fifteen-year-old Marcus had her twenty-year-old sister blushing.

Ophelia inquired, "Marcus, what do you mean?"

Marcus licked his lips, a gesture that all the Leonard men seemed to do habitually.

"Excuse me?" Ophelia still wanted to know.

"Leave him alone. He needs to get started on the yard before it gets too hot."

"No, unhh-unhh. I want to know what Marcus is trying to say." Ophelia moved away from the table, folded her arms, and flashed her eyes at Marcus who glanced at his watch. "I'll tell you after I'm done."

"Yeah, let's finish this talk."

Marcus nodded and stared at her as he walked toward the door; he opened it, and not saying a word, he laughed and went outside.

"I think he likes you," Dorothy said.

Ophelia bit into a peeled orange. "You noticed too, huh?"

"That, among other things."

Ophelia chewed slowly and pondered, "What does he do?"

"What do you mean?"

"How does he make a living?"

"Ophelia, the boy is only fifteen."

Ophelia spit chunks of orange all over the table.

Dorothy found David sitting in the family room, laid back against the chaise lounge chair, listening to Coltrane's *Love Supreme*. Since the Miles Davis incident, David trashed all of his albums and now preferred the likes of Coltrane, Ramsey Lewis, and Thelonious Monk. She sat quietly next to him, took his arm, and placed it around her shoulder. It'd been three weeks since he struck her last, and she was trying everything she could to pacify him. There seemed to be an unspoken rule that in times like this, she didn't initiate a conversation. If David wanted to talk, he would have to be the first to open his mouth. She felt him squeeze her shoulders.

"Guess what," he said.

"What?"

"I'm not a resident anymore."

"Congratulations. We need to celebrate."

"Today was my last day. Now it's time to get the practice off and going."

"If you need a receptionist, I can answer the phones for you."

"I'm not having any wife of mine working outside of this house."

Dorothy raised herself up to get a better glimpse of David.

"You heard right. My mother never worked outside the home, her mother never worked, and my father's mother never worked."

"So you expect me to sit here all day and stare at these walls?"

"You better be thankful you have a husband like me to take care of you. I know women who would love to be in your place." He squeezed his eyes shut. "Damn this headache." He rested his head on the ball of Dorothy's left shoulder. "Massage my temples."

Without a word, she did just that. Inside, she was screaming. She got tired of hearing how fortunate she was and how lucky she was to have a husband like him. If that was the case, why did she feel so worthless? She proceeded to massage his temples, trying hard not to bury her nails into his skull.

"Massage my back and shoulders."

The nerve of him, she thought. But she played the actress role. "I'll do anything you want me to, honey," she said aloud.

Later that evening, Dorothy lit every candle in the bedroom while David poured scotch into a tumbler. It ached

Dorothy's mind to think that all David wanted was a "house-wife." David gulped his scotch and set the glass on the table next to the bed. He removed his robe and stretched nude across the bed. Dorothy's gaze traveled from the crown of his natural, to the tautness of his honey-colored pectorals, down to the ripples of his stomach, and even farther down to the veins that held up his erect penis. Dorothy opened a bottle of Johnson's baby oil and rubbed her palms until she generated heat. She applied oil on David's horizontal body, starting first with his shoulders. She had so much she wanted to talk about. She wasn't feeling very sexual, but she played the actress role, anything to pacify him and keep him happy. Her oily hands traveled down to his chest. They traveled down a little farther to his abdomen. She moved her hands in a circular motion. A light moan escaped from David's lips. Then in one motion, he grabbed her and laid her on her back. She stared silently at the flame from the candlelight in David's brown eyes. He came closer and kissed her lips.

"Dorothy," he whispered against them.

"Yes," she responded.

"Be gentle with me," he said. The request caught Dorothy off guard, and both of them laughed and held each other in a tight embrace.

Later that night, Dorothy was awakened by the sound of laughter and screaming. Dorothy thought it was coming from the neighbors next door, but then she realized, they lived quite a distance apart from them, so it couldn't have been them. She turned to David beside her breathing deeply and sleeping like a baby. Dorothy tried not to think about it and tried to go sleep. Then she heard it again, and it sounded like it was inside. She immediately shook David.

"Honey, wake up." She flipped on the lamp switch. The glare from the light blinded him.

"What?" He squinted.

HAPPILY NEVER AFTER   111

"Listen."

"Listen to what?" He wiped his eyes.

"Shhh."

They listened out for it and heard it once more. David glanced at Dorothy, and without saying a word, they got out of bed, slipped on their robes, and went down the hall. David knocked on Ophelia's door.

"Ophelia." There was no answer. He knocked again. "Ophelia."

Dorothy opened the door and walked in to find an empty room.

"You sure you heard something?"

There was another crying outburst. "See, did you hear it?"

They listened intently and sure enough they both heard it. It sounded like Ophelia's voice, and it was coming from the family room.

"What the hell is going on?" Dorothy asked.

"Only one way to find out."

Dorothy followed David into the family room, flipped on the lights, and lying on the floor were Marcus and Ophelia butt naked.

"Oh my God!" Dorothy covered her mouth in shock.

Ophelia quickly grabbed her robe and covered herself. Marcus grabbed some pillows and placed them over himself.

"Excuse me. I'm going to the bathroom."

David stopped Marcus. "Hold on. I want to have a few words with you when you get back." Marcus disappeared with the pillows shielding his valuables. "And hurry up. I haven't got all night." David glanced at Dorothy; she could tell he wanted to laugh.

"So what are you gonna talk about?"

"The talk." He disappeared down the hall. Dorothy glanced at Ophelia, unable to grasp a definition of how she felt.

"Dorothy, whatever you do, don't tell anyone about this."

"Child, please. I'm embarrassed for you. You are hard up."

Ophelia held up her hand in mere protest. "Save it. I don't want to hear it."

Dorothy tied her robe and sat on the sofa across from her sister. Over and over in her head, she kept getting flashbacks of the expression on Ophelia and Marcus's faces when she switched on the light.

"Go ahead," Ophelia said, nodding. "Laugh."

"Ophelia, all the men in Houston, and you want a fifteen-year-old?"

"What's age got to do with it?"

"That's a boy, you're an adult."

"Marcus is not a boy."

"You are sick." Dorothy imagined what her sister was thinking.

"Maybe I am." She buried her face in her hands. "Let's not talk about it, okay?"

Dorothy sat there in silence for a brief moment. "Damn. I can't sleep. I'm tossing and turning in bed, I hear you screaming and I immediately assume the worst."

"So? I heard you and David in the room earlier, so don't blame all the noise on us."

"This is our home. We will scream as loud as we please. I feel like screaming right now."

Ophelia waved her hand.

"They lock people up for doing what you did. You ol' pedophile."

"You can call me what you want, but I can tell you this, I wasn't disappointed."

"You are sick."

Ophelia crossed her legs and twisted her fingers into her hair. "The boy is blessed at his age. I never thought a fifteen-year-old could feel so good."

"Will you stop it?" Dorothy felt disgusted even being in the same room with her sister. "I've heard enough. Good night."

She smiled and untwisted her fingers from her hair. "Don't tell anyone about this."

"About what?" Dorothy pretended she had forgotten about the situation. "Come on, girl."

Ophelia examined her protruding butt in the mirror. "Marcus said I had the kind of ass to ride on."

"Good night!"

When David got in bed that night, he was still amused by the incident. "You talk to Ophelia?"

"She's sick."

"Marcus told me it started when they were outside by the pool. Ophelia kept flirting with him and telling him how good he looked. You know, the older, more experienced woman, and the younger naive boy routine?"

Dorothy stared speechless at him.

"Well, you wouldn't know, but anyway to make a long story short, Marcus said she asked him to put some lotion on her, she asked him to give her a massage, she asked him to stay over for a movie and some popcorn. After the movie, they started to kiss, she asked him how many times he had done it, he told her about ten, and she asked him if she could be number eleven. They kissed once more, they screwed for about five minutes, we caught them, and that's pretty much the story."

Dorothy sighed. "For some reason I wish I were a fly on the wall of that girl's mind. Just imagine what that would be like."

"Dark, gloomy, perhaps. Empty, maybe?"

"There's no maybe to it. Anyway, finish telling me about you and Marcus."

"I gave him the lecture. Told him that if he screwed up and got her pregnant, I'm giving him the abortion."

"That's why these young boys' minds are so corrupt, like that new movie *The Graduate;* about that older woman who has an affair with the neighbor's son."

David chuckled and pulled Dorothy's body next to his warm flesh. "I don't want to think about that. Instead, think about this good loving I'm going to give you." Dorothy felt his penis harden against her leg. He pulled the covers over their heads and they wrestled with each other until Dorothy went down for the count.

Chapter 10

"Dorothy, stop crying. You'll be fine," Katherine said as she held her sister's hand. "When I was pregnant with Richard, I admit I was frightened. I didn't know exactly what to expect. But now as I look back, I realize I hadn't anything to be afraid of."

Dorothy felt ten pounds heavier than usual, and she wasn't even showing.

"When did you find out?"

"Today."

"Does David know?"

Dorothy blew her nose. "No."

"He's going to be so happy. I know when I told Ricky I was pregnant, he didn't stop until he told the whole neighborhood."

Dorothy blew her nose again and pondered her situation. Here she was, nine weeks pregnant, and she already pictured herself with sagging breasts full of milk and ugly stretch marks on her stomach. Dorothy remembered when Katherine was pregnant; she had a lot of fluid in her body, causing her to have a swollen face, swollen feet, swollen arms, and a huge nose.

"I would love to stick around and see the look on David's face when you tell him."

"I think he knows. He's just not saying anything about it."

"Nonsense. You're just saying that because you're afraid to tell him."

"No I'm not," she said abruptly. "Doctors know the obvious signs, like morning sickness and swelling."

"He's been too busy to notice."

"I don't know."

Katherine grabbed Dorothy's hand. "What are you waiting on? Tell him."

Dorothy rubbed her stomach, unable to grasp reality. She still couldn't get over having another individual growing inside of her.

"I love my child so much," Katherine gushed. "Once you have a child, your whole world revolves around him. Whenever you go out, say shopping for instance, your child will always be in the back of your mind." She grinned. "Dot, just the other day, Ricky and I went to town to make groceries, and we passed by this cute little baby shop. I couldn't resist the temptation to go inside and buy something for my baby."

"So?"

"I damn near bought the whole store."

"Get outta here."

David entered the room with a colorful glow on his handsome face. Dorothy sighed and silently thanked God that he was in a good mood.

"Katherine, it's good to see you. How have you been? Where're Ricky and the baby?"

"I'm handling motherhood well. I wish I could say the same for Ricky. He and the baby are upstairs sleeping."

"Not adjusting to fatherhood too well, huh?"

"He's getting a dose of what we have to go through."

David kissed Dorothy on the forehead. "Hello, honey. I have something to tell you."

"That's great because I have something to tell you, also."

"You do?" He sat down on the recliner and gave Dorothy his undivided attention.

"You tell me your news first," Dorothy said, trying to buy a little more time. She glanced at Katherine, who sat mild-mannered, withholding a smile. David eyed them suspiciously.

"What's going on? Why are you two smiling like that?"

"Honey, go ahead with your news," Katherine said. "It's okay if I hear it too, right?"

"I don't see why not, Katherine," David said.

"Well, go on," Katherine urged him.

"My publisher called me at the office and informed me that the book just sold 50,000 copies. He just offered me another deal worth $35,000 for the upcoming book."

Katherine and Dorothy both screamed before they reached out and embraced David.

"The earnings from the last book were really good, and they keep growing." He pranced around the room. "Just think, 50,000 more copies and I won't ever have to worry about getting my practice going." He picked up the phone.

"David, who are you calling?"

He continued to dial. "I'm calling my agent. Hello, Ted?" He disappeared into the kitchen. "This is Dave, how are you?"

Dorothy and Katherine had puzzled looks on their faces.

"He didn't give me a chance to share my news." Dorothy sounded like she was on the verge of whining.

Katherine rubbed her knee. "Don't worry. He will. He's just so happy and excited."

"I know. I'm happy for him. He's doing so well. He's getting calls from everybody wanting to do interviews—*Ebony*, the *Defender*."

"Imagine getting interviewed by *Ebony* magazine. That's all right."

David entered the room once more, smiling as big as ever.

"Congratulations are in order," he shouted as he strolled to the bar to grab three glasses and a bottle of champagne. He popped the top and filled each glass. Katherine slapped Dorothy's hand. "Tell him," she whispered. David did a little dance and gave Katherine a glass. Dorothy declined hers.

"Come on, what's the matter?" David sipped. "This is a 1965 bottle here. That was a damn good year." He poured more into her glass until it bubbled over with foam. "Drink up."

"I can't right now."

"Why not?"

"It's not good for the baby."

"What are you talking about?"

"Our baby." She paused. "I'm pregnant."

David paused and stood there for a moment with the bottle in one hand and glass in the other. He swallowed so hard, Dorothy noticed his Adam's apple bobbing.

"You're kidding, right?"

"No kidding."

He put the bottle and glass on top of the table and kneeled in front of her. Taking her hands into his, he smiled. "Stop pulling my leg."

"Why would I lie?"

He glanced at Katherine. "I take it you knew about this already?"

"Yes." Katherine took Dorothy's hand. "And I'm so excited because I'm gonna be an auntie."

"So that explains why the both of you were grinning like the joker. How far along are you?"

"Nine weeks. I went to the doctor today."

"How do you feel?" He rubbed her face with the back of his hand.

"I don't know. Happy." She giggled nervously, trying to figure David out. She knew if he was angry, he wasn't going to show it in front of company.

Dorothy often found herself watching Katherine and seeing how she nurtured her baby. She held him and talked so softly and gently to him. Every so often she would hold him high above her head and bounce him up and down until he blessed her with a smile. Whenever he cried, she held him against her cheek and shushed him until he stopped. Dorothy took her turn holding him and imagined herself holding her own baby. A girl, maybe? A boy, perhaps?

"What's on your mind?" Katherine asked, her eyes sparkling. Dorothy held Richard in her arms and stared at her reflection in the mirror. "I'm just waiting to see my own baby."

"You know when I was pregnant, I often wondered how my baby would look."

Dorothy held him so close she could smell his soft, delicate scent.

"You'll be a wonderful mother, Dorothy."

"I know I will."

"Children are God's precious little gifts to us." Katherine's voice was filled with compassion. "I love those night feedings, the caring and the nurturing. I wouldn't trade it for anything in the world."

"I know, Katherine."

She kissed Richard's head and gave him back to Katherine who cooed and kissed him before she nursed him off to sleep. While Katherine nursed Richard, Dorothy examined her own breasts. Her size 34 C-cups weren't huge and sore just yet. She had so much to look forward to.

*　*　*

Mrs. Leonard telephoned to inform Dorothy of a dinner party she was hosting in her home. Dorothy realized that it didn't have to be a special occasion in order for Elizabeth Leonard to have people in her home. The company kept the house alive, and music shut out all the emptiness she had been feeling for some time. An emptiness that started the day she brought her newborn son home from the hospital. Mrs. Leonard didn't know a thing about changing diapers, burping babies, or what it was like to baby-sit a child. She was an only child born of privilege, sheltered until the time she met and married David Leonard, Sr. She didn't like being alone with the baby, so she got David to hire help. When Edna West came into the home, she was a single mother. Edna needed a place to stay, and Mrs. Leonard needed a live-in nanny/house-keeper. Elizabeth never cooked, so Edna did the cooking for her. Elizabeth needed a shoulder to cry on. Edna West was there. They raised their sons as brothers, but Edna couldn't possibly sense the loneliness that Elizabeth had been feeling. She didn't want anyone to know that sometimes she had to laugh to keep from crying. She had to bring life into her home. She needed more laughter. She needed the comfort of other privileged ladies whose husbands didn't give a damn about how many Dior and Yves St. Laurent couture outfits they charged on their accounts.

David walked into the kitchen. "Who are you talking to?" he asked.

"Your mother."

David waved his arms and shook his head. He didn't want to speak to his mother.

"May I speak to my son, please?"

Dorothy gave David the phone. "Your mother said please."

He frowned and held it in his hand before he placed it against his ear. "Hello." He leaned against the island in the center of the kitchen.

"You don't sound happy to hear from your mother."

"Why do you say that?"

"What have I done to you, son?"

"Nothing."

"You know, I could use another spa treatment. I'm not getting any younger dealing with your father."

"I told you what you should do, but you don't listen to me."

"I won't do such a thing. What kind of mother do you think you have?"

"Is there something you want to say? Because I gotta go."

"I wish you would come to my dinner party tonight."

"I'm not staying long."

"You may just have a good time."

"And listen to all those hens? Please, I'd rather eat cat shit with a knitting needle."

Dorothy frowned at David. "Don't talk to your mother that way."

Mrs. Leonard sighed. "Think about it. I'll see you and Dorothy around seven."

David put down the phone. "I swear, she gets on my damn nerves."

When Mrs. Leonard opened the door, she immediately looked strangely at Dorothy.

"What's wrong?" Dorothy asked.

She eyed Dorothy from head to toe. "You look so . . . so different."

"Different in what way?" Dorothy asked.

Mrs. Leonard blinked her long, false eyelashes and opened the door wide enough for Dorothy to come in. As they walked through the lavishly decorated dining area, Mrs. Leonard kept naming reasons for Dorothy's change in appearance.

"You've gained a little weight."

Edna West, the housekeeper, checked her out as well.

"Don't mean to pry, but you look like you may have a little company in a few months."

"Nonsense." Mrs. Leonard cut her off.

"She's telling the truth," Dorothy proclaimed, rubbing her stomach, which had yet to develop.

Mrs. Leonard couldn't close her mouth. She stood there, wide eyed, with her arms open. "Dorothy," she cried. Her *café au lait* complexion was bright crimson with chill bumps forming on her forearm. She blushed, grabbed Dorothy's hands, and squeezed them tightly. "You told David?"

"Of course I did."

"How did he take it?"

"He was happy." Dorothy forced herself to smile.

"I'm going to be a grandma." She took Dorothy's hand. "I'm letting you know right now that I'm gonna spoil that rascal."

"That's what grannies are supposed to do."

"I'm so happy for you. Are you happy?" she asked, her eyes probing Dorothy's for the truth.

"Of course I'm happy."

Dorothy could sense that Mrs. Leonard was reading right through her. She knew if David was anything like his father, living with him was a struggle, but they were going to deal with the struggles like mighty women. They weren't going to throw in the towel; they were going to their graves, holding steadfast to their vows.

Seven months later, when David stood in the doorway, he found his wife sprawled across the bathroom floor in a pool of water.

"Your water broke."

Dorothy nodded. It seemed like the only thing she could do. That, and praying to God to give her strength to endure several more hours without shitting all over everything.

"Baby, stay calm."

A twinge struck her, and at that moment for the strangest reason, it made her wish she could fly. David grabbed a handful of towels and wrapped them around her. She could see in his eyes he was wondering how in the hell was he going to carry her to the car.

"You think you can move?"

Dorothy couldn't talk, let alone move. Her left leg caught a cramp and it began to tighten up. She screamed and grabbed the nearest thing—David's shirt collar.

"Just breathe deeply. Each time you feel a contraction, I want you to breathe deeply from here." He laid his palm on her chest. Dorothy closed her eyes and braced herself, remembering what she learned in Lamaze. She learned deep chest breathing, shallow chest breathing, panting, and expulsion. Just the sound of expulsion made her want to explode into a million pieces.

David managed to carry her to the car. Once they got going, he held her hand and coached her each step of the way. "Hang in there, baby. You're doing good, baby. Don't stop breathing, baby. Don't give up, we're almost there." He sped through stop signs and traffic lights. "That's the second one you've ran. I want to get to the hospital in peace, not in pieces."

"Shhh, don't talk, just breathe."

Dorothy promised herself that if she got through this pregnancy, she would never have another baby. Once they were on the freeway, she felt a contraction that felt like it ripped through the walls of her uterus, causing her to sit up straight.

"Calm down, baby."

"I can't, dammit!" Before she realized it, she was squeezing the blood out of his thigh. Luckily for David, they were turning into St. Joseph's Hospital. From that moment on, Dorothy remained in a horizontal position, gazing teary-eyed at the bright fluorescent lights. She heard David's authoritative voice, his reassuring voice, telling the receptionist that his wife was in labor. He held her hand when the doctors came out and rushed her down the corridor, stretched out on a gurney. When she looked into his eyes, he kept saying, "Hold on, baby. You're doing wonderful, just breathe."

"Dr. Leonard, how far apart are her contractions?" Dorothy heard a doctor ask.

"Five minutes."

Moments later their journey came to a standstill. Dorothy opened her eyes and saw David standing to her right holding her hand. He wore surgical gloves, and his mouth was covered with a surgical mask. Another contraction hit. She wanted to die. She heard one of the doctors mention the baby was in a transverse position and that a cesarean delivery would have to take place. The doctor covered her mouth with an anesthetic cone. Afterward she was talking and laughing. Then the room began to fade to black.

When she regained consciousness, she was in a different room surrounded with flowers and balloons that read *Congratulations. It's a boy.* She took a look at her stomach and saw the swelling had gone down but a sharp, needlelike pain remained.

The door opened. From a side view Dorothy saw a white spot. It was the nurse.

"I think she's awake now," she whispered and opened the door wide enough for the other person to enter. Her head felt so heavy that turning it meant more pain, so she lay still, staring straight ahead. A familiar scent of cologne rushed over her senses and she felt the soft, sweet, gentle touch of familiar lips brush against her forehead. David looked into her eyes and held her hand. The twinkle in his eyes made her heart pound.

"You look beautiful." He pulled up a chair. "It's a boy. His name is Ahmad. He was born at 2:45 this morning. He was seven pounds, six ounces and he's twenty-one inches long."

Dorothy pressed her eyes shut. That was music to her ears. At last, her baby was here. She wanted to talk and ask David how the baby looked, but the excruciating pain prohibited such measures.

"Shhh, don't talk. Too much pressure on your abdominal area."

Dorothy mustered a small grunt.

"I'm so proud of you." He leaned forward and kissed her again. "I bet you're wondering whose idea it was to name the baby Ahmad, aren't you?"

Dorothy closed her eyes again.

"Before you jump to any crazy conclusions, let me explain to you why I named the baby Ahmad." Dorothy braced herself; she knew she was in for quite a long story.

"In med school," David began, "I had an instructor named Dr. Abdul Ahmad. Now he wasn't Arab, and he wasn't black—he was white, believe it or not. No one at Tulane liked him because he had a reputation for being difficult. Many a man has contemplated homicide against this man because they failed his class. He was difficult, not to mention arrogant, but in some aspects he regarded me as his prized pupil. I will never forget the day Dr. Ahmad was paged to the maternity ward at Charity Hospital. Now I was the only student who generally stayed after a lab, asking questions. Well, one day I was present during the time he received a call. Dr. Ahmad asked me to accompany him to the maternity ward. When we get there, he turned to me and said, 'Leonard, I want you to deliver Ms. X's baby.' When he told me that, I stood back and examined him, and I thought, *This man has got to be insane. Does he not understand the risk he is putting us all into?* Dorothy, I had never in my life delivered a child, and I asked him, 'Doc, do you know how serious this is?'"

David paused and stared quietly out toward the window. "He said, and I'll never forget it, he said, 'Look, Leonard, I'm serious. I want you to perform the procedure. I want you to prove to me that you are worthy of being a good physician.' So I went into the delivery room, shaking like gelatin and walking barefoot on pins and needles. After three and a half hours, I delivered my first child. The patient was so impressed with me that she named the child after me. Dr. Ahmad believed in me. My own father never had that much belief in me. Dr. Ahmad gave me the confidence I needed to become a world-class physician, and if he said it, it actually meant something. I made a promise to him. I told him that if I had a son, I would name him Ahmad, which means 'worthy of praise' in Arabic." David's astounding testimony nearly put her to sleep. He studied the identification band on her wrist in silence. "Honey, I wish you could see him now. I believe he's going to be a ladies' man. He's got your green eyes."

Dorothy smiled.

"Ma and Dad called this morning. They telephoned the whole block. Now everyone knows our baby's name and weight."

David placed Dorothy's cold hand next to his cheek. "The boy isn't in the world a good seven hours and people already know him."

A Catholic nun entered the room, quietly smiling at both of them. "God bless you both." Her eyes sparkled. "I'm Sister Rose. I'm here to pray for Mrs. Leonard. You must be Mr. Leonard?"

"Yes, I am."

"You can join us, too."

David laughed and shrugged. "You leave me no choice."

Sister Rose bowed her head and proceeded to pray. Once she finished she took Dorothy's hand. "Call whenever you need me. I'll be in the chapel. God bless you both."

Dorothy was standing outside the window, gazing misty-eyed at his diminutive form all bundled up and asleep like the world was at a standstill. Looking at him she thought, *So, you're the little fellow who kept me up all night tossing and turning and craving for food. I gained fifty pounds of fluid and fat, and I kept getting rashes and yeast infections. You made my nose expand all seven continents, my thighs rubbed, my feet were swollen, my mouth was so fat that I talked with a lisp. Your little mind can't possibly imagine all those times you had me wishing I hadn't gotten into this predicament in the first place. But looking at you now, I see it was all worth it. Every gut-aching pain, every single stitch was all worth it. You are so beautiful.*

Everyone loved you before you were even born. Grandma and Grandpa Leonard said they are going to spoil you. Can you believe it? Mémère *Cleo said it, too. She's coming all the way from New Orleans to see you. Your Aunt Katherine and Cousin Richard and Cousin Tiny are coming, too. You know, you are so blessed to have wonderful parents like your father and me, who love you so very much.*

Cleo saw Dorothy staring through the plate glass window at her baby.

"Dot."

"Hello, *Mère*."

"Which one is he?" Cleo asked.

"There. See right there, wrapped up in blue with his thumb in his mouth?"

"Yes. Oh, he's a biggun. Look at how big that boy is."

"He has an appetite a mile long."

"I can see it right now, that boy is going to eat you out of house and home. How much did you say he weighed?"

"Seven pounds, six ounces."

"You weighed eight pounds when you were born, and I didn't have no C-section."

Dorothy perished at the thought.

"How do you feel?" Cleo asked.

"I feel better. Today is my last day. We're leaving first thing tomorrow morning."

"Are you excited?"

"Oh yeah. I can't wait to show him off."

"I went on a shopping spree for the baby."

"*Mère*, you didn't."

"I dropped off most of his things at the house."

"Don't spoil my child."

"That's what *Mémères* do." She tapped the glass and stared cheery-eyed at her grandson. "Look at him, looking like a Buddha doll." Out of the corner of her eye she noticed Doc Sr. and Mrs. Leonard. "Here comes that mother-in-law of yours."

"Be nice, Mama."

"I'll try, but when you leave the hospital, I want to be the first one to keep the baby, you hear?"

Dorothy paid no attention and focused it on Doc Sr. and Mrs. Leonard, who were dressed elegantly. Doc Sr. was whispering something to her and looked perplexed at the stuffed teddy bear he was holding. Mrs. Leonard, on the other hand, was carrying a blue blanket and flashing her ivories.

"Ms. Lacroix, it's good to see you again," Doc Sr. said as he put the teddy bear aside and gave Cleo a hug. "How was the drive?"

"Uneventful."

"That's a good thing."

"Cleo, if I may say so, you are looking more youthful than ever," Mrs. Leonard said as she approached Cleo. "No one would suspect we're grandparents." She winked her long eyelashes and playfully nudged Cleo with her elbow. Cleo forced herself to laugh. "Thank you, Elizabeth. You don't look a day over forty-five yourself." Mrs. Leonard wasn't sure whether or not to take Cleo's remark as a compliment. She stepped aside and glanced at Dorothy. "How are you, princess?"

"Anxious, excited, glad." Dorothy thought about taking her baby home.

"Look what I've found." She held up a pastel blue chenille blanket. "David's baby blanket."

"Where did you find it?" Dorothy retrieved it and cradled it right under her nose. She was surprised that after twenty-eight years it had a delicate, soft odor.

"Edna found it in the linen closet."

"Isn't that something?" Cleo sounded amused. "How long have you had it?"

"Since 1940, almost twenty-eight years ago." Mrs. Leonard fingered it. "I bundled David in this very blanket when he came home from the hospital."

"That's amazing," Cleo said before she sniffed it. "Did you wash it?"

"Of course I did." Ms. Liz snapped. "You think I'd give my grandson an old dirty blanket?"

Dorothy could hear the baby crying inside the nursery. She looked inside. "See what you two did? You upset the baby." A nurse rushed to pick him up.

"I hope she doesn't do that every time he cries," Doc Sr. began.

When the nurse rocked him in her arms, he stopped immediately. Doc Sr. chuckled. "He reminds me so much of David."

"Yes, he does," Mrs. Leonard replied. Both of their eyes were fixed dreamily on the baby. "When do you leave, Dorothy?"

"Tomorrow morning."

"Is David picking you up?"

"Yes, if there isn't a change of plans."

The four of them stood there gazing at Ahmad through the window, anticipating the hours before he came home.

Chapter 11

Dorothy didn't recognize Ophelia until she spoke to her. She stood in Dorothy's doorway, accompanied by a yellow-bearded white fellow. Both appeared as if they had joined the cast of *Hair*. Ophelia had a daisy tattooed under her left eye, a tattoo of a red rose exposed on her right hip, and one of a Buddhist monk on her right arm.

"Hello, my dear sister." When she kissed Dorothy's cheek, Dorothy stood there frozen solid. Ophelia had really gone off the deep end this time.

"What's the matter? Looks like you've seen a ghost."

"What have you done?" Dorothy bypassed the small talk. She asked with a nasty attitude, "And who is this?"

"My ace boon coon, my lover, my friend, my muse, Professor Ra." The man she referred to was dingy with yellow hair that dreaded into long thick, turdlike braids. Even his beard was mangy, streaked yellow and silver, and held together with a rubber band.

"Pleasure to finally meet you." His voice resonated loud and clear into her home.

Dorothy couldn't find words. She couldn't believe her sister would be seen in public with him. She wished her mother were here to see it—-or better yet, her papa. She knew he was turning over in his grave. Dorothy would give anything to see the look on his face.

Ophelia shifted her weight from one leg to the next. "So aren't you going to let us in?"

Dorothy opened wide enough for them to enter.

"Professor, honey, let's sit on the floor," Ophelia insisted.

"Sure, no problem." They sat Indian style with erect posture. *Hallelujah!* Dorothy thought. She sat on the sofa across from them and took a good look at her sister and this Professor Ra.

"Ophelia, tell me about Chicago and how you came about meeting . . . I'm sorry, what is your name?"

"Professor Ra." He and Ophelia looked at each other and laughed like they shared a little secret.

"What's so funny?" Dorothy asked, not in the least bit amused.

"Dorothy, Ra belonged to this group that promotes peace and healthy living. We believe that with everything that's going on with the war and the riots, we're all doomed."

"Doomed?"

"Yes. I met Professor Ra at the Democratic National Convention during all the demonstrations and chaos. He was sitting Indian style in the doorway of the Hilton, meditating and reaching the state of nirvana. He looked so peaceful sitting there so I joined him, and we sat there for hours until those fascist pigs loaded us into a paddy wagon and took us off to jail."

"You were in jail, Ophelia?" Dorothy jumped to her feet.

"I was fighting for my rights."

"We didn't send you to Chicago to waste our money fighting for your rights."

"I felt it was the right thing for me to do."

"Let's see how you like it when you start paying for your own classes."

"I've got her covered, Mrs. Leonard." Professor Ra took Ophelia's hand.

"You're not responsible for her. We are."

"I understand your angst, Mrs. Leonard. Ophelia is hundreds of miles away from home and she's demonstrating, she's in jail, and she's heavy in the movement, but you have my word. Ophelia is in good hands."

The key latch clicked and the front door opened. David arrived, yawning and throwing his coat on the hanger. He noticed Ophelia and Professor Ra sitting on the floor. They both stood to greet him.

"Hello, David."

"Ophelia?" David was baffled by her appearance. "What happened? You got caught in the riot?" He gave her a hug.

"Believe it or not, those riots made me a better person."

"Is that so?" He glanced at Professor Ra. "David Leonard." He extended his hand.

"Pleasure to finally meet you. I'm Professor Ra."

"You teach art?"

"Yes."

"Ophelia's a wonderful artist. She's our next Picasso," David said, still shaking his hand.

"She definitely has what it takes," Ra replied.

"Make yourself at home. I've just spent fifteen hours in the delivery room, and I need to freshen up." He spoke to Dorothy. "How are you?" He beckoned with his eyes for her to follow him. "Could you come here for a second?"

Once they entered the bedroom, David closed the door. "What in the hell happened to her?"

Dorothy shook her head. "I don't know."

"Is she on drugs?"

"She's always been out there doing her own thing."

"I've always wondered about her," David said as he unfastened his tie. "I've spent a lot money on your family. I'm not going to sit around and let them waste it."

"I should've listened to Ma. She told me not to send Ophelia off to school. But I thought I was doing the right thing."

"Now you see? You try to help family and they end up letting you down. I'm not sending any more money to Chicago. She can do like everyone else and work."

"I told her that."

"First it's your father, then your mother, now this."

Dorothy thought she heard right. "My father? What does he have to do with this?"

"When your father died, he didn't have a cent to his name. They didn't know how they were going to pay for the funeral."

"That's a lie, David."

"Tiny told me she overheard her mother talking to your mother on the phone. So I took the initiative and paid for that funeral."

The news sent Dorothy's ears ringing. That was low of him. After five years, her father's death was still a sensitive subject. It brought tears to her eyes. "Why would you bring that up?"

"You need to know who's running things around here."

"You help people because you care about them. You don't do it to rub it in their faces every chance you get."

They heard a sharp knock on the door. "Dorothy, it's me."

Dorothy wiped her eyes immediately. "Just a minute. David's getting dressed."

"We're not through with this conversation." David threw on an old Tulane T-shirt and some pants and opened the door for Ophelia to come in. Dorothy noticed her fingernails were painted black, and covering her right hand was a tattoo of a butterfly.

"Look at you," Dorothy began. "You look like a damn fool."

"Are you finished?"

"David said he's not paying for your schooling anymore."

"I'm not surprised. I just wanted to tell you that I was dropping out, anyway. Ra and I are getting married and we're moving to California."

"No you're not."

"I'm twenty-one, Dot. You didn't just give birth to me." Ophelia's voice was loud and firm.

"You don't know this man. He could be a con artist who takes advantage of gullible country girls."

"He's the best thing that's ever happened to me, Dot."

"One of these days you are going to wake up and realize that when it comes to marriage, there is no such thing as happily ever after. Marriage is work, it's sacrifice. You give up so much of yourself."

"We live in a new day and age, sis."

"You keep thinking that way."

"I have a man who loves me." Ophelia pointed to her heart.

"What do you know about love?"

"I know that I listened to Papa a lot, and I remember him saying to get someone who respects me, and Ra respects me. He respects my body. We haven't even had sex yet."

"Wow." Dorothy giggled.

Ophelia waved her hand in the air and whizzed out of the room.

"Ophelia!"

Dorothy ran after her. Ophelia opened the front door, flashed her eyes at Dorothy and rolled them. Outside, Ra stood near the car.

"Ophelia!"

"Do you hear your sister?" Ra asked.

Ophelia crossed her arms. "Hurry and get me away from here."

Ra looked perplexed at David and Dorothy. "I don't know. She gets that way with me sometimes." He extended his hand to David. "It was a pleasure meeting you, Dr. Leonard."

"Likewise," David responded.

"It was a pleasure meeting you too, Mrs. Leonard. Peace." He held up two fingers.

Dorothy stood in the doorway, her heart as heavy as the ground beneath her slippers. David walked up to her and shoved her inside.

"How dare you call me a liar?" He backed her up against the wall. Dorothy closed her eyes, anticipating a slap to the face. "You apologize to me."

Dorothy thought about her baby in the other room and surrendered to him. "I'm sorry."

"You better be." He backed away and walked out of the room. Dorothy wanted to get her baby and get out of that house, but there was only one car and David kept a tight reign on the keys.

David tried not to involve Dorothy in his personal affairs, but for three days parcel delivery trucks were pulling up, bringing certified letters for him to sign. David opened one and it was a check made out to him for $25,000. After talking to his agent, he informed him that his manual was three thousand sales away from achieving bestseller status.

David wanted to smooth some rough edges between him and Dorothy. With the hours at the hospital and coming home to listen to the baby cry, he needed a vacation. They drove two hours south to Surfside, and he made a cash purchase on a beach home. They got out of the car, and about twenty feet away stood a magnificent 2,600 square-foot structure, about two-and-a-half stories high with double doors and windows so clean they cast a mirror-image reflection when you looked through them. The living room contained a spiral staircase leading to a second level overlooking the massive room. Floor-to-ceiling glass gave breathtaking views of the ocean. David wanted to hire the best damn interior decorator to give it life just in time for the party he was planning to give to celebrate the success of his book, as well as the opening of his practice.

David invited both colleagues and personnel from his practice to attend the party. Dorothy had already met some, and others she had no clue existed. She met two people in particular who entertained her. Sadaria McCloud was a receptionist. The Southern Comfort made her a feisty character, and she enlightened Dorothy and Myranda Corbin by talking about her ex-husband. Drunk as hell with tears in her eyes, she told them her life story.

"I never knew the true meaning of the word hate until I met my ex-husband and my ex-daughter-in-law."

Dorothy and Myranda listened. "I came home one Friday evening. I put in eight hours, and I was dog-tired. My husband and I were on shaky terms, but I was still willing to do whatever I could to keep him satisfied, you know? So I come home to get me a shot of penis-cillin, because it's been a long time, you see. And girls, you know how it is when you ain't had none in a long time. Anyway, I wanted to surprise my husband and I came home a little early to change into something a little sexier, you see. I be damned if I don't come home and find that son of a bitch in bed with my daughter-in-law." Her conversation caught the attention of a couple of others.

"So what happened next?" Myranda asked. She had gotten caught up in the story.

"Baby, I didn't say a word," she began. "I went outside, went in my glove compartment, brought out my .38, went back in the house, stood in the door, and dared the sons of bitches to move."

Dorothy covered her mouth in shock. Myranda was trying not to laugh. "So what happened then?"

"I got tired of standing at the door and left the house my damn self. I said 'Fuck her, fuck you, fuck this damn house 'cause it wasn't in my name anyhow, and forget you ever knew me because I want a divorce, and I want my half of the shit.'" She drank more and swallowed hard. "Y'all just don't know how much that hurt poor Sadaria." Her mouth was watering with saliva, and she showered Dorothy and Myranda with her spit. "Say it, don't spray it," she told herself and wiped her mouth, not hesitating to stop the waiter for another shot.

Myranda, on the other hand, was less talkative about what went on behind closed doors. She mainly talked about her husband, Dr. Corbin, who also worked out of David's practice, and her students at Texas Southern, where she taught history.

"I'm involved with this program called Operation Goals, and its aim is to teach underprivileged and at-risk youths about Negro history. Some of our kids don't know that once upon a time they were kings and queens and built pyramids. All they know is what they see in old beat-up textbooks, all those pictures of slaves wearing tattered clothes without shoes."

"Where did you go to school?" Dorothy asked.

"Xavier."

Dorothy noticed from a pendant she wore that they belonged to the same sorority.

"You may know my cousin, Christine Lacroix."

A smile lit up her face. "Yes. She was my big sister when I was on line."

Dorothy was glad she found a soror in the bunch. No wonder they hit it off so well.

"You know, Faye Kent is here," Myranda said.

"Isn't she the secretary from the national chapter?"

"That's her. She was my line sister."

"Where is she? I can't believe I missed her."

She and Myranda walked upstairs to the second level where there was yet another crowd of people standing around sipping champagne and acting convivial. Dorothy glanced near the champagne bar and spotted David talking to an attractive woman. She was about Dorothy's height, except she was a little on the stout side. Dorothy wondered what they were talking about. David held a glass of champagne in one hand and was gesturing away with the other. The woman, on the other hand, stood there absorbing every moment and every word. Dorothy didn't hesitate to walk in their direction. Myranda said, "That's Mrs. Kent." Dorothy wondered if she was referring to the lady talking to David. She had never seen Mrs. Kent before, only her signature on a few documents and periodicals distributed throughout the sorority. Before Dorothy opened her mouth, Myranda tapped Faye's shoulder. David glanced up and acted surprised to see Dorothy.

"My soror, Myranda Reece, it's good to see you again," she said in a loud and articulate voice.

"It's Myranda Corbin now." Dorothy watched them exchange compliments about each other's dress. David slid his arm around Dorothy's waist. "Faye, I want you to meet my better half, Dorothy."

"It's so nice to meet you, Dorothy."

"Same here."

"Your husband's family and my family go way back. His father delivered my brothers and sisters, and in exchange, my father got him out of loads of trouble."

David chuckled. "You talk too much."

"Dorothy, this is a wonderful man." Faye pointed to David. Dorothy forced herself to smile convincingly.

"Where's Bill?" David asked Myranda.

"He's probably on the beach, who knows?"

"I'm surprised you two managed to separate. Talk about lovebirds," David said and Myranda chuckled.

"Dorothy, Myranda and Bill got married after three months."

"Wow." Dorothy was amazed.

"Bill was my roommate in college. This woman had him missing curfew constantly."

Myranda blushed.

"If I recall correctly, Mr. Bill was a playboy. That is, until he met this woman."

Mrs. Kent took a sip of her champagne and glanced at Myranda. "I know I haven't been keeping in touch with you like I should because I practically live on the road now."

"Did you know Dorothy was a soror?"

Faye's expression lit up like early dawn. "Fantastic. What chapter?"

"Theta Chi."

"Did you go to Xavier?"

"No. Southern in Baton Rouge."

"The Boulé's gonna be in New Orleans this year."

"That's my hometown."

"I love that place. I live in Chicago now and I try as often as I can to get back."

"Excuse me, ladies." David's eyes were fixed across the way. Dorothy watched him strut his six foot-one frame across the terrace and disappear into the crowd.

Faye sipped from her champagne glass. "Hmm, this is good."

Dorothy and Myranda sipped daintily from their glasses.

"Dorothy, you and David have a wonderful vacation home."

"I love it here," Myranda responded.

"Myranda, when are you and Bill going to have children?"

"When I'm forty."

"Forty?" Dorothy and Faye said in unison.

"By then I will have retired from teaching, but right now, it's just not in the cards."

"I had a cousin like you. She waited until she was forty-two to have her first child." Faye shrugged. "At forty-two what little energy you have left is zapped. This is my opinion, Myranda— you know how I like to express my opinion. I like to grow with my children."

"What do you mean?"

"I want to be able to run around with my kids without running out of breath. You know, the older you get, the shorter your patience becomes. When you turn fifty your child will be ten. My cousin is fifty-two, her oldest daughter is ten and the youngest is six. My cousin never popped a single pill until she had these kids. You talk about an old witch. She had to hire a nanny."

Dorothy thought of her own mother and how at thirty-seven she gave birth to Jacqueline. To Dorothy, that was pretty old. Before long they were off on another tangent dealing with their husbands. Dorothy felt really close to Faye and Myranda, as if she had known them all her life. After the party they exchanged addresses and anticipated getting together to pick up where they left off at Boulé in New Orleans. Dorothy could hardly wait.

David was cleaning the lens on his handheld camera and checking the focus with stern concentration. He did not want to miss a single moment of Ahmad's first birthday party. It amazed Dorothy to see her son walking around, trying to put everything in his mouth. Dorothy lost count of how many times she'd pulled paper, dirt, pennies, nickels, dimes, cotton, or whatever he could get his hands on out of his mouth. He really had Dorothy going when he somehow unfastened the pin on his diaper and stuck it in his mouth. Ahmad poked his small tongue and came wobbling to her with blood trickling down his mouth. What really frightened Dorothy was that he didn't shed a single tear, and just had a look of guilt. Since the incident she nicknamed him Man because he was one tough cookie. He could take bumps, bruises and scrapes like a starving person could a free meal, and he hardly ever cried.

For the party, David and Dorothy turned their recreation room into a miniature Disneyland with hats and party favors containing all the Disney characters. When Dorothy walked into the recreation room, David was filming Ahmad through the camera.

"And what does the birthday boy have to say?"

"I feel grrreat!" Dorothy spoke for Ahmad in a high-pitched voice and scooped him up in her arms. It tickled him, so he couldn't stop drooling.

"Look into the camera and say something mushy," David said from behind the lens. Dorothy bounced her son up and down on her lap and coaxed him to look into the camera to flash his million-dollar smile. "Look at Daddy." She took his small hands and kissed them, tasting the combination of sweat and clean Johnson's baby lotion.

"I want a quick 'Da Da' for me," David said with one eye hidden behind the camera. "Come on, say Da Da."

"Tell him to say Ma Ma," Dorothy said jokingly.

"Put him down so I can get a shot of him walking."

David ended up following his son around the recreation room and down the hall to the other rooms. Dorothy rested her chin on the arm of the sofa and watched the two of them. David was enjoying the last of his mini-vacation. Since day one, most of his time was spent with Ahmad, filming his every move and taking him around to show him off at work. The day before, the weather was unusually warm for February, and the three of them went to Hermann Park. There were times when Dorothy got jealous because he didn't say much to her at all.

David put his camera aside and held Ahmad in the palm of his hand. "It's a bird! It's a plane!" David glided him around the room like Superman, taking him up high and down slowly. He played for about five minutes and plopped down with Ahmad secured in his arms. David had never had this much fun with his son since he was born, because of his long hours. He missed out on a lot of precious moments in Ahmad's life. Dorothy wanted David there with the camera to video Ahmad's first step and had seen the look on his face when Ahmad uttered "Da Da" for the first time. It hurt Dorothy's feelings that she was the one who listened to him cry and doctored his gums when he was teething, not to mention changing his diapers.

Ahmad looked at her with glistening green eyes. He was so precious, all dressed up for his birthday party in a Mickey jumpsuit, wearing the shiny white high-top shoes she had just gotten for him the day before. The telephone rang. "I'll get it," she said, reaching to pick it up. "Hello."

Cleo was on the other end, screaming, hollering and yelling.

"She's dead, my baby is dead. Lord have mercy." Dorothy's heart rate sped up, and the saliva in her mouth all of a sudden began to taste like chalk.

"*Mère, Mère!* What's wrong, *Mère? Mère!*" Blood rushed to her ears, and for a moment Dorothy thought her head was going to explode. David saw the look in Dorothy's eyes, and he quickly grabbed the phone. Dorothy grabbed Ahmad and held him in her arms like a teddy bear.

"Hello. Hello, Cleo?"

Dorothy could hear Cleo's shrilling voice screaming through the receiver; it made her tremble. Her teeth chattered uncontrollably, and the first thing that came to mind was that something horrible had happened to Jacqueline. Ahmad turned and looked at his mother with a confused expression in his sad eyes, wondering what in the hell was happening to Ma. Why was she shaking?

David shouted, "Are you sure?" He stared blankly at the floor. "Are you sure about that?"

"Who is it?" Dorothy screamed.

David paced the room with the phone. "We're on our way, I know. Don't panic. Don't panic in front of her. She doesn't need to see you panic."

Dorothy's heart was coming out of her chest. Something must've happened to Jacqueline.

"What's wrong with Jacqueline?" Dorothy screamed. "I want to talk to *Mère!*" Dorothy reached for the phone. David pushed her with his sharp elbow.

"Get back. I'm trying to calm your mother."

Ahmad burst out crying. Dorothy did, too.

"Cleo, listen to me. Do this." Dorothy couldn't understand how he could sound so confident and calm at a time like this. "Call your neighbors and tell them to take you to the airport immediately. I'll take care of the tickets, you hear me? I'll take care of them for you. Bye."

He hung up the phone and looked at Dorothy.

"What's wrong with Jacqueline?"

"She's fine."

Dorothy grabbed her heart and rested her weight against the arm of the sofa.

"It's Ophelia."

Dorothy's heart raced up again. "Ophelia! Is she dead?"

"I wasn't able to calm your mother long enough to find out. But as far as I gather, she's either dead or barely clinging to life."

Dorothy immediately shoved Ahmad into David's arms and ran toward the bathroom. Unable to retain her sick feeling, she hurled into the toilet. She had a guilt-ridden feeling, like somehow Ophelia's accident was her fault. She remembered the last time she had seen her and the way she had looked. When Dorothy closed her eyes, she couldn't help but see the angered look in Ophelia's eyes when she stormed out the door for the last time. They hadn't spoken to each other since. Thanksgiving and Christmas came and went without so much as sending a card. Dorothy felt the tension mounting in her stomach and threw up once more. She heard David shushing Ahmad, who was wailing. Dorothy's throat was raw afterward, but she managed to crawl to the edge of the tub to rest her head there. Moments later, she heard Mrs. Leonard and Doc Sr. behind her, talking.

"I got her," David said to his father. He picked Dorothy up from the floor.

"I'm sorry." Dorothy started wailing like Ahmad.

"You didn't do anything wrong. Why are you sorry?" He held her in his arms.

Dorothy lost the feeling in her legs and fell to the floor again.

"I can't make it."

"Yes, you can."

She shook her head. "No." Saliva dripped from her bottom lip.

They caught a 5:30 flight to Chicago. The whole time on the plane, Dorothy kept having crazy thoughts and visions of Ophelia's funeral. At the airport she was too weak to walk, so David pushed her around the terminal in a wheelchair. She stopped crying once they got in the cab. But when Sam and Dave sang "Something is Wrong With My Baby," she started wailing again.

Once they arrived at Cook County Hospital, they dreaded hearing the news. A physician by the name of Dr. Mercer approached them. "Dr. Leonard, Mrs. Leonard."

"How is she?" David asked.

"She's listed in critical condition."

"What happened?"

"She and a companion were headed southbound on I-55. Somehow they lost control of their vehicle and collided with the northbound traffic. It killed the driver. Miss Lacroix suffered a few broken ribs and a concussion. She had some internal bleeding."

David squeezed Dorothy's shoulders as a sign of relief.

"Miss Lacroix was also eight months pregnant."

Dorothy's eyes widened.

"Any word on the condition of the child?" David asked.

"We're monitoring the child. It's a miracle it survived."

Dorothy grabbed her chest. "There is a God."

"Miss Lacroix is right down the hall. Would you follow me, please?" a nurse said.

In the other reception area, Cleo visited with another nurse. She was dabbing her eyes. Dorothy embraced her mother like she had never seen her before. "*Mère*, I thought she was gone," Dorothy cried.

"I did too, baby."

Dorothy sniffed. "Have you seen her?"

Cleo blew her nose. "No, baby."

"Who was the other person in the car?" David asked.

Cleo shrugged. "I don't know." Cleo rubbed her nose until it was crimson.

They spent the remaining part of the day in the reception area, talking and checking the clock while Ophelia underwent surgery. A physician would give them an update on her condition. It went from very serious to serious to stable.

They stayed overnight in Chicago so they could observe her condition. When Dorothy finally saw her sister, her heart sank to her knees. Ophelia was bruised and bandaged with IVs running through her veins. Her left eye was so swollen and purple that it looked about the size of a plum. Dorothy whispered softly, "Hi."

Ophelia slowly opened her right eye; it was moist with tears. Dorothy was grateful to God that she was alive, though it upset Dorothy to know her sister was pregnant and didn't bother to tell anyone.

"I saw your baby," Dorothy said, trying to attempt a decent conversation. Ophelia closed her right eye and slowly turned her face toward the window. She seemed upset when Dorothy mentioned him.

"Ophelia, I still love you. Although I don't always approve of what you do, I still love you." Dorothy looked at the snow falling outside the window. "I love you very much, and I want you to get well, you hear?" Dorothy stood there for a moment to get a response from her; she got none. Ophelia's eyes were glued to the life outside the window.

Ophelia totally lost her mind after discovering Professor Ra was dead. At first, she lived in complete denial, but when it finally hit her, it got so bad to where Dorothy had to send her to a hospital to keep her under close surveillance. The baby was healthy and living with Cleo in New Orleans. Cleo named him Lucky because he survived the accident and he was premature.

After a month in the hospital, Dorothy moved Ophelia into her home. Dorothy didn't have anything else to do, so she played nurse and made sure Ophelia took the right amount of her medicine at the right time. Ophelia was capable of doing anything and Dorothy didn't want her to overdose. Each morning at 6:30 they swam five laps in the pool and walked about two miles in the neighborhood. Dorothy did everything constructive to keep her sister's mind off the accident, though sometimes late at night, Dorothy would hear her crying. Her doctor said it was normal for her to have long periods of grief. The million-dollar question was just how long.

Mrs. Leonard and Dorothy sat on the patio by the pool, gazing out into the backyard. It was a peaceful morning, and the only noise came from the chirping of the birds.

"I know it's none of my business," Mrs. Leonard began over a cup of hot lemon tea, "but maybe you ought to send her back to the hospital. She's not ready."

Dorothy stared into her cup at the bleak expression on her face. She tapped it, amusing herself with the ripples she created. Mrs. Leonard added as an afterthought, "Have you thought about Ahmad? She could possibly hurt him."

"That's nonsense, Ophelia wouldn't hurt anyone." Dorothy sipped the tea as if it wasn't still hot. "Except for herself, maybe." Her tongue was scorched.

Myranda Corbin, who'd become Dorothy's new best friend, sent Dorothy a letter. She didn't have very much to say, only that the Operation Goals kids went on a field trip to Chicago to the Johnson Publishing Company and they were going to be featured in a *Jet* magazine article. Reading her letters about school got Dorothy thinking about enrolling. The next day she went to the dean, whom she met at one of Mrs. Leonard's parties. He was a giant of a man with sparkling eyes. Dorothy remembered him being extra touchy-feely and smiling at her suggestively every chance he got. She didn't want to be alone in his office, but there she was, staring at him sitting no more than a few feet in front of her with that same look in his eyes.

"What took so long?" he asked.

"I just had a baby."

"That's right. What's your major?"

"I majored in history when I was at Southern."

He looked at Dorothy's file. "Most of these classes won't transfer. You know that, right?"

"No sir, I didn't."

"Look here, I'm gonna cut you some slack. But I'm not going to let you off too easy now."

Dorothy feared this was coming. "Don't worry about it. I'll take the classes I need to take."

"I'm trying to make it easy for you, Mrs. Leonard." He stood and walked next to her chair. Dorothy was eye level to his rotund waist. She stood immediately.

"That's okay. Forget about it." She ran out of the room. Once she got to the car, she felt a combination of hurt mixed with anger. She started up her car and went home.

When David came home, he stormed into the room where she was and slammed the door.

"What the hell were you doing in the office with the dean?"

"What?"

He slapped her across the face and pushed her on the bed. Dorothy touched her stinging face with her hand and looked him in the eye. "Nothing. I didn't do anything."

He stood towering over her like a giant. "You calling me a liar again?" He took his large hands and contorted her face inside them. "I heard you were in the office with the dean for a long time."

"I was trying to get back into school and he kept trying to—"

"Kept trying to what?" he screamed in her face.

"He kept looking at me strange."

"What did you have on?" He towered over her.

"I don't remember."

"You know what? Stay your ass in this house! You don't leave until I say it's time to leave." He left, slamming the door behind him.

If she had the strength, she would have charged right after him, but she didn't. Her pride and self-worth were at an all-time low. Everyone kept singing to her like a broken record of how fortunate she was. Little did they know, she would trade places with a poor woman in a heartbeat if she were rich with independence and peace of mind.

Ophelia opened the door minutes later and glanced at her sister on the bed. "Uh, Dorothy. Could you come here?"

"What do you want?" Dorothy snapped.

She hesitated. "That's all right. I guess I can get it myself."

Dorothy cursed herself before she got out of bed. Ophelia was in the bathroom, holding a glass of water and inspecting the glass for what she called microorganisms.

"You didn't take those pills, did you?" Dorothy asked.

"Remember? You locked them in the medicine cabinet." Dorothy grabbed the keys and unlocked the medicine cabinet. Watching Ophelia was like watching Ahmad, and God knows she didn't need another child on her hands. Ophelia stared at her sister's face.

"I talked to *Mère*," Ophelia said, not delving into her sister's personal affairs. She popped a couple of pills. "She said Lucky was doing fine and . . ." Ophelia burst out crying and stopped. "I miss him so much, Dorothy. Half of me wants to see him and half of me says you don't need to see him. You know he's all I got to remind me of Ra." Tears went dripping off the tip of her nose. Dorothy grabbed some tissues.

"Here, wipe the snot off your top lip."

Ophelia blew her nose and wiped it.

"I'm going to *Mère*'s this weekend. Do you want to go?"

Ophelia continued to dig deeper into her nose. "Yeah, I guess." She pulled out the tissue to inspect it.

"When did you talk to *Mère*?"

"This afternoon when you were out."

"What else did she talk about?"

"Lucky, mainly. She said she got him some clothes. She was going to take some pictures of him and send them to me." Ophelia's bottom lip trembled again. "When I talked to her this afternoon, I heard him crying in the background." She erupted again. "I felt so helpless, Dorothy."

"I know. Come on." Dorothy grabbed her arm and escorted her to her room. It was cluttered with drawings of men: blue men, green men, red men, and all of them had vague and colorful eyes. Dorothy sat on her bed and looked on the floor to discover Ophelia had the plate from yesterday's dinner with crumbs of dried food stuck to it.

"Dorothy, could you take my plate to the kitchen for me? I forgot where it was." Dorothy pulled back the covers so Ophelia could get underneath them.

"How could you forget where the kitchen is?"

Ophelia settled underneath the covers like a two-year-old and blurted out, "Dorothy, it sure is good to be alive." Dorothy smiled; she couldn't agree with her more. Dorothy glanced at another sketch of a man that Ophelia was currently working on. He had a beard and sorrowful blue eyes. Dorothy didn't bother to ask her who the person was.

"You know, Dorothy, I am living proof that there's life after death."

"Really? Tell me about it."

"It's really hard to explain, but this feeling came to me when I was riding in the car. I blacked out right before the impact and I saw this magnificent glow. Dorothy, it was so bright that I couldn't look directly into it. But I felt my way to it. Like something was pushing me. Now that I think about it, Papa was pushing me."

The hairs on Dorothy's arms stood erect.

"So when I got past the light, I ended up in front of a tall golden gate, and standing at the gate was a man with a long golden beard."

"Who was it?"

"Hell if I know. He scared the shit out of me because he appeared from nowhere. He took one look at me and asked in a loud, deep voice, 'Are you lost?'"

Dorothy laughed. "You sure this wasn't a dream?"

"I'm sure. I'm not playing. I actually saw a place that looked like heaven and I saw a man who I believe was God."

Dorothy yawned and continued to listen. "So you think you saw God?"

"I'll be damned. You don't believe me?"

Dorothy didn't want to argue with her, so she pacified her sister, asking her questions to give Ophelia the impression she was interested.

"Dorothy, I swear, everything was white and gold and it smelled like honey, like they say in the Bible."

Dorothy nodded. "Go on."

"He asked me," Ophelia tried to imitate a loud, deep voice. "'What is your name, child?' I told him Ophelia Lacroix. He had these reading glasses and put them on the tip of his nose, and out of nowhere came a huge scroll. He scanned the scroll for about twenty minutes searching for my name. He called out Labarre and Lacoste. He even called out Aunt Vivian's name, and Tiny's papa, and someone else's name that ended with Lacroix, then he went to LaRue. I said, 'Hold up. What happened to my name? You called damn near everybody with a La-something on that list and didn't call me.' He said," Ophelia imitated the voice, "'I'm sorry, child, but your name isn't here.' I said, 'Give me a pen and let me sign it.' He laughed in a sort of jolly, wicked ol' way and said, 'Sorry, we don't allow fornicators, idolaters, and liars through these gates.' I said, 'Hold it, hold it just one goddamn minute' and before I could say anything else he went *presto*. And I found myself in another place. There was fire everywhere, and it seemed like everywhere I stepped, there was a snake."

Dorothy's blood crept underneath her flesh. She hated snakes. Ophelia continued with the story.

"From what I gathered, this place was hell. There were people standing everywhere, cursing and screaming and calling me names. I almost got into a fight, but the man at the gate stopped me. He was an ugly man with a receding hairline and chin longer than eighty cents in pennies."

"You sure this wasn't a dream?"

She raised her right hand. "I swear to God on Professor Ra's grave this wasn't a dream."

Dorothy urged her. "Go ahead."

She stared at Dorothy for a moment. "This wasn't even a damn nightmare. I swear to God this was real, Dorothy."

Dorothy chuckled. "Okay."

"The man at the gate didn't ask for my name. He just asked me was I Negro or white."

"Why did he ask you that?"

"He said if he let another Negro enter through his gate, he was going to have to relocate because the Negroes he had were down in the furnace trying to put the fire out."

Dorothy laughed so hard tears came to her eyes. "Ophelia, what am I going to do with you?"

Ophelia kept a straight face the whole time, which made it even funnier. Dorothy laughed until her stomach was in knots. Ophelia reached out and tapped her sister's hand. "If you don't want me to say anything about it, I won't."

Dorothy stopped laughing. "What are you talking about?"

"I'm talking about you and David. I won't mention anything about it."

"There's nothing to tell."

"Look, I may be loony and on medication, but I ain't too far gone to see what's happening, so you don't have to pretend with me."

"Everybody argues sometimes."

"He's not supposed to hit you."

"Things'll get better, Ophelia."

"They won't if you don't start fighting back. You remember what Papa told us that night?"

Dorothy wiped her eyes. "Yes."

"You don't have to put up with it."

"I know." Dorothy sniffed. "I know."

Dorothy spotted Tiny at the end of the stairs when she stepped off the plane in New Orleans.

"You look so pretty," she gushed. "It's still hard to believe you have a kid."

Dorothy checked out Tiny. She lost a little weight. She used to be short and plump, but now she was svelte and petite. The teal green outfit she had on accentuated all the right areas.

"Tiny, I can tell you lost some weight. You look good."

Tiny did a runway model turn for her cousin.

"And you are really wearing that dress. Just look at you."

Dorothy glanced at Tiny's narrow hips and slim waistline when she sat down.

"There's a saying: when ya got it, ya flaunt it."

"Well, you better keep it, is all I'm saying."

"I've got to, honey. I have my reasons now."

"Mike wouldn't happen to be one of those reasons?"

Tiny gave her cousin an ugly stare. "Give me a break. Mike is old news."

"What happened?"

"I'm tired of games, Dorothy, you know? Some people just go too damn far."

"How long were you together?"

"Seven years. I wasted seven years of my life with him and what do I have to show for it?"

"But y'all break up and get back together. How long do you think you can be without him?"

"For as long as heaven is happy and hell is hot," Tiny said.

Tiny couldn't fool Dorothy.

"So how are David and my little cousin Ahmad?"

"They're fine. His book is selling like crazy."

"Yeah, a friend of mine from law school just had a baby and read it. She said she's never known a physician to know so much about a woman's body and emotions. You'd swear a woman wrote the book. She had a lot of good things to say about it."

Dorothy chuckled quietly. If they only knew what she endured living with David. "So she really liked it?"

"Of course. She's even recommending it to her friends."

"That's great. You should see the letters he receives."

"Where's my free copy?"

"Speaking of which, I have one in my suitcase you can have."

"I'm gonna level with you, Dorothy. Since your baby shower, all I think about now is having a kid."

"You know it takes two to tango."

"Hell no, that's out of the question. I'm not having Mike's baby," Tiny convinced herself. "Tell me what's going on with Ophelia. Katherine told me she was nutty as a fruitcake."

"You got that right."

"How's her baby?"

"He's fine. *Mère* keeps him. Ophelia won't even see him, says he reminds her of the father."

"She needs to get over it." Tiny's eyes wandered into the crowd of passersby. Someone or something caught her eye.

"Oh my goodness, will you check out sister girl?"

Dorothy giggled and searched for the guilty party. She gave up because there were hundreds of people roaming around the terminal.

"Well, cuz, what's on your agenda for today?" Tiny asked.

"I'm going shopping and I'm grabbing a bite to eat at Dooky's."

"Sounds like a winner to me."

Dorothy and Tiny met up with Myranda Corbin at Dooky Chase. Myranda and Dorothy acted like two old biddies and stayed in their corners, while Tiny flirted with every pair of pants that waltzed by her. It mattered not what color they were or whether they were single. Once she got on the tipsy side, there was no point in stopping her.

"I don't give a damn if I don't ever hear from Mike again." Tiny wrapped her ruby-red lips around a shot glass of scotch and water and tilted her head back to finish it. She thought about what she said and stared at the flickering flame burning from the candle. "He could come through that door right now carrying fourteen bars of pure gold, a red '69 Corvette convertible, singing 'Please, Please, Please' like James Brown, and I still wouldn't go with him."

A tall, dark gentleman happened to walk by their table. He caught Tiny's attention. "Say, tall, dark and handsome, what are you doing tonight?"

He wiggled his tongue in a sexy, suggestive way and continued walking about his merry way.

"Oh no, he didn't." Tiny nearly fell out of her seat.

Myranda took her napkin to fan the air around her. Dorothy sipped from her champagne glass.

"He's too dark, and besides, I don't want nothing that black but a Cadillac, and it's got to have some white-walled tires."

"Amen," Myranda replied, which was one of the few things she said all night.

"Let's toast," Tiny began. She stood holding her glass. Myranda and Dorothy stood and did the same.

"First of all, I'd like to propose a toast to the sorority for bringing us here together." Tiny rubbed her temples. "A toast to our chapters, our families, our friends, our men—that's if you claim one." Tiny looked at Dorothy. "No, it's not Mike, thank you."

"Did I say anything about Mike?"

"In case you were entertaining the thought."

"Go on with the toast, cuz."

"I want to toast to everything and everybody that made this occasion possible. I love you girls."

"Someone bring out the violin," Myranda added.

They giggled and drank up before they checked into a hotel on the French Quarter and spent half the night talking and laughing. Not once did Dorothy think about David.

David's nurse, Ms. Johnson, was happy to see Dorothy when she arrived one afternoon with Ahmad in tow. Dorothy thought she was by far the sweetest person to ever walk God's green earth. They met for the first time at the beach house and clicked like birds of a feather.

"There she is, Miss America." Ms. Johnson's face glowed when Dorothy entered the place. Dorothy noticed quite a number of patients from all ethnic backgrounds waiting in the lobby. They all looked at her, wondering who she was, strutting in wearing a charcoal gray Yves St. Laurent suit with the pumps to match.

"Is my husband in?" Dorothy smiled, giving Ms. Johnson a peck on her cotton-soft cheek.

"Did you see that lobby?"

Dorothy sighed. "Busy place."

Ms. Johnson played with Ahmad before she motioned for Dorothy to follow her down a corridor to another waiting area where a couple of patients sat.

"Now, you'll have to wait right here. I think he's in with a patient right now."

"Sure, no problem." Dorothy sat down and helped Ahmad into the seat next to her. "Ms. Johnson, if he has fifteen minutes to spare, that'll be fine."

"Okay, sweetie." She winked before she disappeared down the hall.

Dorothy glanced at the other ladies sitting across from her who appeared to be around her age, in their mid-twenties.

Both had huge sandy-brown naturals, or Afros crowning their heads. Dorothy checked out their attire. They looked like they were going to a club rather than to the doctor's office. The light-skinned sister was dressed in a paisley mini-dress with black patent-leather platform boots, while the dark chocolate sister was blazing from head to toe in a brick-red jumpsuit with brick-red platform boots to match. The light-skinned sister leaned forward and waved her hand at Dorothy. "Excuse me. Which doctor are you waiting to see?"

Dorothy took her time before she answered, "Dr. Leonard."

"Honey, you'll be waiting all day to see that man. He's always packing the house."

"Why?" Dorothy asked, anxious to find out.

The dark-skinned sister added, "All the ladies come here just to see him."

"Why?" Dorothy opened her purse and pulled out a box of animal crackers for Ahmad.

"Because he's easy on the eyes, and I just love the way he examines me, don't you?"

It was obvious that neither she nor the light-skinned sister could read the shock on Dorothy's face, for they went on telling her how they would achieve orgasm just from the touch of his large hands when he examined their breasts.

"If that nurse wasn't in the office, honey, that man wouldn't stand a chance with me." The dark-skinned sister slapped high fives with the light-skinned sister. Dorothy was steaming underneath her suit. She wanted to burst their bubbles, but at the same time she wanted their stupid asses to keep on talking.

"So you get orgasms?" Dorothy asked.

"Right on, and honey, it's good enough to smoke a cigarette once he's done." They laughed and slapped high fives again.

"Excuse me sister, what is your name?" Dorothy asked the dark-skinned sister.

"Lisa."

"And what is your name?" Dorothy asked the light-skinned sister.

"Monique."

"Well, I'm Mrs. Dorothy Leonard, Dr. Leonard's wife."

Lisa and Monique's eyes resembled a deer's caught in headlights the second before impact.

"Well," Monique responded before she glanced at Lisa for her reaction.

"Thank you ladies for shedding some insight on what really goes on at the doctor's office."

"No disrespect." Monique's complexion was the color of Lisa's jumpsuit.

Dorothy felt some gratification seeing the disappointment in their eyes.

"You enjoy being married to him?" Lisa asked.

Dorothy thought of the awkwardness of the question and of the life she had with David up to that point.

"I love it," she lied. "I'm not worried about what goes on up here because I know at the end of the day, he's coming home to be with me and his son, whom he absolutely adores." Dorothy emphasized the point by kissing the crown of Ahmad's curly head and flashing her diamond wedding ring when she crossed her legs. Ms. Johnson appeared in the doorway.

"Follow me, Mrs. Leonard."

Dorothy gathered Ahmad and flashed a phony smile at the two ladies. "It's been charming," she said before following Ms. Johnson into David's office. He was sitting behind his massive mahogany desk with his eyes buried in a stack of papers.

"Dr. Leonard, someone's here to see you."

He looked up, his eyes narrowing on Dorothy and Ahmad just over the top rim of his reading glasses. "What a pleasant surprise."

Ahmad abandoned Dorothy and jumped into David's lap. David bounced him up and down on his knee.

"I came by to see if you wanted to join us for lunch," Dorothy began.

David's eyes traveled from Dorothy's to Ms. Johnson's. "Ms. Johnson, would you close the door on your way out, please?"

"Sure." She smiled and gave Dorothy a pat on the shoulder.

David's smile vanished once the door closed.

"Have you been paying attention to that waiting area?"

"Yes, I know, but Ahmad cried all morning after you left."

David looked into his son's eyes. "Ahmad, did you do that?"

To his surprise, Ahmad nodded.

"For you, I'll take thirty minutes."

He placed Ahmad on the floor. At one year old, Ahmad could sense he had his father wrapped around his little finger. He became chipper. Dorothy remembered the girls sitting in the waiting area. Once inside the car, she couldn't bite her tongue.

"Are you having sex with your patients?"

"What in the hell . . ." David realized Ahmad was sitting in the backseat. He lowered his voice. "What would make you say a stupid thing like that?"

"Two of your patients gave me an earful, said they get orgasms when you examine their breasts. Explain that."

"That's my fucking job. I examine women's bodies. I am not responsible for their orgasms. That's on them. When I examine these women, my nurse is present, my gloves are on, I do my job, and that's that."

"You and Bill need to enforce a dress code. These women are coming to you dressed like whores."

"My job is not to tell my patients how to dress."

"You are supposed to be running a respectable practice, but

from the looks of your patients, you're running a whore-house."

"I expect you to say something like that."

"Dammit, I don't like it."

"Lower your voice when you're talking to me."

"I'm not your child," Dorothy fired back.

David stopped the car in the middle of the busy street. Horns blared from other cars as they swerved around them.

"I swear to God, I will kill you right here, Dorothy."

Dorothy looked out the window at all the cars swerving around them. She reached for Ahmad in the backseat. "If you hurt my baby, I swear there won't be enough bullets in the world for your ass, David Leonard."

David looked into her eyes and saw that she meant every word of it, and just when she thought he was going to back-hand her, he backed off.

Chapter 12

Four years had come and gone. Four reunions had come and gone, and Dorothy's marriage to David was not without its highs and lows. For a young girl of twenty-eight, she found herself plum exhausted. She was a nervous wreck, walking on pins and needles, trying to make everything appear happy from the outside, when it really wasn't.

The only joy she got was getting Ahmad prepared for private school. She spent her days on the sofa reading to him, and when she wasn't doing that, she was making out a list of things to buy him for school.

David, on the other hand, ran across the country. If he wasn't at the hospital, he was in the office. And if he wasn't in the office, he was checking out the site of their new home. It was almost finished, and the only things needed to make the 8,500-square-foot structure complete were the furnishings.

David started plans for the house back in 1972. He wanted the locale in a retreat-type setting, so he found thirty acres of land southwest of Houston in a small sleepy town named Richmond. He talked all the time about building the ultimate dream home, and it seemed his dream was just days away. The home had six bedrooms; five baths; a five-car garage; a game room; a library; a Jacuzzi room; a tennis court, which Dorothy thought was a little extravagant; a library; and a huge kitchen with a sunroof. Dorothy counted sixteen rooms.

Dorothy was pondering really hard on what she needed to get Ahmad for school when the telephone rang. She picked up. "Hello."

She heard absolute silence on the other end.

"Hello."

Still silence, so she hung up. That was the second time that day it had happened. The first time occurred that morning, right after David left for work. Dorothy guessed someone felt the need to call and make her hold the phone to her face like an idiot. She pulled out a writing pad and pen and started listing the things Ahmad needed: shoes, pants, shirts, socks, drawers, undershirts and sweaters. Ten minutes passed and *ring*. Dorothy let it ring three more times before she picked up and held it.

"Hello."

Silence.

"Hello."

Silence.

"Hey, get a fucking life and stop calling here." She slammed down the phone and unplugged it. Ophelia entered the room and stared at her rather strangely.

"What was that all about?"

"Just someone with nothing else better to do."

She sat on the sofa across from Dorothy and twiddled her thumbs around her knees. At twenty-six, she was still lacking a year of art credits at the Art Institute of Chicago, still jobless, and still depressed about stuff that happened five years ago. Lately she'd been in and out of rehab. What started three years ago as a minor accident resulted in a freaking head-on collision.

Ophelia started experimenting with drugs. Dorothy blamed herself partially; she shouldn't have let her sister tag along with her to the Ali-Frazier fight. David threw a wild after party, and Ophelia dabbled a little snow here and there. Locking herself in the bathroom with Norm Prejean, she tried marijuana initially, and when that didn't satisfy her, she turned to heroin. Dorothy discovered this ugly side of her sister when she came home and heard the stereo blasting Jimi Hendrix's *Are You Experienced?* Dorothy thought the Vietnam War had moved into her bathroom when she rushed in and found her sister sitting on the floor looking like a zombie. Dorothy went hysterical.

When the drugs started, the stealing started. Money came up missing from Dorothy's purse. She didn't have to tell Ophelia but once to get out. If she didn't give a damn about herself, Dorothy didn't either. Ophelia wasn't gone but three days when the Houston Police found her wandering around town, barefoot and crying with a purse full of stolen credit cards, all in Dorothy's name. The officer asked Dorothy if she wanted to press charges. Dorothy's mind said, *Yes, take that hussy away from here*, but she heard herself tell the officer, "No."

When Dorothy picked her up, she took her straight to rehab. Not a word was exchanged between them. All Dorothy could remember was how she wanted to strangle her sister and get her out of her misery. She was running from rehab to rehab, spending unnecessary money. Dorothy even sat in on some sessions and offered to counsel. She managed to do all this while at the same time dealing with her problems with David. His beatings grew less. Nowadays he talked more, telling her things like, *Nobody wants you*, and *You're nothing without me.*

"Dot, I think I'm ready," Ophelia blurted out.

"Ready for what?" Dorothy was anxious to know.

"I think I'm ready to go back to school."

"And I think I'm ready to have the big one. Ophelia, who in the hell do you think I am?"

"I need you right now, Dot."

"I'm not spending another dime on you, Ophelia Lacroix."

Ophelia nodded and bit her bottom lip, acting as if Dorothy made her feel two feet tall. "That's cold. I'm your own flesh and blood."

"Ophelia, get out of my face."

"If I can't get help from my own family, who can I turn to?" Ophelia said aloud. "Everybody wants to dwell on what I did in the past. I know I fucked up, but that's behind me. I'm clean. I know what that junk does to you. It destroys your mind, it destroys your soul; Dot, it destroys the people you love, it destroys everything."

Dorothy blocked Ophelia from her mind and continued to write the list she had been trying to write for thirty minutes. Dorothy heard her get up and run down the hall. A few minutes later she heard the door slam.

Dorothy must've spent hours deciding on food, alcohol, and Fourth of July decorations. That night she was hosting a soirée, and she had just the right foods, the right decorations, and the right music to spice it up right.

Claire flew in from California and arrived around 9:30.

"Where is everyone?" she asked, looking around the room. Dorothy ushered her to a seat.

"Give them a few minutes, they'll show up."

"I just envy you, cuz. You seem to have everything: a man who brings home a good steady paycheck, a gorgeous home, a beautiful child. What more could you ask for?"

Dorothy sat down in her white Oscar de la Renta halter dress. "A bigger set of these," she said, pointing to her breasts.

"Here, you can have mine," Claire added. For a woman

who couldn't have weighed more than 110 pounds she had a voluptuous bustline, just like the actress Pam Grier, towhom she bore a striking resemblance.

"Stand up, girl, let me see that dress."

Dorothy stood and modeled for her cousin.

"I like that skirt. Does it unfasten? And check out that split, uh-oh. Is this couture?"

"Yes."

"Now that's what I like," Claire began. "A man with taste."

Claire, who worked as a photographer with *Life* magazine, brought her portfolio. Dorothy was pretty impressed with her spread, especially the one she did on Billy Dee Williams.

"What was it like working with him?" Dorothy asked.

"I tried so hard not to get star-struck but honey, with Billy Dee, it was hard not to." Claire began to fan the air around her. "But he's such a gentleman, down to earth, a really neat person. It's just too bad he's married."

"Let me show you around."

"Dot, cuz, if you could kindly direct me to the champagne, I'll be just fine."

"Go outside, through those double doors, dear."

"Thank you, cuz. I love the place." She strutted outside in her skintight blue demin bell-bottom suit.

More guests arrived. Some from David's practice, and some Dorothy didn't recognize but who knew David. One person stood out, and Dorothy hadn't seen him since the night of her wedding almost ten years back. He was dressed in white linen and was smelling like Irish Spring soap and expensive cologne.

"Jerome."

"Dorothy."

"Jerome."

Jerome embraced Dorothy, and when it seemed that wasn't enough, he kissed her passionately on the lips. It caught

Dorothy off guard. It took a minute for her to gain back her composure. She kept looking around for David, remembering how wired he was the night of their wedding.

"Look at you." Jerome stood back and admired her outfit. "You haven't changed one bit. You still look the same as you did ten years ago."

"Thank you, have a seat." Dorothy checked out his appearance. He changed a lot, especially in the hair department. Jerome was bald like Isaac Hayes and was a little on the stout side, too. He was always handsome with tell-all eyes.

"So, were the directions hard to follow?"

"Not at all. I checked on my ma and talked to her for about an hour and caught up with some friends from med school. I would've been here sooner, but hey, I'm here." He smiled and gave her a pinch on the jaw. "Where's my frat at?"

"Upstairs."

"What's he doing upstairs? The party is down here."

"Good question."

"Tell him to come down. His long-lost frat is here."

"I sure will."

"Where's the restroom, Dorothy?"

"Down the hall, first door on the right."

When Dorothy entered the bedroom, it was empty. She noticed the light from the bathroom was on. She walked inside and stood frozen in her tracks. David was hunched over the marble countertop.

"David!" She said it so fast.

He raised up quickly and wiped his nose.

"What?" he answered, sounding aggravated.

"Tell me that's not what I think it is."

With a smile emerging from his lips he remarked, "It's not what you think it is." His voice was deep and breathy.

"What in the hell are you trying to do?" She was enraged.

"Look."

"I don't want to hear it."

She turned and walked away. Before she opened the bedroom door, from out of nowhere he jumped up, slammed it shut and turned her around. His hands were cold as ice.

"Let me explain."

Dorothy fought against his grip. "Let me go. I don't want to hear it."

"Dot, dammit, let me explain."

She just looked at him, her eyes in contempt.

"When you've gone through as much as I have and seen as much as I have, the pressure, Dorothy . . ." He stopped. The look on his face was so intense, it had her shivering.

"I'm tired. I get tired a lot."

"Why?"

He held up his hand. "Let me finish. In college, I used to brag about how long I could go without sleep. Take bets on it, but now." He shook his head. "It's wearing on me, and all I ask is that you bear with me."

"You've got to make a decision."

He took his fingers and squeezed his eyelids. "Look, I promise I won't do it again."

"That's what you said ten years ago when I saw you in the room with Emma Prejean."

"Why are you bringing up old shit?"

"Because I'm still dealing with the shit. I'm tired of you making empty promises. I'm tired of it."

"All I needed was one blow—just one—to get me through tonight. But after tonight, no more."

This episode was all too familiar. Dorothy heard "no more" enough times to send her to the moon and back. "You and Ophelia. A junkie and a cokehead. How did I get to be so damn lucky?" She laughed for it seemed like the only thing to do to keep from crying. "Just a minute ago, my cousin was saying, 'Dorothy, you seem to have everything: a handsome hus-

band, a beautiful home, and a lovely child. You have everything you want.' I just wish she could see this."

David turned and walked without emotion toward the bathroom. Dorothy opened the door. "You coming down, or what?"

"I'll be down in a minute."

"Jerome's here."

"I said, I'll be down in a minute."

Dorothy closed the door and stood there, holding the knob
in her hands. She didn't know how to feel and didn't know
what to say. Something told her to forget about it, shut it off,
because it would only get uglier the more she thought about
it. She walked with calmness and laughed louder than she did
before.

The band was outside under the gazebo playing, "Let's Get
It On," and anyone who could was out on the terrace dancing.
The atmosphere reminded Dorothy of *Soul Train*, the way
everybody dressed and moved, even the way their Afros
swayed. Dorothy picked up a bottle of gin and played bartender. If she saw an empty glass, she was filling it to the rim.
She spotted David's brother, Marcus, and his girlfriend, Mercedes, smooching in the corner.

"Hey, give her some breathing room."

"Hello, Sis." Marcus' eyes widened when he saw Dorothy's
halter dress.

"You look hot," Mercedes began. She was Marcus' main
flame, a professional model from a small town on the Mexican
Yúcatan. Mercedes herself looked elegant and sassy, plus she
recognized a hot item when she saw one. "Where's your husband?" she asked.

"Yeah, where is he?" Marcus began. "Doesn't he know his
wife just started a four-alarm fire out here?"

Dorothy thought about David and faked a laugh. "He'll be
down in a minute."

"Must've been another long day at the office."

"So Marcus, are you still hanging in there with L.A.?"

"Of course. L.A.'s my second home."

"When does training start?"

"Next month."

Marcus had gotten larger, musclewise. He had turned pro about a year earlier, and things were going pretty well for him. Since high school, he dreamed of going to the NFL, but Doc Sr. and Mrs. Leonard and the rest of the family doted on intellectuals, not jocks. They wanted Marcus to focus on law and do football for the sake of recreation. To Marcus, it was more than that. Football was his life; he wanted to tackle the gridiron and follow in the direction of Jim Brown and O.J. Simpson. Since his sophomore year in high school, Marcus was determined to get into a top-notch university, so he chose USC. While in college, Marcus was an All-American, setting and breaking school records in football and track. He was a natural-born athlete who dabbled in a little soccer, too.

"So, Sis, why are you holding that bottle?"

"Where is your glass, Marcus, and yours, Mercedes?"

"Come on now, you know I don't drink," Marcus declined.

Dorothy held up her index finger. "Just one swig."

"No," Marcus protested.

"You're a party pooper."

"Here, I'll have some." Mercedes held out her glass.

While Dorothy poured, Marcus gave in to the peer pressure and decided he wanted some.

"I thought you didn't drink."

"One swig wouldn't hurt. Damn."

Dorothy made her way to the band, which was now playing "I'll Take You There" by the Staple Singers. The bass player was making cute faces as he thumped the strings. Dorothy entertained him and the rest of the band with her so-called dancing. She heard Claire and the others behind her, urging her to do all kinds of dances like the Funky Chicken and the Watusi.

Dorothy spotted David laughing and talking with Myranda and Bill. She didn't want to be anywhere near him, so she went out back and danced until sweat flew everywhere. She stopped long enough to get another shot of gin. When that wasn't enough, she got two more shots, then three shots. She grew tipsy and mellowed out poolside. After a while she felt strong, masculine hands encircle her body and a penis bulge against her spine. She smelled the old familiar scent of Irish Spring and she knew it wasn't David.

"W-w-w-wait a minute," Dorothy stuttered.

"Dorothy," she heard him whisper against her earlobe.

She turned around and saw Jerome."You better stop."

"I wanted to mention it to you earlier, but then I thought, nah, bad timing."

"Say what?"

"Are you okay?" He looked into her eyes and saw that she was in a daze.

"I'm fine," she said.

"I wanted to tell you how fabulous you look in that dress."

"Thank you, Jerome."

"I talked to my frat. He's a very, very, very, very lucky man."

She giggled. "Thank you. I'm a very, very, very lucky woman."

Her mind rewound to what she saw earlier and she didn't want to think about David anymore.

"Have you eaten?" Dorothy grabbed Jerome's hand and led him to the buffet table. "We have honey-glazed chicken, bar-becued chicken, smoked turkey, crawfish."

Jerome picked up a turkey drumstick and bit it. "Hmm. You smoked this?"

"I had it catered. Here, try some of this." She took a small slice of potato pie and allowed him to sample it. He bit it and didn't stop until he licked all of her fingertips.

"And there's plenty more where that came from," she said.

"I see." Jerome's stare was seductive. He took her hand. "Can we go somewhere and talk?" he asked.

"Jerome, no. Look, why are you doing this?"

"I just want to know one thing."

"What?"

"Are you happy?"

"Is that why you came all the way from California?"

"You invited me, remember?"

Dorothy took a little time before she answered. "Yes, Jerome, I am very happy."

"You got me convinced." He stood back, skeptical.

"I couldn't get any happier," Dorothy responded, trying to sound upbeat.

"I grew up with him. I know everything there is to know about him. I know his thoughts and his weaknesses. I've seen him make love to the prettiest women and kick them at the same time."

Dorothy wanted to explode and tell everything to Jerome, but felt it best to just leave well enough alone. He leaned forward to give her a kiss on the cheek, but Dorothy turned her head.

"You better leave," she managed to say.

He nodded, and without looking back, he strolled through the crowd. Dorothy had a million and one thoughts race through her mind. She was on the verge of tears when she retreated inside the house. She picked up another bottle of gin and poured herself a drink. By now her insides were burning and throbbing like someone poured acid in her. Then suddenly the room started changing colors, and she swore she had infrared vision. She didn't even see the photographer standing just a few feet in front of her.

"Mrs. Leonard, I'm from the *Houston Defender*. Would you and Dr. Leonard care to pose for some shots?"

"Sure. Where's my husband?" She squinted and looked for David. "I'm sorry, I didn't catch your name?"

"Carlton." He extended his hand. His grip was strong and firm.

"Carlton, excuse me. I need to freshen up."

"Oh, go right ahead."

"There's plenty to eat and drink out back. Make yourself at home."

Dorothy's head throbbed and pounded harder when she walked into the bathroom. She closed the door and picked herself apart in the mirror. Her hair, makeup and lipstick were still in place. But she felt like shit. Her head was swimming in thoughts, crazy thoughts. She felt good some of the time and felt like shit all of the time. Half of her wanted to break down and cry, the other half wanted to forget about all of life's troubles and party like there was no tomorrow. She turned on the faucet, grabbed a towel and wet it just a little to rid some of the perspiration on her skin. She turned off the light, walked outside, took the photograph with David, and danced until her legs were sore.

Two hours later . . .

"Psst, Myranda, I want to talk to you." Dorothy's head was spinning uncontrollably.

"You okay?"

Dorothy's mouth was hanging a mile and she could barely walk. Myranda caught her before she fell. "Where's David?" Her voice echoed, just like the other voices around her. Even the music echoed.

"Myranda, help me."

"You have to help me and take at least one step."

Dorothy's legs were numb. "I can't walk."

"Can I get some help?" she shouted.

Dorothy closed her eyes and sang Aretha Franklin's "Day-dreaming." She didn't care how it sounded, so long as some-body heard it. A familiar voice took her from Myranda. "I got her." He swept her off her feet and carried her upstairs. Dorothy heard the door open and close and the sound of laughter and music dying in the distance. She knew she was in her own bed when her body hit the firm mattress. The lamplight came on and blinded her. "I don't need that damn light. Turn it off."

The smell of Lagerfeld cologne crept into her nostrils. She opened her eyes.

"David?"

David leaned forward and kissed her lips. That was all she needed, a lousy kiss from him. She wiped it away because it was cold and wet and fuming with rum.

"Why don't you go on and leave me alone," she said.

"I've been thinking," he began.

"Oh really?" she said. "You still manage to think?"

"I deserve that," he said. "I'm sorry about everything. I never really meant to hurt you."

"But you have."

"Shhh." He put his finger over her lips. "I'm putting it all behind me—the drugs, the beatings, everything. You willing to give me another chance?"

Dorothy thought about it; he really sounded sincere. "Okay," she mumbled.

"Thank you." He put his arms around her and kissed her lips. "I love you." Pretty soon the rum on his lips began to taste sweet and she closed her eyes.

The next morning she woke up, naked and in great pain. *My God, what on earth?* She looked around and saw the top of her outfit lying on David's pillow. She tried to get up, but her head felt ten pounds heavier and her neck was sore. She fought the pain and raised herself up anyway. Her stomach and breasts were covered with small red passion marks. She took the sheets from her bed and wrapped them around her. When she put her feet on the floor, she noticed her panties lying beside David's wallet. Her body struggled to fight another bout with pain before she picked them up. David's wallet came open and out fell a fifty-dollar bill and a yellow piece of paper with the initials C.G. and the number 777-7713 underneath it. Dorothy wondered what C.G. stood for. There was no need to fight unnecessary bouts of pain, so she crawled back into bed.

Chapter 13

Dorothy was shaking her head. Her doctor told her some news she didn't want to believe.

"Are you sure?"

"I'm positive, Mrs. Leonard."

"How far along?"

"Twelve weeks."

Dorothy sighed and stared at the ceiling, silently praying to God. Abortion came to mind, but she convinced herself she had a conscience and couldn't continue life with the dark cloud of abortion suspended over her. David didn't want another child—he'd told her that on numerous occasions. When she got home, she cried and cuddled herself between the pillows atop her king-size bed. She blamed the melancholy on hormones, remembering how she went through a bout of it during her first pregnancy. But during that period, it came and went suddenly. This time it lingered.

David came home that evening around nine and flicked on the lights. He paused when he saw Dorothy balled up like a bug on top of the covers. He slowly took off his brown leather jacket and hung it in the closet, along with his white medical coat. The embers in the fireplace were almost out, so he opened the fireguard and turned the charcoal-and-ash covered logs over. He wasn't satisfied until the fire had rebuilt itself into a row of flames. He then walked in the bathroom and opened the seat on the toilet and laughed quietly to himself, recalling a joke Dr. Corbin told him during lunch. After the toilet splashed and gurgled, he washed his hands and wrestled with his conscience. He was dying for another blow, but instead he undressed down to his boxers and slid underneath the covers next to his wife's warm and soft body. Dorothy opened her eyes when she felt the hairs from his chest brush against her back. She turned to face him.

"Hello," she said.

She closed her eyes when David brushed his lips against hers.

"How was your day?" he asked while pecking softly around her neck.

"Okay," she mumbled, feeling her body tighten when David pulled her closer. He couldn't help but notice the dismal look in her eyes.

"What's wrong?"

"I went to the doctor."

David waited in anticipation.

"We're having another baby," she said.

"Are you serious?"

"I'm afraid so." Dorothy examined the look in his eyes; she couldn't tell whether he was happy, but to her surprise he planted a congratulatory kiss on her lips.

"You're not mad?" she asked.

"Why should I be mad?"

"You said you didn't . . ."

"I know what I said, but you know what . . . Ahmad could use a brother or sister."

"I know," Dorothy heard herself agreeing.

"We need some more life in this house. Hell, I like hearing the pitter and patter of feet." David turned her face and body away from his. "I love you, woman," David said as he kissed the nape of her neck and rubbed the long cesarean scar underneath her navel. A minute later he was asleep.

"*Mère*, it's me. How are you?"

Cleo was ironing Lucky's pants when Dorothy called.

"Hi, *bèbe*, I'm fine, just ironing Lucky's and Jacqueline's school clothes."

Dorothy leafed quickly through a Sears catalog. "Guess what?"

"Don't tell me nothing else about that damn Ophelia. That child got more problems than a chicken got feathers."

"This ain't about Ophelia."

"Good. Don't tell me nothing else about that girl. Ol' wench."

"Now, *Mère* . . ."

Cleo was so steamed she forgot about Lucky's pants and burned an ugly brown hole in them.

"I'll be goddamned!"

"What happened?"

"I burned a hole in this *bèbe*'s pants."

"I'm pregnant again."

"Ah, shit."

"*Mère*."

"I didn't mean you. I'm still pissed off about these pants. I spent too much money on them."

"You can just buy another pair."

Cleo balled up Lucky's pants in frustration and threw them on the floor.

"So you and David got another baby coming?"

Dorothy released a tired sigh. "Yes. It's due in April."

"I thought you said he didn't want any more children."

"He didn't. That's why I was shocked when he responded the way he did."

"Look at it like this: You and David aren't getting any younger. Plus, you got a lot of money. You got a nice house. You fly first-class around the world. One more child wouldn't hurt. As a matter of fact, three more wouldn't hurt."

"I don't think I can take any more cuts after this one. That scar from Ahmad looks so ugly under my navel."

"Speaking of Ahmad, how is he?"

"He's doing real good in school. He's in first grade but reading at the second-grade level."

"That's good. Lucky just learned how to write his name. He's so smart. You know, I enrolled him in day school."

"How is Jacqueline, Little Miss Fancy-Pants?"

"That little heffa loves to play with my makeup and stuff toilet tissue in her blouse. I say, keep on, one of these days you gon' have titties so big, you ain't gonna know what to do with them."

"All little girls go through that stage."

"I know, you did the same thing."

Dorothy glanced at her chest. "I guess I didn't play it enough. Mine are still the same as they were before I had Ahmad."

"They usually get bigger after the second child."

"I've known women to have four children and still have small breasts."

"That doesn't stop them from sagging."

Dorothy thought about that. "I guess you have a point."

Dorothy thought about her older sister. "*Mère*, how's Katherine?"

"I assume things between her and Ricky have gotten better."

"I know they were on shaky ground for a moment. I remember her telling me Ricky got laid off and she was the only one bringing home a steady paycheck."

"I don't know what to say about Ricky. I don't understand him. He got an engineering degree. All these engineering jobs around Texas and Louisiana."

"Nobody hires Negroes. I don't care how many degrees he's got."

"That motherfucka is lazy, too."

"Stop it, *Mère*. That's ugly." Dorothy was tickled.

"Let's talk about your man. Did the stuff work for him?"

"I hope it did. I followed your directions. I prayed over it for ten minutes and sprinkled some under his pillow."

"Did you take his picture and pray over it?"

"Yes, I did."

"Did you take his drawers and rub them in olive oil?"

"Yes, *Mère*."

"Sister Devereaux told me if there's anything else you need, let her know."

"I hope I never have to ask for anything like that. *Mère*, I can't help feeling . . ."

"Feeling like what?"

"Like I deceived him."

"Deceived? If anything, you helped him. What's wrong with putting a little herb under the pillow? Now the last thing you need is another dopehead on your hands. Ophelia is enough worry, and besides . . .it's better to stop him now before he snorts your house, you, his job, and my grandbaby up his nose." Cleo lamented for a second. "When you first told me about David, it really hurt me. I don't normally let stuff bother me, but that did. With everything good going for him, why would he mess it up?"

Dorothy released another tired sigh and checked the time on her watch.

"My God, what's next?" Cleo asked.

Dorothy remained silent.

"I'll burn a few candles of my own and say a prayer for you."

"Thank you, *Mère*. I could use it."

Outside, Dorothy's driveway looked like a luxury car lot. Inside, the aroma of pastries, finger sandwiches, and cream of broccoli soup meandered about the kitchen and overflowed into the den, which was cluttered with opened packages of baby gifts. Dorothy was well into her third trimester. She knew she was going to have a girl this time, so she told everyone to buy soft feminine colors.

"You ladies are too much," she said after opening a package that contained a baby book with her sorority's colors. Five of her sorors were there, along with Tiny and her mother, Carolyn; David's nurse, Ms. Johnson; Cleo; Aunt Ruby Jewel; Mrs. Leonard, Katherine; Marcus's girlfriend, Mercedes; Myranda Corbin; Sadaria McCloud and Chanel Gainous.

Chanel was the newest member of the Leonard practice who started working as a receptionist the previous summer. After severing ties with her family, and after a semester of college, she left New Orleans I-10 bound west for Houston. It was during a visit to David's office that she decided she wanted to work. She noticed Sadaria was overwhelmed with paperwork and tried to convince David to hire her. David was impressed with her persistence, not to mention the creamy white tank mini dress that covered her mahogany complexion. He told her to be at the office at eight o'clock sharp. It was 7:59 when she stepped off the city bus and showed up for her first day wearing a short black spandex skirt with a soft pink, low-cut blouse. When she introduced herself to Sadaria and told her that she was working, Sadaria thought it was a joke.

"Where you going?" Sadaria had asked.

Chanel took one look at herself. "I'm coming to work. Do you have a problem?"

"Honey, you're gonna have a problem if you don't go home and change clothes."

Pointing to her attire, Chanel had asked, "What's wrong with this?"

Sadaria couldn't believe this girl had the audacity to ask her that with a straight face.

"You really want me tell you?"

"I asked, didn't I?"

"That outfit has 'coochie for sale' written all over it." Chanel had thought it harsh coming from someone who didn't know her, but she learned very quickly that Ms. Sadaria McCloud didn't bite her tongue.

"And another thing, Miss Chanel, if you're trying to entice Dr. Leonard or Dr. Corbin, I got news for you: they're both happily married with beautiful wives." Chanel's expression didn't change on the outside, but inside, her heart fluttered at the thought of David. From the moment she'd seen him almost ten years ago, she still held on to the bouquet. Although the flowers had long withered, she kept the frozen bouquet as a reminder that accompanying her half-sister Whitney to the wedding and catching the bouquet was no accident. Now she had her foot in the door of opportunity and the only thing standing in her way was a nosy-assed, juicy-mouthed receptionist and "two beautiful wives."

David had invited the staff to his house for an annual Christmas dinner, and that's where Chanel first became acquainted with Dorothy. Chanel found they had a lot in common. They were both Tauruses, both were crazy about their fathers, and like Dorothy's father, Chanel's had passed away when she was eighteen. Chanel liked to plan parties, and Dorothy thought it was nice of her to help organize the baby shower. Chanel was low-key and quiet. She preferred to stay away from everyone else and busy herself serving punch and cutting slices of cake. Chanel eventually made her acquaintance with everyone, and everyone seemed to think it was nice of her to go beyond the call of duty.

"Cuz, who is she again?" Tiny asked, biting into a teacake.

"Who are you talking about?"

Tiny nodded in Chanel's direction. "The girl serving the punch."

"That's our soror Whitney's half-sister, Chanel Gainous."

"Name doesn't ring a bell. Make me know her."

"That's all I know about her."

"I don't consider myself a mind reader, but I am getting some very unusual vibes."

"From Chanel? Why?"

Tiny paused from chewing on her cookie and gave Dorothy a questionable stare. Dorothy noticed it.

"I'm confused, Tiny. What are you getting at?"

"Watch her. I don't know what it is, but something about her just isn't right. I got a bad feeling in my chest."

"You sure that's not acid reflux?"

Tiny chuckled.

"You know, Tiny, Sadaria told me the same thing, but I'm not feeling any bad vibes. I think she's good people."

"You know, Caesar felt that way about Brutus, and Jesus felt that way about Judas."

"I think you've had too much to drink. You are way out in left field with this Brutus jive, and besides, Chanel's got her own thing going. She has a good man."

"Have you met him?"

"No."

"Hmmph." Tiny replied.

After the baby shower, Chanel lingered and helped Dorothy clean up.

"You've done enough, sweetheart. Go home," Dorothy insisted.

Chanel plopped down on the couch. "I would, but there's nothing to do there."

"Your man will keep you company."

"He keeps me bored, that's what he does. Half of the time I end up going out." Chanel looked at Dorothy. "Do you go clubbing?"

"No," Dorothy replied.

"I forgot, you don't party."

"It's not that I don't party. I just don't go to nightclubs. My parties are mainly potluck dinners and soirées around the house. David and I used to host parties all the time," Dorothy said, reminiscing about the Ali-Frazier fight. "One time we flew to New York to the Ali-Frazier fight. David and some of his colleagues rented a suite at the Marriott, and we threw the loudest, rowdiest, baddest after party. We rocked all night long."

Chanel was impressed, at least on the surface. But down underneath, she melted with envy. Chanel savored the opportunity to tell her friends the same kinds of stories—her true stories of how it felt to make love to a married man and go on with life as though nothing happened. To have to face that person every day and not think about the evening before when he whisked her feet off the floor and into the stirrups of his examination table, and ignited passions within her she never knew existed. To have to face that person every day and not think about their evenings after five-thirty when they made his desktop a bed of roses and made sweaty, hot, passionate love with pictures of his wife and small son staring at her and her staring back, gloating.

Chanel eyed David closely when he leaned over and gave his wife a tender kiss on the cheek. She smiled quietly to herself, recalling the moments her lips, breasts and other parts of her body were the proud recipients of those same lips.

"How are you, Miss Gainous?" he asked, sounding formal.

"I'm fine, Dr. Leonard," she replied.

"How was the baby shower?" he asked Dorothy.

"I got Ophelia to film it, but halfway through, the camera started acting up."

"Acting up? How?"

"It kept getting out of focus."

"You sure it wasn't her who was out of focus?"

"I checked. It was your camera," Dorothy said.

"Where is it?" David asked.

Dorothy stood. "In the family room. I'll go get it."

When she left, David and Chanel sat in silence.

"Why are you still here?" he hissed once Dorothy was out of sight.

"I wanted to see you. Is that a problem?"

Before David said any more, Dorothy entered the room again carrying the camera. "I think you need a new one. If you ask me, this baby here is old and worn out."

David couldn't stop kissing his little girl's cotton-soft cheeks.

"This is Daddy's little girl," he said to the nurse who was there with him in the nursery. "She'll always be Daddy's little girl." He held Nia's diminutive form in one palm and kissed her good night. Dorothy couldn't let the moment pass without grabbing the camera. "Give her another kiss," Dorothy said as she held the camera over her eye. Through the grainy screen, she saw David plant a soft kiss on Nia's forehead.

At three months, Nia was already sitting up without her parents' assistance. Dorothy ran around screaming, "David, quick, go get the camera. This isn't normal."

David assured her it was a sign of maturity and independence. At ten months she was walking on her own. At her first birthday party, she was singing and miming all the songs to

Stevie Wonder's *Songs In the Key Of Life* album, not to mention pulling herself up to play Ahmad's piano in the process.

When Nia turned fifteen months, Dorothy was pregnant again. That was the only explanation for her queasy feelings and crying spells. Chanel was pregnant, too. When Dorothy asked her if the father was just as happy as she was, she hesitated. "I've seen happier people at a funeral." Her eyes filled with tears when she explained to Dorothy that the man, whom she called Linus, insisted she get an abortion.

"Don't do it, Chanel," Dorothy told her. "I thought about it once and God forbade me to think about it again."

"I can't support a child. I can barely support myself."

"That's what David and I are here for."

Chanel cried. "Thank you. I don't know what I'd do without you. You and Dr. Leonard are good people." Chanel quickly dried her large, brown, almond-shaped eyes.

"You have my word on that," Dorothy said.

"I really do appreciate this. I really want this child."

"I know you do, sweetie," Dorothy said before giving Chanel a hug and a warm rub across her back. "The less stress you have, the better off you and your baby will be."

Chanel nodded and wiped the snot that tickled the tip of her nose with a tissue. Dorothy picked up a *Cosmopolitan* magazine and flipped randomly through the pages. "You are my soror's half-sister, and I'll do my best to help you." Dorothy spotted a svelte and energetic-looking Mercedes splashing in a fountain, showing off her wide million-dollar smile.

"Chanel, Linus is meaningless. He's dead weight, and the last thing you need is dead weight."

Chanel rubbed her abdomen—she wasn't showing quite yet. "You're right. Me and my baby deserve better."

Chapter 14

Edna, the Leonards' housekeeper, ushered Chanel outside to the pool. With her eyes covered by large sunglasses, she found a seat near the back on the edge of the row. At the altar, David and Dorothy stood saying their vows to each other. Dorothy, along with a priest and fifty other guests, listened as David stumbled over promises and lines. Chanel had taken a half bottle of Pepto Bismol just before she came. She knew her stomach wouldn't be able to take the garbage she was about to hear. And to think Dorothy asked her to help plan it. She even asked her to be a bridesmaid, but Chanel told her that she might have to go to New Orleans for the weekend.

"I haven't reneged on any promises. Sure, our marriage hasn't always been perfect." David looked into Dorothy's eyes. "We've had our disagreements, but after every rainy day comes a day filled with sunshine. I've come to realize when you have a love as strong as ours, it can withstand the tests of time." They kissed like a scene right out of a soap opera. "For ten years, you have been the only woman for me." David kissed her again.

Chanel felt her stomach churning into knots. She was on the verge of throwing up, so she stood and made a brisk walk away from the ceremony. She didn't stop walking until she found a bathroom and closed the door.

"Fake son of a bitch! He can't be serious." Anyone within earshot would've thought she was crazy. Chanel began thinking about the times she and David spent together. For three days the week before, he stayed all night at her house, and each night around eleven, he called his wife to tell her he was staying at the hospital a little bit longer.

For two years, Chanel had made him forget he had a wife. She made him happy, very happy. She turned that world of his inside out, doing things to him Dorothy couldn't imagine doing. Sure, Dorothy was his wife, but Chanel was his lady, not to mention a freak in bed. They went to Las Vegas, it seemed, every weekend and gambled away hundreds of dollars and enjoyed countless hours of sex. They slept, got high, ate fabulously, and had more sex. David made her feel special, as if she was the one wearing his wedding ring. Sometimes Chanel had to catch herself because she forgot he had a wife and two kids to go home to. There was a song that best described Chanel's situation, "If Loving You Is Wrong, I Don't Want To Do Right." To Chanel, it was all about her; she wanted the same first-class treatment with which Dorothy was often pampered. To Chanel, it was becoming an obligation for David to satisfy her the same way he satisfied his wife, or more so. In her mind, she could have David all to herself and make life a living hell for Dorothy.

Chanel realized she was on the verge of crying and stopped herself before she allowed the salty taste of tears to fall down her flushed cheeks.

Outside, David picked Dorothy off her feet and carried her laughing and crying down the aisle. He put her down and picked up Nia, who was dressed in a red suede dress trimmed in white ruffles. Her soft, wavy, black hair was gathered at the crown of her head with a red-and-white ribbon tied in a bow. She was adorable in her father's arms. He carried her almost everywhere he went. Ahmad was dressed in a black tuxedo with a red tie and small cummerbund that he occasionally wore for a bra because it wouldn't stay around his waist.

Dorothy's cousin Claire snapped two shots of David and Dorothy with the children in front of the fireplace. When midnight arrived, Edna put the children to sleep. Dorothy recalled what happened ten years back. For obvious reasons the second time around seemed so much sweeter, and she was thankful she lasted that long.

"Happy New Year," she shouted before giving David a kiss. The deejay cranked up the music and Dorothy did the oddest thing by leading the guests in a traditional New Orleans dance called Second Line.

Across the room in a secluded corner, pretending to be elated, stood Chanel. She glanced at David and Dorothy and shook her head. She grabbed her purse and made an exit into the darkness and loneliness that awaited her.

After just ten hours of labor, Dorothy gave birth to her third child, a boy this time whom she named Jamal. Dorothy was still lying in the hospital, drifting in and out of sleep with extremely high blood pressure. Her face was swollen to twice its normal size. Dorothy told David that out of the three pregnancies, this was by far the worst. She forgot all about the trouble she went through once she saw Jamal; he was wide awake, staring at her, smiling.

Chanel had a little girl named Danielle, whom she absolutely adored and couldn't let out of her sight. David cherished her, too. He even purchased a house for Chanel and Danielle. It was a spacious three-bedroom house with a huge backyard and a swimming pool, where he and Chanel often swam naked.

Dorothy invited Chanel to go shopping with her. She couldn't pass a store without going in and purchasing something for the kids. Ahmad needed a couple of pairs of slacks. Nia needed a couple of dresses, and Jamal needed an outfit and a pair of patent-leather shoes. Dorothy picked out a pink-and-white dress for Nia.

"How adorable," Chanel said. She was eyeing a similar dress for Danielle.

"This is absolutely adorable."

When the register attendant totaled Dorothy's receipt, she held it up because it appeared it would never stop feeding from the register. There must've been a foot of paper.

"Lucky kids," the attendant said. "I wish you were my mom."

When Chanel arrived home, David was sitting there.

"Hi, baby." She rushed up to give him a kiss, but he turned his head.

"We need to talk." His voice sounded hard, his stare was cold.

"About what?" With her large eyes still on David, she put Danielle down in her bassinet.

"About you and my wife," David said. "I want the non-sense to stop."

"What nonsense?"

"Stay the hell away from my wife."

"Dorothy is my friend."

David frowned at her in disgust. "Friend? You call yourself a friend?"

"You're not making sense to me."

"I'm going to put it to you this way. You can have this house. I'll see to it that Danielle has a roof over her head. If she needs anything, you know how to find me. Am I making sense now?"

"So in other words?"

"Quit this dog and pony show. Enough is enough."

Chanel was motionless for a few seconds, hesitating and trying to find her words. "So you mean—"

David interrupted. "You and I are done."

Chanel shook her head slowly. "So that's how it is? You gon' walk out on me and Danielle?"

"I'm not walking away from Danielle."

"What about me, David? What about my fucking needs?"

"You knew my situation when you got involved with me."

Chanel's eyes were watering with tears. "You told me that you were unhappy and you needed me to fix things. Now that it's fixed, you don't need me anymore. Is that what you're saying?"

"You got cute, and it's my fault I let you get cute. But if you keep this up, it's not gonna be so cute anymore." David turned and walked toward the door.

"If you leave, I swear I will call Dorothy and tell her everything."

He turned around. "You what?"

"You heard me, I said I'm gon' tell her everything."

"You wouldn't."

"You try me."

Without thinking, David grabbed Chanel's neck and pushed her slender little body up against the wall. Her face was contorted inside the palms of his large hands. "You listen to me and you listen to me good. If you fuck with me or my wife, or my children, I will kill you."

Tears poured like a dripping faucet down her cheeks, stopping just short of her trembling mouth. David released her. She put her arms around his neck; he removed them and walked toward the door. When he opened it, he turned and looked at Chanel.

"Give all my love to Danielle, will you?"

Chanel burst out crying when she picked up her shoe and threw it, almost hitting him when he closed the door.

David arrived home to find Ahmad entertaining Dorothy and Nia with a storybook. Dorothy noticed a faraway look in his eyes. He managed to smile and sat on the sofa next to her and the children.

"What's this you're reading, son?"

"*Sounder*," Ahmad said while flipping the pages.

"Good book; good movie, too," David responded.

"I checked it out at the library," Ahmad said. He held up another much larger book. "I checked this book out, too."

"This is thick. You sure you can read all that?"

"Of course, Dad."

David smiled cheerfully at his older son.

"You finish reading to your sister. Your mother and I need to talk."

Dorothy didn't like the tone of his voice, but without hesitation she stood and followed him into the kitchen.

"How was work?" she asked, trying to sound chipper.

"Not bad, not bad," he replied. He noticed his wife had gained some weight with the last pregnancy. She wasn't the petite size she was when they married, but more like a size sixteen.

"What have you been eating?" he asked.

Dorothy looked at herself. "That's what happens when you stay at home all day with three children with huge appetites."

"Yeah, I guess. Well, anyway, I got my American Express billing statement in the mail today. I noticed last month you spent thirteen thousand dollars. You spent thirty-five hundred at Macy's, another fifteen hundred at Baby World and eight thousand at the furniture store. What did you buy?"

"I bought those Queen Anne chairs in the hallway upstairs."

"Those ugly-ass chairs cost eight thousand dollars?"

"They were imported from London."

"I don't give a damn if they came from Timbuktu!"

"Stop yelling!"

David opened his medical jacket and pulled out a Southwestern Bell phone bill.

"Do you have any idea how much the phone bill was last month?"

Dorothy folded her arms and sucked her breath. "No, David, I don't know."

"Forty-five hundred dollars. I see calls to New Orleans and calls to California. You been talking to Jerome?"

"No. My cousin Claire lives there, remember?"

"What do you talk about for three hours, Dorothy? Write the bitch a letter!"

Dorothy felt a lump of hurt developing in her throat.

"You think my money grows on trees?"

"You won't let me work. You keep me in this house all day."

"Starting now there are going to be some changes, you hear?"

"What changes?"

"Number one, stay off the phone. Number two, no more going to the mall. Number three, lose some weight. That yellow smock makes you look like a damn school bus."

"What's next? You want me to jump off a bridge?"

"Oh, you want to be funny? Go get your credit cards!"

"What?"

"Did I stutter?"

"You're not being fair!"

"No shit. Were you being fair to me when you squandered

my money? You act like I got money to burn. I ought to make you take the shit back!"

Dorothy stood with a menacing look in her eyes.

"Your ass is going on a two-hundred-dollar-a-month allowance. Is that understood?"

Dorothy shook her head.

"Now stop stalling like you got a stick up your ass and get me those goddamn credit cards!"

Dorothy shook her head. "No!"

"Stop playing with me!"

"I don't say anything when you waste your money on drugs."

"It's not your business what I do with my own money."

David began to unfasten the belt around his waist. In a rage, Dorothy stormed past her husband and made her way to the spiral staircase that led upstairs to their bedroom.

"You better be back by the time I count to twenty or I'm coming up there to whip your silly fat ass."

Dorothy slammed the door to her bedroom and ran to the closet where she kept the credit cards. In a crying rage she rummaged through her clothes and shoeboxes. She paused when she came across a .22 caliber handgun. Crazy thoughts began to dance through her mind as she held the shiny black gun in her trembling hands. She thought about the last twelve years of her life with David. She didn't want to kill him; she wanted to scare him, though. She didn't know how to express to him how unhappy she was, but oh boy, she could show him with the gun. She put the gun inside the box and placed it back in the closet. Slowly, she stood and retrieved the American Express and MasterCard and walked downstairs like a child who was about to be punished.

Dorothy tried so desperately to squeeze into the size sixteen gown David had purchased for the United Negro College

Fund gala. Just days earlier she and David were arguing about credit cards and telephone bills. Like clockwork, he made up for it by lavishing Dorothy with gifts. This time he purchased a twelve-thousand-dollar Cartier necklace to wear with her too small Valentino gown.

When David walked into their bedroom to adjust his tie, he saw Dorothy stuffing herself into the dress.

"You need some help?"

"No," she snapped. "I'm in it, see?"

David noticed how her stomach and hips protruded. Her once Coke bottle figure had transformed into a pear. To David, she just wasn't the same; their lovemaking wasn't the same. David could recall the times when her breasts fit snugly into his mouth. Now he had to lift them into his mouth. At times he wondered whether Dorothy cared how she looked anymore. He had grown tired of seeing her dragging her feet and dressing so slovenly.

Lately he had been fantasizing about Chanel and how delectable she looked and how wonderful she felt. Although three weeks had passed since he last confronted her, he had arranged for her and a friend to attend the UNCF benefit gala that tonight.

At the gala, he couldn't keep his eyes off her. She wore a red sequined gown with a low neckline, enhancing her brown 36 D-cups and making the evening much more pleasurable to the many men in her presence. Her black wavy hair was in a French twist, her large eyes were sparkling, and ever so often she would glance seductively in his direction when Dorothy wasn't looking. She even engaged in a little foot action underneath the table, running her toes along his legs.

David fantasized about the hours they would spend together afterward. He even made plans to whisk her off to the house in Surfside to enjoy countless hours of nonstop lovemaking. *My God*, he thought, *I can feel her right now.*

Chanel was thinking about the hours that lay ahead. She glanced at the diamond watch on her left wrist. It was ten after nine, which meant they weren't scheduled to leave for another two hours. *I knew he couldn't resist this*, she thought. *I knew he was coming back to me. Damn, he looks good; feels good, too. I don't know if I can wait any longer. A good quickie is what we both need before we get on the road.*

Dorothy was too busy enjoying the swordfish and chardonnay sitting before her. She was thinking, *Lord, if I could only get the recipe from the chef.*

Chanel's date, a resident who worked with David in the maternity ward, was too busy thinking about Monday morning. Now and then he would strike up a conversation, other times he was daydreaming and staring into space, though occasionally thoughts of Chanel's breasts came to mind.

That night Dorothy went to bed alone. David told her he had paperwork to deal with at the hospital and assured her he would be home as soon as he finished. When Dorothy woke up the next morning, she was in bed alone. She dialed the number to the hospital and asked for David. When no one could locate him, she concluded he was on his way home.

PART THREE:

AFTER

Chapter 15

"Honey, what's on your mind? You haven't uttered a word since we left Houston."

"Nothing. I'm thinking about nothing. Now stop bugging me."

"You need to stop taking that stuff."

"You don't know what you're talking about."

"You give me the silent treatment, and you walk around here like a zombie. Why is that?"

"As usual, you're overreacting."

"Is there somebody else?"

"Now, you know better than to ask me some shit like that."

"Shhh." Dorothy glanced over her shoulder. "The kids."

Nia and Jamal were asleep in the back of the RV. Ahmad amused himself with a book.

"Will you stop bugging me and let me drive, all right?"

"But—"

"Look," David said cutting her off in mid-sentence, "what did I tell you? I don't want to talk. Period. End of discussion."

Dorothy stared silently at David. His cavalier attitude only frustrated her; she literally had to bite her tongue to keep herself quiet. She gazed at the sign that read, NEW ORLEANS, 66 MILES. She forced herself to remain quiet for the remainder of the ride.

The minute Cleo opened the door, she could sense right away that something was troubling Dorothy.

"Dorothy, why you let this child leave the house with her hair all over her head?"

"*Mère*, how are you?" Dorothy pecked her mother on the cheek.

"I'm fine." Cleo studied her daughter closely.

"I need to talk with you."

"You sure do. Look at you . . . you're all fat and slouchy. You don't try to keep yourself up anymore, do you?"

"*Mère*, are you finished?"

"No."

"Yes you are. Let's talk."

"Wait a minute, don't rush me off. Let me enjoy my grandchildren."

She grabbed Jamal and Nia. "Give *Mémère* some sugar." Dorothy stood in the doorway of her mother's dining room and watched David sit in silence in the living room. He glanced at his watch. "I'm gonna gas up the RV. I'll be back."

Dorothy watched him exit the room. At that moment she felt like the weight of the world was on her shoulders. She pondered away at her thoughts. She wanted to ride with him and talk to him without the children or her mother around, but when she finally managed enough nerve to walk out the door, the RV was gone. Dorothy found a spot on the porch swing, nestled in the corner of her mother's large veranda. She cursed herself for being so afraid. She felt like she was on her own, and to her, that was the emptiest feeling in the world. She didn't want to tell her mother just how miserable she was inside because her mother would say she was weak. So she sat rocking on the swing before Ahmad joined her.

"Hey, Man." She smiled when he sat next to her. Her little boy was now twelve years old and three inches taller than her. He had her emerald green eyes, sandy brown hair, and her complexion, and a smile that melted his mother's heart. At the moment, he wasn't smiling, and that bothered Dorothy.

"Talk to Mama."

"Are you and Dad getting a divorce?"

Ahmad's question left Dorothy speechless for a second.

"Honey, no, of course not," she responded.

Ahmad sighed. "I hear you and Dad arguing all the time."

"When you're married as long as we've been, you encounter problems. But the good thing is, you talk out your problems, find out what's causing them so you can find a solution."

"Mom, if you decide to get a divorce, I'll stay with you."

Dorothy looked into her son's eyes and saw he was serious.

"Man, honey, I love your father, and I love you too, and I'm not going to get a divorce. I promise."

Ahmad's eyes showed wonderment, as if somehow his mother's voice and smile offered assurance where there once was doubt.

Dorothy and her mother finally found time to themselves to talk. She was tired of hearing about Jacqueline's boyfriends and Lucky's sissified ways.

"Mama, can you for once, today, listen to what I have to say?"

"What, child?" Cleo replied as she thumped her cigarette ash.

"My marriage is falling apart." Dorothy retrieved a cigarette from her mother. "I can't please David, no matter what I do." Dorothy lit her cigarette and took a long drag as if she had been smoking for years. "You know, Mama," she exhaled a cloud of smoke, "I believe David is seeing another woman."

"What would make you say something like that?"

"Somebody is always calling and hanging up. David stays out all night. I call the hospital and they don't know where he is. I call the office and he's not there. Now what does that tell you?"

"You're overreacting. That man is in love with you."

"Like hell he is." She took another drag. "David is jealous, he's abusive, he's controlling, he's manipulative . . . oh, he can charm the pants right off you and slit your throat at the same time." Dorothy said it before she knew it. Cleo looked at her daughter as if she was a total stranger. "You talking about your husband?"

"Yes."

"Your children's daddy?"

"I'm talking about David."

Cleo frowned. "Why are you just now saying something about it?"

Dorothy hesitated as she tried to think of something to say. "I just kept thinking things were going to get better and one day he'd stop."

"How long has this been going on?"

"A long time."

"How long?"

"Since before we got married."

"I knew it. I didn't want to see it, but I remembered that time when he asked you to marry him in New Orleans and when you dropped out of school. He wouldn't let you get two cents in before he was all over the place. Son of a bitch." She lit another cigarette. "Do your children know what's going on?"

"I try not to let them hear us."

"Has he hit you?"

Dorothy closed her eyes. "Just one time," she lied.

"Why in the hell didn't you tell somebody, Dorothy? When was this?"

"A long time ago, before Nia and Jamal were born."

"I'm angry at you for not telling me this sooner. I could've gone to Sister Devereaux and we could've done something about it."

Dorothy shook her head. "*Mère*, no. I don't need that. I thought her stuff would help the last time, but it didn't."

"You didn't pray hard enough."

Dorothy waved her hand in protest and took a long drag on the cigarette.

"*Mère*, I came this close—" she indicated with her thumb and index finger—"to killing him." Her eyes watered with tears.

Cleo smashed her cigarette butt in a nearby ashtray and blew out a cloud of smoke. "You know, I don't like this. I don't like it one damn bit, Dorothy."

Cleo knew what type of person her daughter was. She didn't deserve what was happening to her, and she wasn't one to fight back. She needed somebody to do her fighting for her, and Cleo was more than willing and able to. "I'll kill that son of a bitch for you."

"No." Dorothy snapped. "That's why I never wanted to tell you." Dorothy felt a tear fall from her eye.

"Stop crying."

Dorothy wiped the tears with a handkerchief that Cleo provided for her.

"Listen to me. You got to fight back. Right now you're trapped in the corner, and as long as you're there, you are going to get kicked around and beaten like nobody's business."

Dorothy listened to her mother. She made it sound so easy, but Dorothy didn't have the nerve.

"Let me tell you something, Dorothy," Cleo began. "Don't

let this marriage get the best of you. You have three beautiful
children who love and adore you."

A smile rushed over Dorothy as she got a mental picture of
her three babies. "Ahmad asked me if I was leaving David."

"See! He knows that shit ain't right. What did you say?"

"I told him that I loved his daddy and I wasn't ever gonna
leave him."

"Are you serious?"

Dorothy finished off the cigarette. "Yes, I am."

"You're crazy if you stay there."

"I'm going to try to make things better."

"Listen to me and listen good. If Mama ain't happy, ain't
nobody happy."

Dorothy blew her nose. "I hear you."

"You're much better off leaving," Cleo added.

"I can't just up and leave like you did, *Mère*."

"I got Sister Devereaux's number."

"No, thanks." Dorothy was firm. "I don't need that."

Three months passed, and Chanel was sparkling like a
chandelier in her jade green silk pantsuit. David stood in her
doorway, dapper and crisp wearing a black Armani suit, holding two long-stemmed roses.

"You look like a million bucks," he said before planting a
kiss on her lips.

"You like?" Chanel asked. He held her hand while she did a
turn for him. David's eyes danced up and down her slender
frame. "Yes, Lord," he replied.

Danielle came screaming and running into her father's
arms.

"How's my little angel?" David picked her up and kissed
her forehead. "Look what I have for you and your mother."
David gave her a rose.

"Thank you, I drew a picture of you. Do you want to see it?"

"Sure, can we see it after we come back from the restaurant?"

"Yeah, let's go. Hurry up!"

Danielle was a miniature version of her mother, all dressed up in jade green.

"You heard her, didn't you?" Chanel asked.

"We see who's running things around here." David said before giving Chanel another kiss on the lips. Chanel grabbed her purse and locked the door behind her.

During the ride to the restaurant, Chanel smiled to herself as she stared at David. She felt like a princess, and it made her want to giggle like a precocious little girl. She was finally with the man she loved and celebrating their years together with a dinner at their favorite restaurant.

"I made reservations under the name Chanel Gainous," David explained to the maître d'.

"Follow me this way," the maître d' responded. He found a seat near the center of the restaurant.

"How's this?" he asked David, regarding the seating area.

"This is fine, thank you." David pulled out a chair for Chanel and a high chair for Danielle.

"Here are your menus. There will be a waiter here shortly."

Chanel glanced at the menu. "Good choice, David."

David glanced at the menu. "I know."

The Houston Room was one of the city's premiere spots, known for its fine dining and live entertainment, in addition to its host of famous patrons.

Across the room, unbeknownst to David and Chanel, sat Sadaria McCloud with Ms. Johnson.

"Ms. Johnson, will you look." Sadaria tilted her glass across the room in David's direction.

Ms. Johnson stopped chewing, glanced over and quickly turned her head. The sight was unbearable. David and Chanel were engaged in a kiss.

"I knew it." Sadaria stood.

"Where are you going?" Ms. Johnson asked, alarmed.

"I'm going over there."

Ms. Johnson sat her down. "Mind your own business."

"We need to tell Dorothy. We can't sit back and pretend this isn't happening."

"And like I told you, missy, mind your own business."

"Ms. Johnson, Dorothy called me at work yesterday, crying about how distant and cold David was to her and how they fought all day and night. Now you see that bitch over there? She's the reason their marriage is in the shape it's in. I think we should tell her."

A waitress approached their table with the check. Ms. Johnson opened up her pocketbook and slipped a fifty-dollar bill into the checkbook.

"It's not right and you know it. If David wanted her to know, he'd tell her. It's not our place to do that."

"Dorothy is just like a sister to me, Ms. Johnson. I don't want to interfere in her marriage either, but she told me some things and I couldn't help but wonder."

"I don't want any part of this."

"Come on, ride out to her house with me. I guarantee you he won't be going out there any time soon."

"No."

"If your husband was cheating on you with your best friend wouldn't you want to know about it?"

"Some things just have a way of revealing themselves," Ms. Johnson explained. "Now if we go out there with this, Dorothy might not ever forgive us, and furthermore, you and I could lose our jobs behind this."

"Truth be told. I'm ready to leave anyway. I've had enough nonsense." Sadaria took one last sip of her rum and Coke.

"How do we leave without them noticing us?" Ms. Johnson wondered.

"I want them to see me." Sadaria glanced over and noticed Chanel feeding some of her salad to David. "Will you look?" They both glanced across the room. "You think David's that little girl's daddy?" Sadaria asked.

"I don't want to jump to any conclusions," Ms. Johnson declared.

"Come on, let's pay Dorothy a visit."

"I'll ride with you, but I'm not getting out of the car."

When Sadaria broke the news to Dorothy, she stood in shock for a moment before she sat down on the edge of the sofa.

"So that's the other woman?"

"Yes," Sadaria said. "I tried convincing myself that it could've been a business meeting, but then again, who does business on a Sunday evening and who brings their child to the meeting?"

Ms. Johnson sat across from Dorothy, angry yet hurt for Dorothy.

"Why didn't I see it?" Dorothy asked. "I invited this woman into my home. I helped her when she was down on her luck. When she was sick, I was the one who fixed her herbal tea and brought it to her bedside."

"I can't understand how some women could stoop so low." Sadaria shook her head.

"She used to come to me crying about all the problems she was having with this man named Linus. It was David all along."

Dorothy took her handkerchief and dabbed at her eyes. She

was fighting with all her strength to be strong. "Sadaria, you didn't see what was going on?"

Sadaria stood. "I always had my hunches, but I knew the minute she stepped into the office, she wasn't any good."

"Thank you, Sadaria. I'm glad you finally decided to tell me."

Ms. Johnson was trying to wipe tears from her own eyes. "Dorothy, we didn't want you to have to find out this way."

Tears began to stream down Dorothy's cheeks like rainfall. Ms. Johnson took Dorothy's hand and held it.

"It hurts. Especially when I've tried so hard to be decent and honest, and I put up with so much, y'all don't understand."

"I know," Ms. Johnson agreed.

"I gave him fifteen of the best years of my life. Only he and God knew just how much I loved him." Dorothy was so overcome with emotion that at times it sounded like laughter.

Sadaria held Dorothy's other hand.

"What did I do to deserve this?"

"Some men are just peculiar creatures. You can be the best woman in the world to them and that's not good enough." Ms. Johnson rubbed Dorothy's hand.

"Dorothy, why don't you come take a ride with us?" Sadaria suggested.

"I need to, but I want to be here when he gets in." Dorothy grabbed a coin purse sitting on the coffee table and opened it. Her Virginia Slims and gold cigarette lighter were inside.

"You smoke?" Sadaria asked.

"You like Virginia Slims?" Dorothy offered her the box.

"Yeah, I'll take one."

"You smoke, Ms. Johnson?"

"No, but give me one anyway."

Dorothy did the honors and lit their cigarettes. "I'm up to two packs a day."

"Two packs? Honey, quit." Sadaria took a drag.

"I can't."

"You drink, too?" Sadaria asked.

"A few shots here and there."

"Don't lose yourself. Get it together." Ms. Johnson held her cigarette, letting it burn and thumping the ashes in a nearby ashtray.

"My roommate from college used to tell me that a long time ago."

"If you need to leave, do so. That's what I did," Sadaria said.

"It was easy for you. Your kids were grown when you and your husband split. I still have babies, Sadaria."

Dorothy took one last drag of her cigarette and smashed the butt in an ashtray. She lamented, "I don't believe this." Her eyes welled up with tears again. "She even asked me and David to be her daughter's godparents, and David, son of a bitch, went along with it, knowing damn well he was screwing her."

"How old is that little girl?" Sadaria asked.

"I think she's Jamal's age." Dorothy's words trailed off and her expression drew blank. "What are you implying?" she asked Sadaria.

Sadaria and Ms. Johnson didn't reply but folded their arms and began to brainstorm. A long silence filled the room.

When David finally arrived, Dorothy was sitting in the dark on a chaise lounge, staring out the window. David unbuttoned his shirt and unzipped his pants. He turned on the lamplight and saw Dorothy sitting quietly across the room.

"Why are you sitting in the dark?" He joined her and examined her expression. "You hear me talking to you?"

Dorothy remained silent. David checked her forehead with the back of his hand. Dorothy moved her head. "How long have you been having an affair with Chanel?"

"What?" he responded defensively.

"How long, David?" She increased the volume of her voice, removing all pleasantness.

David's eyes searched Dorothy's eyes for questions. "It doesn't matter."

"How dare you!"

David sighed; he couldn't deny it. "I don't know, six or seven years."

Dorothy pressed her eyes shut as the tears started to flow. A soft sob escaped her lips.

"She doesn't mean anything. She doesn't compare . . ."

Dorothy cut him off mid-sentence. "You've been with her seven years. Evidentially she means something to you."

"I know whatever I say now won't mean anything . . . you're hurting."

"You have no idea how much. I've been nothing but good to you, David."

"I know, baby."

"I can't trust you anymore."

David shook his head. "I deserve that." He lowered his head.

"There's something else I need to know."

"What is it?"

"Is Danielle your baby?"

David braced himself. He dreaded this moment and had hoped in a million years he never would have arrived at this point. His head told him to *deny, deny, deny.* His heart told him otherwise.

"Yes, she is my daughter."

Dorothy took a deep breath. She didn't want to exhale for fear her heart might jump out of her mouth.

"You're serious."

David nodded. Dorothy picked up a vase and tossed it at

his head before she realized it. It smashed into a million pieces on the floor.

"You son of a bitch! It wasn't enough you had an affair, but you had to get a baby, too! I hate you! I hate you. You are a fucking dog!"

"Calm down!"

"Calm down!" She tossed a pillow in his direction and ran up to him, pounding furiously on his chest. He tried shoving her back but she was relentless.

"You are a low-down son of a bitch!" She fought David, remembering what her Papa said about disrespecting her house. David hadn't seen this side of her, and he didn't fight back. He shielded himself.

"How could you do this to me and your children?"

David couldn't respond.

"So that's where you were when I called the hospital and left messages? You were laying up with that bitch?"

David's temples started jumping, and his silence was too much for Dorothy to bear. "Is that where all your money goes? Do you have her on a two-hundred-dollar-a- month allowance? Fuck you!"

Dorothy dashed across the room and opened the closet door. She got David's suitcase and threw it on the floor. "If you want to be with your other family, goddammit, you get your shit and get out!"

"I'm not going anywhere." He picked up his suitcase and placed it back in the closet and slammed the door.

"I hate you so goddamn much!" Dorothy uttered through gritted teeth.

"No, you don't."

"You don't deserve a woman like me, David!"

"Yes, I do." He started walking toward her. "If you want me to beg, I'm begging you. Let's get this behind us and start over."

"Start over? Fuck you!"

David came closer and reached out for her. She slapped his hand away.

"Please," he whispered.

"Get away from me!"

"I'm sorry."

"You're sorry you got caught!"

"Don't do this!"

"I should've done it fifteen years ago!"

"You don't really want me to leave!"

"You hurt me for the last time, David!"

David came closer; Dorothy could feel his breath on her forehead.

"Get out of my face!"

He stood in front of her, his eyes pleading for her to forgive him. Without another word, he walked out of the room. Dorothy stood frozen; in case he decided to come back in the room she had another vase ready to pound his skull. Her emotions were getting the best of her, she didn't know whether to laugh or cry—all she knew was that at that moment she was miserable, and the only way she was going to be happy would be by getting a divorce.

The following morning, she walked into the kitchen to find David sitting at the table, enjoying a cup of coffee and reading the paper.

"Why are you still here?" she asked.

"Let's talk." He patted the empty spot beside him.

"I don't want to talk, do you understand that? It's best you leave, right now."

David was about to respond when he saw Ahmad walk down the stairs. Dorothy stopped and regained her composure. "Good morning, Man."

"Good morning," he mumbled before opening the refrigerator.

"Honey, do you want eggs and toast?" Dorothy asked, trying to sound upbeat and happy. Ahmad closed the refrigerator and looked at his parents. Dorothy could sense something was troubling him.

"You know, Mom and Dad, I'm not really hungry anymore."

Dorothy and David glanced each other.

"What's wrong, son?" David asked.

"I'm tired of hearing you and Mom argue and fight! Just stop it and get a divorce!" He turned and walked out of the room. Dorothy started after him but David stopped her.

"I'll handle this," he said.

The doorbell rang. Dorothy opened it. Chanel Gainous stood on the other side of the door. She was radiant in her lime green dress and new sunglasses. Her teeth were sparkling white and her lipstick was glistening like a bright red flame.

"How dare you?" Dorothy said through gritted teeth. "You got some nerve showing up at my door, you miserable low-life snake!"

Chanel sensed the tension in Dorothy's voice and switched her approach. "I came to see if David was home. He promised to take his daughter school shopping today. I know it's not a problem." Chanel was brazen with her approach.

"Look," Dorothy began, "if you don't leave my house right now, I swear I will blow you up into so many pieces, they won't be able to identify your teeth."

"I know you're not threatening me. I'm not going anywhere until I see David. Just so you know, he takes good care of me and his child, and I'm here to make sure that he continues what he started."

"Maybe you didn't understand what I said," Dorothy began. "I will hurt you, Chanel. You don't know who you're fucking with."

"You better tell David to come here and see about his child."

Dorothy slammed the door in her face and ran upstairs to find David.

"David!" she heard herself shout. Her bathrobe was swinging carelessly behind her. She found David in Ahmad's room. "David, you better come downstairs quick and tell your friend to leave."

A questionable stare was glued to his face. "Friend?"

"Excuse us, dear," Dorothy said to Ahmad as she followed David out of the room and closed the door behind her. "Your bitch is outside. Tell her to leave before I end up hurting her."

Once downstairs, David opened the door. Chanel was standing with Danielle in hand. David was furious.

"Will you take her and leave!"

"You told me last night you were going to take her school shopping."

Dorothy appeared in the doorway next to David.

"Take Danielle and leave before I call the police."

"What did you tell me last night?"

Dorothy shook her head; it was obvious Chanel wasn't playing with a full deck.

"You need to leave." David tried to appear calm and diplomatic, but a bead of perspiration around his temples and armpits told the gospel truth.

"Tell her which one of us you'd rather be with," Chanel snapped. "Tell her like you told me, how you were going to divorce her fat ass and marry me."

Dorothy shook her head in disbelief. "You have a serious problem."

Chanel added a rebuttal. "You are going to have a serious problem if you don't stop fucking with my man." She lunged toward Dorothy, but David intercepted her.

"Dorothy, go in the house and call the police!" he shouted.

Dorothy turned and left; she could hear Chanel cursing and screaming at David and Danielle screaming and crying. She saw Nia and Ahmad running down the stairs followed by Jamal.

"Man, call the police and tell them to hurry!"

"What's wrong?"

"Just do what I tell you!" Dorothy tried talking over Jamal, who was screaming. Nia was nearby, sniffing and rubbing her eyes. "Is Daddy going to jail?" she asked.

"Your daddy's not going to jail! Shhh."

"I want my daddy!" Jamal cried out.

"Daddy's coming back. Shhh."

Jamal broke out in a tantrum. "I want my daddy!" he cried before he fell to the floor and started kicking. Dorothy scooped him up and shook him without thinking. "Look!" she shouted. "I'm going to spank you if you don't shut up!"

Jamal cut his tantrum down to a low whimper.

When the police arrived, Chanel had calmed down. The police asked if David wanted to press charges. He shook his head.

"Why not?" Dorothy questioned him. "After all the shit she put your children through today, fuck you! I'll press charges on her myself!" David tried to calm her down.

Chanel wasn't making the situation easier. She took Danielle's hand. "I hope you're happy, you son of a bitch. You will see me in court. Oh yes, me and Danielle are gonna have a field day on your funky ass!"

"You can have him!" Dorothy shouted. "He's all yours!" She slammed the door. She turned and looked at her three children. She didn't want them to see her crying, so she ran down the hall to the library and shut the door behind her, locking it. With tears streaming down her cheeks, she rushed to the mahogany desk where she picked up the phone. She didn't know just who she was calling, but she punched in a few numbers and listened to the dial tone. When Tiny answered the phone, Dorothy hesitated.

"Hello," Tiny repeated. "Hellooo."

"Tiny," Dorothy said, sniffing.

"Who is this?" Tiny asked, not quite catching the shivering voice on the other end.

"It's me, Dot."

"Cousin. What's wrong?"

Dorothy broke down. "Tiny, I am so tired. I need out."

"What's going on, Dorothy?"

"It's the last straw for David."

"What has he done?"

"You were right."

"Right about what?"

"About that girl who worked with David."

"What happened?" Tiny asked, anticipating Dorothy's response.

"She and David—"

"Shut up. Get outta here!" Tiny screamed before Dorothy could finish.

Dorothy felt a headache coming on, so she closed her eyes and massaged her temples with her fingers.

"How did you find out?"

"She had the nerve to show up at my door."

"Hold up, back up. She did what?" Tiny asked. She was furious.

"She came to our house talking shit," Dorothy responded.

"Did you kick her ass?"

Dorothy could tell her cousin was no longer sitting down.

"It all happened so fast, I didn't know whether I was going or coming."

"Where's David?"

"Gone."

"Where are your children?"

Dorothy thought about her babies and started crying.

"They're here. God, I wish my children didn't have to see this, Tiny."

"I know. Look, why don't you send your kids here to stay with me until you and David get this situation worked out."

"There ain't gonna be no working out. I've already made up my mind."

"You sure?"

"That's why I'm calling you to see if you can find someone to represent me."

"You really serious about this?"

"There is a child involved. Of course I'm serious."

"A child? She had a child?"

"Yes."

"Hush your mouth," Tiny said gasping. "I don't believe it."

"You see what I'm talking about?"

"I am shocked, Dorothy."

"I swear to God, I hate David. I hate him so much."

"How soon can the kids come to New Orleans?"

"Tomorrow."

"You work on getting them reservations and I'll work on finding you a good divorce attorney, okay?"

Dorothy agreed.

"I love you, cuz, and you're going to get through this," Tiny said.

Dorothy hung up the phone, laid her head down on the desk, and immersed herself in tears. Nothing could heal the large wound in her heart. She looked around the room in search of answers. Then suddenly she felt the urge to get down on her knees. She closed her eyes and said a prayer.

Father God,
I know I haven't talked to You like I should. I have a serious problem that I know only you can help me with. Please forgive

me for all those times when trials and tribulations came into my life, and instead of going to You, I tried to fight them myself. God, please forgive me for not giving you the due glory during good times. God, listen to me, please. I need You, my children need You, and most of all, my husband needs You.

Dorothy paused and cried silently.

God, please give me the heart to save my marriage, because right now I don't have it. Oh God, save my marriage for my children's sake. I don't want them to grow up without their father. They love him so much and I want to love him, but God, it's so hard.

Dorothy wiped the tears from her eyes.

It's so hard. Please give me the strength. Amen.

The days following the discovery left Dorothy on an emotional rollercoaster. She called Tiny and decided against retaining a divorce attorney. She and David hardly spoke to each other, and when they did, it was small talk, as if they were strangers. There were days when Dorothy hated to be in his presence, so she hid whenever he came home. She hid in the poolhouse, she hid in Nia's room, she even spent a night in the RV.

Chanel didn't stop calling, nor did she stop coming to the house and to the practice. She caused so much commotion and confusion that David fired her, then went to court to file a restraining order against her. David paid her a special visit to settle things with her once and for all.

"As long as you live, you are going to regret the day you fucked with me!" Chanel shouted.

David opened up his checkbook and drew out his Cross pen. "Fifty thousand enough for you?"

"I don't want your fucking money."

"You didn't say that last week."

"Me and Danielle need you."

"Cut the bullshit, okay? I'm sorry. When I look at my home, my business, and my children, and I see how far I've come . . . I can't risk losing it."

"You have a good thing with me and Danielle."

"I told you when you first found out you were pregnant to terminate the pregnancy. Now I can't imagine life without her. But I've got to place my priority on the lady who's wearing my ring, and that's Dorothy Lacroix Leonard, not Chanel Gainous."

Tears spewed from her eyes, and before David saw it coming, she up and slapped him. "You had nothing but happiness with me. Go on! We don't need you or your fucking money anyway! Go back to your little happily never after."

David sat calmly. Any other time he would've retaliated, but he tasted the blood in his mouth and sat, engulfed in his thoughts.

"I don't need you!" Chanel shouted with tears rolling down her cheeks. "I hate you. God, I hate the day I met you! Get out!" She pointed toward the door.

David quietly stood and made his way to the door. He opened it and turned to look at Chanel. "Give Danielle a kiss for me," he said before leaving Chanel and a life with her behind him. He convinced himself this time it was for good.

Chapter 16

Dorothy opened her door to see a UPS guy with a notepad standing in front of her.

"Special delivery for Mrs. Dorothy Leonard. Will you please sign here?"

With a questionable look glued to her face and without explanation, she signed the pad. The man presented her with a large rectangular box with a Gucci emblem. She didn't question who sent it. She knew it was from David. She unwrapped it to find a white silk gown inside, accompanied by a small white card that read, *I have a surprise for you,* written in David's handwriting. She took the box with the gown upstairs to her room. For some reason Dorothy couldn't resist smiling, but this time she wasn't giving in. Her feelings could not be bought. She threw the box on the bed.

"Try it on."

Dorothy jumped when she heard David's voice behind her.

"You can't buy me out of my misery."

"I'm not trying to do that."

"Yes, you are, now stop it, okay?"

David stood in silence for a moment. "Why don't you try it on for me?"

Dorothy hesitated before she removed the top from the box and looked inside at the beautiful white silk gown.

"You like it?" he asked.

She nodded.

"I'm stepping outside. I'll see you downstairs, in your dress, in one hour."

"It's going to take more than an hour for me to get dressed."

"Okay, an hour and a half."

"Look, what's going on? I'm not in the mood."

"Get that dress on and I'll show you."

Dorothy walked outside to find David standing beside a black Cadillac limo. He was decked from head to toe in Giorgio Armani. His brown skin had a youthful radiance that reminded her of the day she first laid eyes on him.

"Are you ready?" he asked.

"Yes." She studied his eyes carefully. When he extended his hand Dorothy, although reluctant, reached out to take it. Once she sat inside and positioned herself in the leather seats, her heart began to pound like drums. David wasn't far behind. He signaled to the chauffer to drive off and close the partition, giving him and Dorothy their privacy. He sneaked a peek at his wife.

"You look beautiful," he said softly. "You care for some champagne?"

Dorothy hesitated before she answered. "Yes, thank you."

He poured her a glass of Dom Perignon.

"Thank you," she said.

"My pleasure." David poured himself a glass and placed the bottle in an ice-filled chiller. They both sipped quietly, hardly saying anything to each other. Then suddenly the

opening chords to Teddy Pendergrass' song, "Can't We Try"
began to fill the speakers in a lively surround sound. Dorothy's
green eyes began to glow. She absolutely adored Teddy Pendergrass' music, though the current tune was rather melancholy. It was as if David was speaking to her through this song.
She listened to the words and turned her attention to the life
going on outside the car. It was funny how life continues to go
on as usual, even when there's a death, a divorce, or two people who've come to the crossroads, not knowing which direction to take. She was so engulfed in the song and her thoughts
that she forgot about David. She felt alone.

"Hey." David gently took her hand. "I'm still here."

"I don't know how I feel about us anymore. You hurt me a
lot over the years, and I'm just getting the nerve to tell you
that. You're good one minute, the next, you're like a madman,
and I can't deal with it."

"I love you, Dorothy."

"Don't." She put up her hand. "You don't love me. You love
to control me."

"I know I get a little carried away."

"Seventeen years is a long time, and I can't tell you one
time that I thought I was happy, David. Not one time."

David sat his champagne glass near the chiller. "I never
made you happy?"

"No," Dorothy said before she realized it.

"Did Jerome make you happy?"

"Hell, no. And this ain't about him."

"I know I made my mistakes, but I tried doing the best I
could."

"I feel stupid and vulnerable. I placed my head and my
heart, and I gave up so much to have a life with you, and you
go and you do this . . ." Dorothy wiped away a tear that was
forming in her eye. "Where are we going, anyway?"

*   *   *

Dorothy found herself sitting on the front row facing an empty stage. David sat across from her, checking his watch and eyeing the stage. The atmosphere of the club was lively yet mellow and relaxed, with votive candles burning. An emcee walked on stage to the applause of the crowd. "Ladies and gentlemen, you are going to have an intimate evening with one of the sexiest balladeers in the industry. He gave us hits like "If You Don't Know Me By Now." The audience began to applaud, and the applause grew louder as the emcee continued to name hit after hit. Dorothy found herself on the edge of her seat.

"Club Atlantis, you asked for it, up close and personal. Coming to you all the way from Philly, please give a round of applause for Philadelphia International recording star, Mr. Teddy Pendergrass."

Dorothy stood with applause when he came on stage, dressed in a black tuxedo. He greeted the audience, who greeted him back with thunderous applause. His band started the chords to his first song, and while they played, Teddy improvised. "You look so good, Houston, but I need to set the mood right. I hope you don't mind if I . . . turn off the lights."

The audience, especially the ladies, stood cheering on Teddy while he performed a signature tune.

Dorothy's face was bright like a thousand watts. David was equally pleased. He was pleased throughout the evening as Dorothy sang along and even danced. After five songs, most of which were upbeat, Teddy slowed the tempo and came downstage. The dim lights in the club went completely out, and the spotlight directed its rays on Teddy.

"I want to dedicate this song to a special couple sitting with us tonight. They're going through some problems. The brother approached me and asked if I could put his feelings into words with one of my songs and sing it to her."

David glanced at his wife, whose expression was submerged in deep concentration.

"He said, 'Teddy, I love her so much. We've been married about fifteen years, we have three beautiful children and I just don't want to lose a good thing.' He said, 'Teddy, I did something that I'm really ashamed of, and now everything is all wrong.' He said, 'Teddy, we don't even sleep in the same bed anymore.'"

The audience gasped and broke into scattered whispers.

"This brother looked at me and said, 'Teddy, I love this woman. I love her so much because she's my latest, my greatest inspiration.'"

David closed his eyes and smiled. That was his favorite song. Teddy sang the words.

Dorothy's eyes watered with tears. She knew just whom he was talking about. Halfway through the song, she was so overcome with emotion that she got up and walked away. Through the crowd she went, clearing her path until she made her way outside. She called up the limo and waited, staring at the rain, which was pouring so hard it looked like a thin white sheet. David wasn't too far behind.

"Stop it! It's not going to work out." Dorothy said.

The limo pulled up. "I'm trying to apologize to you the best way I know how, Dorothy." The chauffeur opened the door and closed it immediately after they got in.

"You just had to get Teddy Pendergrass in our business. You think I'm supposed to forget about everything and act like everything is fine and dandy because he sang to me?" Dorothy stopped. "It's not going to change anything, David. I can't deal with this. I want a divorce. I can't keep living like this. I'm tired of sleeping in separate rooms. I'm tired of you using drugs. I'm sick and tired of you treating me like dirt. I refuse to put up with it any longer."

David sighed. "Okay, okay. I'm listening. We'll get counseling, but don't talk about divorce."

"I can't live with you, knowing you have an outside child."

Dorothy paused. "Put yourself in my shoes. Would you be so quick to forgive me?"

"I know I haven't been a good husband, Dorothy." He cupped her face in his hands. Dorothy could see tears glistening in his eyes. "I screwed up, I admit it, but I'm begging you. Don't give up on me."

"You can do all the begging in the world, David. It's not going to change how I feel."

"Dorothy—" David's expression was so intense—"all I want to hear from you is, 'David, I know you're sorry. David, I forgive you. David, I'm not going to leave you. David, I'm willing to give you another chance.'"

Dorothy shook her head in disagreement. The tears in David's eyes were falling down his cheeks.

David cried out in desperation. "I love you and I can't go on without you."

Tears spewed out of her own eyes. "I refuse to let you hurt me anymore."

David got down on his knees. "Dorothy, please."

Dorothy looked at the helpless man at her feet. Deep in her heart, she felt David was sincere. This time he was going to change. Before she even realized it, she took his pitiful face into her hands and began to kiss his lips and respond to his every plea. They became entangled in a web of passion so intense, the windows in the limo became ice white. David unbuttoned his tux and removed his shirt and undressed Dorothy, taking off everything but her shoes. David positioned himself between her large, *café au lait* thighs and made long-awaited love to her. They were both so emotionally overwhelmed and charged, the spontaneity of it surprised them. Dorothy couldn't remember the last time she felt like this with David's lovemaking. Nothing could compare to this strange, intensified moment.

The rays from the morning sun awoke Dorothy. She opened her eyes to see David staring back at her.

"Hey, you," he whispered before he kissed the tip of her nose.

"Good morning." She noticed they were in their bed, together.

"How did you sleep?"

"I slept really good, and you?" she asked.

"I hadn't slept that good since the first time we made love. You remember that?"

Dorothy began to blush. "Yes. It was on my twentieth birthday to be exact."

David stared straight ahead at the ceiling. "I've got so much I want to say, I just don't know where to begin."

"Like what?"

"Why our marriage took a turn the way it did." David thought about it for a moment. "I can't blame everything on the coke. Part of it was due to my upbringing."

"Why would you say that?" Dorothy asked.

"My father wasn't really abusive, but he liked to control things. He liked a lot of order, and he just never wanted my mother out of his sight."

Dorothy opened her mouth in shock.

"Of course they kept it hush-hush. My old man was something else. He was going back and forth between my mom and Ms. Edna."

"Jerome's mother?"

"Oh, yeah."

Dorothy shook her head; she couldn't believe what she was hearing.

"My family had a reputation to uphold. They didn't want to tarnish their image, so my mother allowed him to treat her like shit. She was just like you. Kept her mouth shut, didn't want anybody to know just how bad off it was."

Dorothy rested her chin on David's chest and listened as he went on.

"There were times when I resented her for it. Hell, she didn't teach me any better, so for the longest time I thought a man was supposed to use fear to keep his woman in line."

"Is that what happened with you and Bettye?"

"Yes, sort of."

"Did you ever hit Bettye?"

David hesitated. "A couple of times . . . I don't remember."

"I remember many years ago, Bettye approached me and told me to beware, that things aren't always what they seem."

"She said that about me?" David asked.

Dorothy closed her eyes and pictured Bettye as though it were yesterday. "Yes she had tears in her eyes when she told me."

"That's why I used the drugs—they made me numb, made me forget about all the pain I caused people."

"You and I should've had this talk a long time ago."

David smiled and gazed lovingly into Dorothy's eyes. "I don't know what I'd do without you." He kissed her lips.

"Stop. You'll have me crying in a few minutes." Dorothy fought back a tear.

"I know I tried intentionally and unintentionally to bring you down, but you persevered. You hung in there with me."

Dorothy couldn't hold back the tear from falling.

"I love you so much, woman." He lavished her naked body with tender kisses. "Can I show you something?" He took her hand and led her to their large walk-in closet.

"What are you doing?" she asked.

"Shh, don't say anything, just watch."

She watched him reach inside an old high school jacket of his and pull out a bag of cocaine. She was so alarmed, the hairs on her arms stood up.

"I promise you, this is it. So help me God." He led Dorothy from the closet and into their bathroom where he emptied the bag into the toilet. Dorothy was astonished.

"You probably have another stash somewhere."

"No, I don't."

"You promise?"

"I promise."

"Thank you." She put her arms around him.

"Let's call around for a counselor so we can work on getting this marriage in order. Okay?"

"Okay," Dorothy replied.

There was life and laughter back in the Leonard household again. Dorothy and David entertained their family and friends often with gatherings, which included barbecues and crawfish boils outside near the pool or inside watching television.

"Dorothy, this Easter gathering is so wonderful," Mrs. Leonard said, giving Dorothy a peck on the cheek. "I am so happy for you and my baby."

Dorothy nodded. "I'm happy too."

She tapped Dorothy's hand and proceeded on her merry way. Dorothy was amazed at how Mrs. Leonard aged so gracefully. For a woman of sixty-eight, she still wore high-heeled pumps and fitted A-line skirts.

"How's my angel?" David asked, cuddling Dorothy in his arms.

"I'm really enjoying this dinner. You should've seen those kids trying to find the eggs we hid."

"They were excited, huh?"

"Yes. I'm glad you thought of this dinner, David."

"We need to spend more time with the people we care about the most."

"I couldn't agree with you more."

Dorothy turned and gave him a quick peck on the cheek. She watched him walk away. Her thoughts were interrupted by her daughter's voice.

"Mom! Mom! Lucky and Man are upstairs fighting!"

"What? You go up there and tell your brother I said come here, now!"

Nia turned and walked through a crowd of her relatives. At that moment, Tiny entered the kitchen.

"Hi, cuz, what's ailing you?" she asked.

"Those damn kids. Tiny, were we that terrible when we were their age?"

"I can't speak for you, but I was a good child," Tiny commented jokingly. She noticed the sparkle back in Dorothy's eyes. "How are things going with him?"

"Like it was when we first met."

"I admire you a lot," she said. "You are better than I ever will be in this life or the next."

"You've got to be able to forgive."

"Like I said, after what happened, that bitch is lucky she's not pushing up daisies." Tiny poured herself a glass of lemonade. David's brother Marcus approached Dorothy and Tiny.

"Is he available, Dorothy?" Tiny asked.

"Tiny, please, you know who this is?"

Marcus gave Dorothy a peck on the cheek. "What's happening?" he asked.

"Marcus, this is my cousin, Christine."

They shook hands. Tiny flashed a radiant yet sexy smile. "What are you doing tonight?" she asked.

"Stop it. She's not serious, Marcus."

"Like hell I'm not. Now move, Dorothy. I'm trying to score a touchdown and you're blocking me." Tiny moved Dorothy aside. Marcus smiled and licked his lips. Tiny thought it was a sign of approval, and she glanced at Dorothy.

"He has nice lips. I think I'm really going to like him," she whispered.

Marcus gave her his arm and the pair walked arm and arm

out of the kitchen. Dorothy joined Cleo, who sat near the pool puffing on a cigarette. "You haven't noticed anything unusual, have you?" she asked.

"What are you talking about, *Mère?*"

"With David."

"No, not lately. You noticed something I didn't?"

"No, *Mère*'s just being *Mère*, that's all."

Dorothy proceeded to eat her pecan pralines.

"I went to Sister Devereaux."

Dorothy stopped eating.

"Those herbs really helped."

"I don't see what you find fascinating about that stuff."

"It's powerful. I've seen it work miracles."

Dorothy continued eating.

"I think I need to get some for Lucky. He acts more and more like a sissy every day."

"You talked to him?"

"He's in denial. A boy his age ought to have girls calling the house. He's got boys and sometimes grown men calling the house."

"That doesn't mean he's a sissy."

"Have you seen his ears? Both of them are pierced, plus he wears panties. That's not normal."

"What does Ophelia have to say?"

"Seems to me like she's encouraging it."

"It doesn't surprise me."

"She's been acting strange lately. I think she's back on that stuff."

"Don't say that," Dorothy said while chewing her praline.

"I believe she is."

"What are you guys talking about?" Jacqueline asked, joining them. At seventeen, she had grown into a beautiful, graceful, and intelligent young lady. She was a dance major at the

University of Houston and had a body sculpted by the art form.

Cleo looked at her youngest daughter from head to toe. "Where's Lucky?"

"I don't know. Why?"

"Tell him to come here."

Jacqueline groaned. "I'm tired. I don't feel like it."

"You can dance for ten and twelve hours a day, but you can't even go inside to get Lucky for me? I swear, kids these days."

"Okay, *Mère*. Lord." Jacqueline rolled her eyes and pranced her size four body inside.

The music was jumping and everyone was up trying to dance.

"Go on, Mrs. Leonard, strut your stuff," Jacqueline said, urging her on. Mrs. Leonard waved her hand. "No, I can't."

"Go ahead, Mother." Marcus stood. Only then did she dance and dip a couple of times to the amusement of the audience. David grabbed Dorothy's hand to lead her in a dance. "You remember this?" They cut a few steps that were popular in the sixties.

"Yes," Tiny began. "That's the Squirrel."

Dorothy shook her head. "No, Tiny."

She joined Marcus for a dance. "Marcus, you remember the Jerk?"

"No. That was before my time."

Tiny stopped. "That wasn't funny at all." Marcus' comment struck an age-sensitive chord.

"Backstroke" by the Fat Back Brothers was playing loud and clear over the speakers, and the younger generation got a kick out of watching the older folk laugh and reminisce over dance moves. Even Doc Sr. was enthused and popping his fingers. Moments later, "Forever Mine" by the O'Jays came on.

Everyone stopped dancing, leaving David and Dorothy dancing alone.

"This is the song, baby," David whispered.

"I know," Dorothy whispered back. They closed their eyes and slow danced hand in hand. David opened his eyes and looked at his wife. Her green eyes were staring back up at him. They were more beautiful than ever, and her smile was so refreshing. Dorothy saw a look of love and affection in her husband's eyes. Without hesitation they became engaged in a long, passionate kiss. They were oblivious to everything. Even the wooing from everyone around them didn't stop them from kissing. It seemed the romance was back for now.

About the Author

T. Wendy Williams is the author of *Mile High Confessions* and *Happily Never After*. She currently resides in Houston, Texas where she is at work on her third novel.

EXCERPT

PREVIEW

Holy Hustler

By P.L. Wilson

Coming in February 2007

Chapter 2

"You know, you should really do something about her," Reginald said as he passed his father the financial documents.

Pastor Goodlove ignored his son as he scrutinized the numbers that just didn't add up. They had walked out to the enclosed deck that ran along the backside of the massive house. It's where the pool and hot tub were housed.

"According to these numbers, we're down nearly ten percent. I don't like this," Pastor Goodlove said, still looking at the figures.

"Well, I told you, you need to get a handle on Theola's spending. Just last month, in um, February, she spent something like twenty thousand. Yeah, that's right, twenty thousand dollars on clothes. I mean, I know you want her to have nice things, but that's crazy," Reginald insisted.

Finally his father looked up at him. "Theola spent twenty thousand dollars on clothes in February?"

"Yeah, Pop, that's what I'm trying to tell you. But you act like you don't care what she does. I don't understand it, man.

The tail can't be that good," Reginald mumbled under his breath.

"You let me worry about Theola. You just work on these numbers. I don't like what I've been seeing in the past few months. By August, we're headed to the promise land and we can't go if the finances aren't straight," Pastor Goodlove threatened. "I told you I don't want to take out any loans on this project. You got anything else?"

Reginald looked down at the ground. He used his hand to rub his nearly bald head.

"Well, um, look Gee, you should try to curb your spending a bit, too. I mean, um, at least until we finish the expansion. With gas prices climbing, we should think about you cutting down on using the helicopter. I mean, the pilot's fees alone are crazy. Then the plans for the new beach house down on the west end of Galveston beach." Reginald looked away from his father.

"What are you saying, boy?" Pastor stepped toward Reginald. "Look at me like a man. You saying I don't deserve these things, boy? I don't think you realize just how hard I work. It takes talent to translate God's words into a message you young folk want to hear. Then there's my work with the ill and disenfranchised. The counseling, endless appearances, and let's not forget the weekly radio program. I deserve what I got and then some. Let's not forget, either, it's my talent that takes care of you and yours. But enough about me, at the beginning of the year, you talked about hiring grant writers to secure more money for the AIDS center. I ain't heard another word about that." Pastor Goodlove stepped even closer to his son. He looked him straight in the eyes. "I mean, what the hell am I paying you a whopping fifty thousand dollars a year for if you can't help increase the bottom line?"

Reginald scowled under his father's words.

"I'm still working on the grant writers. I'm meeting with

two next week. They should be in place by the end of March."

Pastor Goodlove started fumbling with his clothes as Reginald went on about plans for the next two months. The pastor pulled his phone from his pocket and dialed his driver.

"I need you here in ten minutes," he said before flipping the razor thin phone shut.

"Is there anything else, Reginald?"

"No, I guess that's it. I'm going to Victoria Tuesday to meet with the developer. Can I take the helicopter?"

"Didn't you just tell me about logging time in that thing? Now you want to hop in it? Drive," Pastor Goodlove snapped.

"Okay," Reginald said.

Pastor Goodlove looked at his diamond encrusted Rolex watch. "Tell Theola I had to go away on business for a couple of days." He left out of the back door to meet his driver.

Damien Goodlove had explained to his wife that he merely ran into Jazzlyn outside the restaurant. He assured Michelle that things were not as they appeared when she walked in on them at the restaurant. He was only trying to comfort her, as he was often called to do since he was a deacon at Sweetwater PG.

Damien had explained that Jazzlyn was having a hard time with the women and men at the church. It seems her reputation was making it difficult for her to make female friends and the men wouldn't leave her alone.

But the minute he was able to coax his wife back to her own table, he convinced Jazzlyn to leave the restaurant and promised he'd catch up with her later. Damien had been working on the sweet little Jazzlyn for weeks, and there was no way he was giving up just because he forgot where his wife and her gossiping friends liked to brunch.

Hours after that near mishap, he was about to reap the benefits of his weeks of wooing Jazzlyn. They were holed up inside a room at the Motel Six off Interstate 45 on the outskirts of Houston.

"I thought we were gonna get a nicer room, Dee," Jazzlyn said.

"Lemme see what you got on," Damien insisted. He felt he had spent enough time and money and he was ready to get some kind of return on his investment. He and Jazzlyn had been sneaking around for nearly two weeks.

Each time he tried to take things to the next level, she came up with some lame excuse about why they couldn't do it. He wasn't about to give her the opportunity this time.

Jazzlyn peered around the corner from the bathroom. "You ready for me?" she teased.

Damien was tired of the games. He wanted her in a bad way and he had the most painful hard-on to prove it. He sat waiting on the edge of the bed.

When Jazzlyn walked out of the room, she was a heavenly sight. She wore a little gold lace number that barely covered her large breasts. Her body was even better than the other deacons had described. Damien could hardly believe his good fortune. He had something for Jazzlyn and he couldn't wait to give all of it to her.

"I really hope this brings us closer," she said.

"Um, yeah, why don't you turn around real quick?" He rubbed his crotch and nearly started drooling when he caught a glimpse of her plump behind and the little tiny gold string that seemed lost between her juicy cheeks. She looked sluttish in the outfit and he liked it.

"Come here, girl," he said.

"Wait, I wanna talk first, Damien. Remember when I was telling you about my experience over at Wilshire Baptist? I guess I'm just um—I don't know, a bit afraid. See, I don't want to make the same mistake again. I'm ready for something real, a husband—you know, a man of the cloth. And I know, well, I know you're not in charge at Sweetwater, but everybody knows you're in line for . . . um, Damien, I can't concentrate when you do that," Jazzlyn said.

"You don't like it?" he whispered.

"No. I mean, it's not that, it's just we got all the time in the world to get to that. I just want to set some ground rules before we, well, you know . . ."

Damien took his thick chocolate finger and forcefully inserted it into Jazzlyn's moist opening.

"Sssssss," she playfully slapped his shoulder. "Will you stop it? I'm, I'm trying to tell you something," she giggled.

Instead of stopping, Damien pulled the crotch of the teddy to one side and rammed three more of his fingers into Jazzlyn. He stared deeply into her eyes as his fingers explored her.

"We didn't come here to talk, Jazz."

"Yeah, but you could at least try to spend some time with me?" She released a heavy breath.

Damien twisted his fingers deep inside her flesh and marveled at the way the feeling made her eyes roll up in the back of her head. She snickered.

"You like that?" he asked, eyeing her closely.

At first she grabbed at his hand. "Wait boo, I'm tryinta' ooohhh, I'm um," she started gyrating her hips against his hand. "Damn Dee, there you go . . . you hittin' my spot already."

"Yeah girl, I'm about to be way up in you in a minute. You like that, huh?"

Jazzlyn bit down on her bottom lip, struggling to stop herself from screaming. She moved her hips and squeezed her thighs together.

Damien, even more excited than before, used his free hand to pinch her nipples. He gently slapped her left breast, watched it bounce out of the teddy, then slopped it with his

moist tongue. He caught her nipple and held it tightly between his teeth.

"Sssss . . . I need you to um, to www-wait," Jazzlyn fought.
"We gotta talk about what this is gonna mean. Oooh wee, you
know, when we're through."

Tired of hearing her talk, Damien took her hand and
guided it to his massive member. At first touch, she pulled her
hand away as if she was touching sheer fire itself. But he easily
steered it back.

"Ooooh, it's soooooo," Jazzlyn struggled to catch her breath
as Damien's fingers moved in and out of her quickly.

Satisfied that she might be ready for what he had to offer,
he removed his fingers, sniffed them, then suckled each one
like he was savoring candy. As he did this Jazzlyn's eyes
locked on to his.

"Pull that chair over here," he demanded.

Jazzlyn did exactly what he asked. When the chair was right
where Damien wanted it, he removed the last of his clothes
and placed the chair a few inches from the bed.

He took Jazzlyn by the hand. "You trust me?" he asked.

She nodded, saying yes, and allowed him to guide her
closer to the chair.

"Okay, look at this. I'm gonna sit on the chair and lean
back." Damien tilted the chair until it leaned comfortably on
the mattress. "Here, push on it, you see how sturdy it is on
this mattress. I'm not gonna let you get hurt, okay?"

"Why we gotta have it leaning like that?" she asked.

"'Cause that's gonna help me get way up in you. Real deep,
that's how you like it right? I just wanted you to see that the
chair is sturdy against the mattress."

"Um, ah, okay," Jazzlyn said.

Damien placed the chair back to its upright position and
pulled his boxers to his ankles. Jazzlyn's eyes nearly bulged
from their sockets.

"You okay?" he asked, beaming with pride.

"Um . . ." Her eyes stayed glued to his member.

Damien stroked himself, hoping she wasn't about to try and back out now that she had gotten him all worked up. "Here, why don't you touch it? I swear it won't bite," he assured.

"I'm not worrying about being bitten," she said.

As soon as Damien's hands left hers, Jazzlyn pulled her hand away from his crotch.

"You not scared, are you?" he asked gently.

"Nah, it's just, um. I ain't never seen one like that. I mean, how it get so big and thick?"

"Good genes, baby. Goodlove genes to be exact. Don't worry, you'll enjoy it," he promised. Before she could say another word in protest, Damien pulled out a tube of KY Jelly. "If you like, we could use some of this, but I think you can handle it."

Jazzlyn looked back and forth between Damien, his large member and the jelly he held in his hand. She didn't say a word.

"C'mon, girl. I promise it'll only hurt for a minute, then it'll get good for you." Noticing the time, Damien sat on the chair and extended his hands toward Jazzlyn.

She stepped toward him and started to remove the teddy that was now completely soaked with her wetness. The smell of raw sex lingered in the air. The room was hot and muggy. Damien pulled out the black and gold condom wrapper. Once it was on as best as he could fit it, she carefully swung one leg over the left side of the chair.

"You ready?" he asked.

Jazzlyn took a deep breath, then exhaled. "Here, play with my titties, that'll help."

"Look don't worry about none of that. I'm gonna take care of everything. I'll help you get on, then once you all comfy, I'll handle everything else. I just want you to hang on and enjoy yourself, cool?"

"Um, okay."

At first the head of Damien's member sat at her opening. She wiggled her hips and worked more of him into her slowly.

But after a few minutes, Damien started getting impatient. He was ready to beat up on her walls. When she was half way on his member, he took her by the hips and shoved himself as far as he could go up into her.

She released a strained yelp, but it didn't take long for her to start moving her hips. After a while, her moans went from belly wrenching gasps to sheer squeals of pleasure, music to Damien's ears.

Attention Writers:

Writers looking to get their books published can view our submission guidelines by visiting our website at:
www.QBOROBOOKS.com

What we're looking for: Contemporary fiction in the tradition of Darrien Lee, Carl Weber, Anna J., Zane, Mary B. Morrison, Noire, Lolita Files, etc; groundbreaking mainstream contemporary fiction.

We prefer email submission to: candace@qborobooks.com in MS Word, PDF, or rtf format only. However, if you wish to send the submission via snail mail, you can send it to:

Q-BORO BOOKS Acquisitions Department
165-41A Baisley Blvd., Suite 4. Mall #1
Jamaica, New York 11434

By submitting your work to Q-Boro Books, you agree to hold Q-Boro books harmless and not liable for publishing similar works as yours that we may already be considering in the future.

1. Submission will not be returned.
2. **Do not contact us for status updates.** If we are interested in receiving your full manuscript, we will contact you via email or telephone.
3. Do no submit if the entire manuscript is not complete.

Due to heavy volume of submissions, if these requirements are not followed, we will not be able to process your submission.